STATE SECRETS

Wendy Charlton

DEDICATION

Honouring a friend, fellow author, and storyteller
James McGrath 1952 -2023

To all my wonderful readers, please remember, I am
writing as fast as I can!

.

Table of Contents

ACKNOWLEDGMENTS

I would like to thank my husband, without whose help this one would not have made it over the line, thank you, Andrew, with much love.

Thanks also to my wonderful beta reader, Elaine Griffiths, who is a wonderful sister and probably my biggest fan.

.

DISCLAIMER

This is a work of fiction.

Unless otherwise indicated, all the names, characters, businesses, places, events, and incidents in this book are either the product of the author's imagination or used in a fictitious manner. Any resemblance to actual persons, living or dead, or actual events is purely coincidental.

Prologue

2nd September 2019

The red light on the speakerphone flashed to let him know that the call he'd been waiting for was about to begin. He pressed the answer button and a harsh electronic voice floated from the device.

"Please enter your 6-digit code followed by the hash key".

He entered the code he'd received earlier that day in an encrypted email.

"You will be connected to the call when the owner starts the session".

The thin metallic strains of Mozart's 'Eine Kleiner Nachtmusik' escaped from the phone's loudspeaker.

He was sitting at his treasured mahogany desk, an exact replica of the one in the Oval Office at the Whitehouse, lightly drumming his fingers in time to the rhythm of the music on the desks highly polished surface. A reading lamp, an aged leather writing pad, an antique silver inkwell and a large cup of coffee were the only other items that encroached on the desktop. The ornate desk, which was symbolic of his status, was the centrepiece of his private den. The walls of the room were adorned with photographs of him standing next to, or shaking hands with most of the world's leaders and top entrepreneurs. He had once believed that being 'leader of the free world' would be his legacy, but now he knew different. Orchestrating control of the global energy markets would be what he was remembered for.

On another continent and a different time-zone, the same process was taking place. However, this man was not relaxed, not waiting patiently for the call to begin. He paced around the dingy back room, an old wooden table stood under a bare lightbulb. It was strewn with spent coffee cups, shot glasses and an array of mobile phones.

"What the hell are we waiting for?" he barked at the phone, in a heavy Russian accent.

'Eine Kleiner Nachtmusik' was not one of his favourite pieces, he preferred something stirring, more powerful.

Something by Tchaikovsky or Mussorgsky. 'Night on a bald mountain'; now that piece had real power.

He was interrupted by the voice from the phone.

"Your call will begin in one minute".

In a study in the basement of a grand Georgian house in Belgravia London, two men, Adam Hunt, a former British Prime Minister, a slim, intense, and impeccably dressed middle-aged man with golden skin pedestal

and clear green eyes that made him difficult to ignore, and Stewart Pearson, his slightly older but nondescript Private Secretary, both looked at the phone, willing the call to begin.

Adam Hunt spoke, his accent was that of a self-made man, typically clipped and British. He had the look of a powerful diplomat, who's every word seemed to have been carefully selected and polished before it was uttered.

"Bloody hell, Pearson, can't they get a move on? I've got things to do …". The telecommunications system worked invisibly in the background, and suddenly with a click, the men were all connected to the call.

His words were interrupted by a deep gravelly voice, Eastern European, and slightly intimidating.

"Gentlemen, I apologise for the lengthy delay. Technology is not my strength. Let us begin".

Hunt was the first to reply.

"Thank you, Mr. Gorski, I do not have a lot of time, so let's keep this brief. The selection committee have completed their due diligence into the Hunt Foundation and are happy with the leading-edge work we are doing as a centre for Climate and Energy Change. They were particularly impressed with our new technologies that can help to tackle the climate crisis. It's clear they see us as global influencers".

Gorski replied, he sounded sceptical.

"And where exactly does controlling the world's energy markets come in that mission statement?"

Hunt sat back in his seat, stretching his long legs out in front of him.

"The worlds' energy markets are a complex mechanism. The economic control it can give us, will allow us to negotiate favourable trade deals. We can influence lesser developed nations who are vulnerable to supply disruptions, geopolitical conflicts, and price fluctuations. We can help them to build resilience.

If our global foundation were to be the 'regulators' responsible for this, then no individual country would have control over energy supply".

Pearson, the older man to his right, who was considerably scruffier, with sparse red hair and a shaving rash, nodded enthusiastically in support and said,

"We are on-track to put in place plans that have been evolving for over two decades. A little more patience is all that's required".

Gorski was deeply irritated and ran his right hand through his greying curly hair.

"Why is your puppet on this call, this is a dangerous conversation to be having, and the fewer people who know about it the better".

"I can vouch for Pearson. He is working behind the scenes and taking the majority of the risks, I want him here".

Gorski was unconvinced.

"If we support this plan, it will give us the control and the power to destabilize energy markets. We could trigger global economic instability".

Hunt gave his sidekick a reassuring smile.

"Don't worry about that Gorski, we already have everyone who matters signed up to our project. Global investors are in complete agreement with the data-modelling that sits behind this. With us controlling energy prices, we can guarantee our influence on the compliance of those in power, as long as they get their rewards".

Former US President, John F. Hudson, the elder statesman who had been silent until now, stopped stirring his coffee.

"If I had to make a prediction, gentleman, I would say that this will not have the galvanising effect that you suggest. It's far more likely to strain international relations, particularly if other countries realise that the controlling entity, namely your foundation, is using energy as a political weapon. It may even trigger conflicts if they seek to blame each other. I like it!"

His southern drawl had an element of excitement and anticipation. Hunt replied,

"Good. So, the next milestone is the appointment of the Diplomatic Envoy to the Middle East. That process has begun, and we should have confirmation in late spring 2020. Once I am confirmed as the envoy, then the final piece of the plan is in place, and we can begin".

The statesman fiddled with the spoon in his saucer.

"How certain is that appointment? If you don't get it, it could seriously compromise the timescale of the project".

A well-practised smile formed on Hunt's face,

"Don't worry about that, Mr. 'former' President, we are confident that it's a mere formality".

"It had better be, we all have a lot riding on this. The special relationship between our two nations, that we used to enjoy, cannot be depended on to get this across the line. My backers will not handle failure in a gentlemanly way, if you get my meaning".

Gorski seized on the message from Hudson,

"Are you suggesting that there may be a problem"?

"No sir, but like you, I have a lot to lose if any of this becomes public knowledge, my involvement, and my investors need to be invisible".

Hunt interrupted,

"Let's not get side-tracked. Everything about this project is beyond secret. There are no records of our conversations, there are no files and nothing in writing to implicate any of us. 'Keep calm and carry on', as we Brits like to say".

Gorski let out an exasperated sigh,

"We will reconvene in three months".

The call was terminated. The red lights on the phones blinked out.

Now they just had to wait for their plan to become a reality, and then ...... they would be the three most powerful players on a truly global stage.

1. Shady Fields:

Thursday 16th January 2020. Midday,

Hilary hated this time of year. Christmas had been and gone, taking all the festive colour and trimmings with it. Shady Fields had looked barren and empty for several days until the status quo was re-established, and the residents had settled down once again. She had decided to work over the holidays, since it was her first year without her beloved Aunt Ada. She had died last year, and Hilary was still dealing with the massive gap her passing had left in her life.

Layla Strong, the recently promoted manager of Shady Fields, had a new man in her life and wanted to spend time with him. Hilary had been happy to oblige her. It also meant that she had been able to spend some time with her boss, Daniel Grant, the Director General of British Security Services. He was one of the main architects of the scheme that was this most unusual residential home.

Hillary had been drawn to him from their first meeting. An intense man with a magnetic personality and a sense of authenticity that was charismatic. She felt there was definite chemistry between them, although she had never acted on it. She had quickly learned that Daniel had lost his fiancé, Martine, during an aid mission in Syria that was ambushed in 2017. The details were sketchy, but her source also told her that while he was investigating the incident, he had been shot and seriously wounded. His retirement from active service was the result. Instead, he had been tasked to create Shady Fields.

The unique residents of Shady Fields shared a common heritage, they had all been active secret agents with MI5 or MI6, they were all still bound by the official secrets act and had extraordinary work histories and skill sets. The end of the Cold War and the shift towards technology-led espionage meant that agents rarely died in 'the field' and were more likely to reach retirement age and draw a pension. Sadly, some of them would suffer from memory problems. Dementia or Alzheimer's presented the security services a tricky problem. What do you do with an ageing secret agent that has lost control of their inhibitions and talks openly about their secret past?

Many of them had been involved in some of the most significant historical events in living memory; the subterfuge, intrigue and plotting by world governments was well known to them. You could not allow that sort of sensitive information into the public domain without some safeguards. Shady Fields was that safeguard.

Hilary sat in her office mulling over the care home's financial reports. They were managing to keep their heads above water, but it wasn't easy. It was an expensive service to run, and although they were profitable, they struggled to keep ever rising costs under control. Daniel had handed over the operational and managerial side of the business to her completely since his promotion, and now preferred a hands-off approach, keeping it under observation as a strategic asset rather than having direct involvement in daily operations.

Hilary had joined the team at Shady Fields in 2018, shortly after it opened, and if she was honest, was quite sceptical about the need for such a place. However, in the last few years, Shady Fields has experienced a murder, a kidnapping, and an armed attack by a gang of Eastern European criminals. She was no longer sceptical, but mindful of the value of her residents and of the secrets they held.

Hilary needed to concentrate and clear her desk in the next thirty minutes. They were welcoming their latest resident at 11 am this morning. She was special for several reasons. Firstly, she had once been the Director General of British Security Services. Celia Browning had spectacularly smashed through that glass ceiling by being the first woman to be appointed to the role. Secondly, she had been one of the youngest to get the top job, and more recently, she had been the instigator of Shady Fields, a solution to a problem that the civil service would much rather pretend did not exist. Hilary had not discovered whether Celia had formulated the Shady Fields plan because she knew she had Alzheimer's or whether it was karma that she had been diagnosed with the disease now.

Since her retirement, Celia had lived alone, her husband had passed seven years previously and her grown-up children now lived abroad. Her daughter in New York, with an investment banker, and her son in San Francisco, working for a trendy marketing agency. From what Hilary could gather, there had been much discussion between them about Celia's future, but Celia was resolute. She had no intention of being a burden to her children. Her condition was deteriorating quickly, and she would soon need full time supervised care. Her particular history meant that the missions she had sanctioned, and the secrets she was party to, were too sensitive to run the risk of becoming public knowledge.

Hilary had been present at a fiery meeting between Celia and Daniel. Celia had decided to make the decision that would dictate how she experienced the time she had remaining, whilst she still had capacity. Daniel was quite shaken when he saw the physical and mental deterioration in her condition in just a few short months. Her children had both been consulted, and Celia's mind was made up, she would move to Shady Fields sooner rather than later. Her condition could be managed more effectively, and strangely, she felt comforted by the level of control she still had in the process.

There was a light knock on the door and Layla popped her head in.

"Hilary, she is here. Just arrived by car, and the removal men have taken the packing cases up to her room. I have given Deborah the job of helping to unpack her things".

"Thanks Layla, I'm just coming," Hilary quickly saved the document she was working on and logged out of her computer. She picked up her key card, slipping it into her pocket, and followed Layla out of her office.

"Did you enjoy your break?"

Layla smiled.

"It was great, we walked by the sea, ate great food and read books, just what I needed".

"That's good, so pleased you enjoyed it. I'll follow you down, I just need to let Daniel know she has arrived". Hilary sent Daniel a brief text to that effect, smoothed her skirt and set off along the corridor and down the magnificent staircase into the imposing entrance hall.

Celia stood in the hall, looking around blankly. She had been here a couple of times since it opened, and it all looked familiar, but if she was honest with herself, she wasn't sure how long ago that was. When she first conceived Shady Fields, it was as an altruistic response to some in the civil service who were happy to take chances and leave ex-agents to their own devices.

For her, there was too much risk in that approach. The world was changing, espionage wasn't the same and what had been acceptable fifty years ago, was certainly not acceptable now. The drive for public transparency had left many of their old agents exposed, compromised and vulnerable. The secrets they held could still cast long shadows. They had all carried out dubious missions, brokered clandestine deals, been involved in deaths and betrayals, and Celia was no exception. But she had no idea that she would end up here quite so quickly.

She left the service, taking early retirement, but was pleased to have had a significant role in the appointment of her successor. Daniel Grant had been one of the best agents she had ever worked with. He was honest, principled, and extremely capable. She had been more than a little surprised that the 'powers that be' had accepted her recommendation and appointed him. Maybe he would succeed where she had failed. He was certainly no pushover and would not be manipulated by politicians. She smiled, knowing her parting shot was to put a very sharp thorn in their sides.

Hilary walked over to her, reaching out a hand to shake.

"Welcome, Celia, did you have a good journey?"

Celia smiled back and knew that she had forgotten this woman's name. Her face was familiar, she could even place her in this building, but her name remained stubbornly just out of reach.

"Yes, it was fine, thanks".

She shook the offered hand and waited for the name to come, but nothing happened.

Hilary watched Celia closely.

"It's Hilary Geddes, we have met a few times before, briefly".

Celia had been on the interview panel with Daniel when she had applied for the job here just a few short years before. She hadn't realised how quickly Alzheimer's could progress, or the physical effects it had on a sufferer. Celia was most definitely thinner and less 'pristine' in her appearance.

"I have arranged for us to have tea in the library, then you can go up and settle into your apartment. Deborah will help unpack your things, and if there's anything else we can do for you, just ask".

Hilary felt slightly uncomfortable. She had done the 'welcome meet' several times, but it had never felt like this before. Hilary remembered her interview and how intimidated she had felt by the formidable woman with a grey, precision cut bob. For all her subtlety, perfect makeup, and steel grey designer suit, she oozed power and authority.

Hilary had been a fast-track civil servant, advising government ministers on policy and strategy, until that fateful White Paper on the state of care provision for the elderly, frail and vulnerable. The one that exposed the massive flaw in public spending allocations. She had uncovered documents that revealed a £30billion shortfall that the government had forgotten to mention in their last election campaign. In fact, Hilary's white paper had gone further. She forensically deconstructed their spending plans, highlighting 'misinformation and statistical manipulation' which, had the truth been made public at the time, would have undoubtedly lost them the election. It had been made crystal-clear to her that she needed to go before she was pushed.

Then three years ago, at about the same time, her Aunt Ada had been diagnosed with stage four cancer and scheduled for an operation with chemotherapy to follow. She needed specialist care and time to recover, and Hilary had found herself visiting Ada in this unusual residential home called Shady Fields, deep in the Home Counties countryside.

The surroundings were outstanding, a huge and beautiful mansion house of cream stone. It looked more like a country hotel than a residential care home, and Hilary had wondered what it must cost to spend your twilight years in a stately home like this.

What Ada had described as simply a job in the civil service after the war, had, in fact, turned out to be highly sensitive missions for the security services involving, spying, secret agent training and a high level of expertise in weapons training, all tied up in a neat parcel of the Official Secrets Act.

Little did Hilary know then that just months later, her world would be transformed by taking on a senior role in the running of this unique place and all that it entailed. She was now a member of that exclusive club complete with a government ID card, a signatory to the Official Secrets Act and the experience of two missions, where she had been exposed to betrayal, violence, and death.

Now things had come full circle, meeting the woman who had sanctioned her appointment and transformed her future. She was now protecting the woman who had employed her.

They stood for a moment in an awkward silence before Hilary ushered Celia into the library where an open fire and a tray of tea things stood waiting. The walls were lined with dark wooden bookshelves filled with everything from leather-bound first editions to a well-thumbed paperback collection. There were comfortable reading chairs dotted about the room, with accompanying tables that accommodated stylish reading lamps. In the middle of the far wall there was a striking marble fireplace flanked by two leather chesterfield sofas, facing each other over a solid oak coffee table. Hilary crossed the room to the settee on the right of the fireplace. Sitting, she poured two cups of hot, strong tea. Celia followed her lead, absorbing the sights, sounds and smells of the library, occasionally experiencing glimpses of time previously spent here.

The building had a long and distinguished history. It had been used by the Secret Service during the second world war as a base for early electronic surveillance but fell into disrepair after the war. However, it was ideal for Celia's purpose. The refurbishment had not been cheap, but was beautifully done. It had four floors, with lift access to the upper floors; while the ground floor included the resident's communal rooms; TV lounge, dining room, library, activity room, bar and wellbeing room, used for yoga, relaxation, and mindfulness classes. A large glass and brick garden room ran almost the full length of the rear of the house, overlooking the gardens and woods. The utilities were also situated at the rear of the building, with kitchen, laundry, cleaning services and reception all running from the ground floor.

The upper floors housed a number of one or two-bedroom apartments, and there was also a kitchenette and a quiet lounge for residents. The main staff office and meeting room was on the first floor, with smaller staff offices on the second and third floors. Hilary couldn't be sure how much of the homes' layout Celia could remember, so she ran her through a quick overview, more as an icebreaker rather than for something to say.

Hilary explained that as a resident's condition became more complex, their needs were met with more intensive care and increased security. The top floor was reserved for those who needed twenty-four-hour nursing care, those who were virtually bedridden or who needed secure facilities due to their challenging behaviour. Hilary knew there was a strong likelihood that Celia may well end up there, but she didn't say that out loud.

They chatted amiably until they had finished their tea, and Hilary noted that Celia's attention was beginning to wander.

"Now everything's signed, would you like to go in for lunch? It's served between 12.30 pm and 1.30 pm in the dining room just across the corridor".

Hilary watched the woman's reaction carefully. She detected a slight hesitation.

"Or, if you like, you can go up to your apartment now and have a lunch tray delivered instead. It would give you a bit of time to settle in before you come and meet everyone else".

Celia relaxed her shoulders a little.

"Yes, I think I would prefer that".

Hilary nodded to Deborah, who had inexplicably appeared in the doorway at exactly the right time and was now crossing the room to Celia's side.

"Follow me, Celia, I will take you upstairs. Here is the key to your apartment, your belongings have already been taken up".

Hilary watched this once authoritative woman meekly follow her care assistant out of the library.

She glanced down at her watch; damn. She should have been in the clinical suite with Dr Arnot for the resident reviews five minutes ago. She swept up her folder and headed for the first floor, making her way up the stairs and along the corridor past the offices that faced the back of the house. She arrived at the clinical suite door and entered without knocking. The clinical suite sounded very grand, but it was just a small office with a desk set against a wall and two low armchairs set to one side with a small coffee table in front of them that Dr. Arnot used for consultations. The obligatory box of tissues sat, stranded alone, on the tabletop.

Her apology for being late spilled from her lips, but it was delivered to the back of Dr Arnot's head. He was busy updating his records on the large screen on the desk in front of him.

"Don't worry about it, come and catch your breath".

"I was just welcoming Celia to Shady Fields; she arrived about an hour ago".

"Such a shame, she was a force to be reckoned with when she was Director General. Alzheimer's certainly does not discriminate; it can hit anyone, and it's happening to a much younger age group, too".

He shook his head almost despairingly.

"Are you ready for the update, then?"

Hilary settled into one of the low armchairs, took out her pen, and writing the date and time in the header on a clean sheet of paper, Said,

"Ready"

"Okay, in no particular order, let's start with the medication reviews. Bill Tandy is getting on fine and is responding really well to the new drug regime. We seem to have halted his memory loss, or at least slowed it down considerably. I know Ben will be really pleased, particularly after the events of the last few months".

Hilary sighed. Bill and Ben, the Dynamite Men, as they were affectionately known, had played a major role in protecting Shady Fields from an armed attack six months ago, and if she were honest, she had worried that it could have a major impact on Bill's condition. They came as a pair, lived in adjacent apartments on the first floor, and could be a bit of a handful at times. The fact that Shady Fields now benefitted from a deep ornamental pond in the grounds was the result of Bill's over-zealous approach to removing a tree stump using a home-made bomb.

Their background was in military intelligence as bomb disposal specialists. Not normally a long-term career choice. But they had excelled in their jobs and when they retired from the service, they worked as private contractors for more than a decade.

They had put their unrivalled knowledge of explosives to very effective use, and their company had become extremely successful. It seemed like the sky was the limit until Bill was diagnosed with Dementia. Ben, who had always looked out for his best friend, persuaded him to sell up, and they went on a world cruise to enjoy countries they had visited before, this time as tourists not to blow something up. It had become clear then that Bill would need specialist care when his condition deteriorated, so they took the decision to move into Shady Fields. They were privately funded and a very welcome source of external revenue for Hilary. She had grown extremely fond of the unconventional pair and their combustible hobbies.

"Charlie Bingham is as fit as a butcher's dog and ticking the others off with his stories and name-dropping, so no change there then".

Hilary stopped taking notes.

"How's he doing mentally, though? He's lost a couple of friends while he has been here, is he adjusting?"

Dr Arnot partly swivelled around in his chair, so he could make eye contact with Hilary.

"I would say that he has adjusted okay. He was very cut up about William's death, particularly the way it happened, but he dealt with it. I think reconnecting with his granddaughter has had a positive impact on him. He seems to have a spring in his step when she comes to visit. Yes, I think Charlie is just fine".

Hilary could not suppress a smile.

"Is he still convinced he is Lord Lucan?"

Dr Arnot just stared at her.

"It's not as outlandish as some of the thing's others in here utter. And I think it's highly likely that he's the only man left standing who knew what really happened to Lucan. He certainly moved in the same circles, he was a contemporary of his and there may have been a family connection too. To be honest, nothing that happens in this place would surprise me any more".

"What about Jon Dowie-Brown, how's he doing?"

Hilary had been pleasantly surprised when Jon came to Shady Fields to recover from his recent illness. She had never met anyone quite like 'Dowie-Brown' as he insisted on being referred to. He was a dapper man, flamboyant, bordering on being a dandy. Tall, slender and with a shock of snowy white hair, complete with an impeccably trimmed beard and waxed moustache. His designer glasses always matched his outfit, which was usually a tailored three-piece suit in a loud colour or a bold check, with a handmade shirt and silk cravat or neck-tie, depending on his mood. Hats were also a great indicator of his disposition on any given day, if he was sporting a fedora, then he felt confident and happy to attract attention, a newsboys cap, and he was feeling playful, a Homburg, and he meant business, but never a bucket hat, as he had once told Hilary, he was not a heathen! He would never blend into the crowd, wherever he was.

By today's standards, his label would be a 'metrosexual' with an eclectic sense of style. Though a few brief conversations with him had taught Hilary that he never thought of himself as any of those labels, he just knew what he liked. He was an individual who had never followed the masses. She found him fascinating. He had been a military cartographer who was seconded to the intelligence services, to build detailed maps of strategic territories and sites of conflict. He was also a strategist of some renown and a great chess player.

"Hmmm, he is interesting. He had a serious illness and a few complications, which is why he needs to be here. He needs to build his strength before going home. The man lives on his own, very independent and a bit of a loner. He's been here four weeks and expected to be here another four, but I'm struggling to get a measure of him. He can be quite abrasive, easily offended and can be quite argumentative, but then in a blink he can be quite charming and excellent company. It's the way some people react to being faced with their own mortality. He seems angry with the world. The difficultly is that unless we can get him to deal with the emotional side of things better, it could well hamper his recovery. I thought you might get the staff to build a connection with him. He should be relaxing and taking light exercise; recreation to rehabilitate. Can you see what they can do, I've done everything I can medically, it's up to him now"?

Hilary nodded,

"I've asked Ben Faulkner to keep an eye on him and to spend a bit of time with him. I'll also have a word with Layla and see what else we can arrange".

She made a few more notes.

"Is that it, then?"

"No, there's still Kitty Oliver. Hypertension, Osteoarthritis, and type two diabetes. Her osteoporosis is quite advanced, she has lost an inch in height in the last few months and her chronic back-pain is getting more difficult to manage with standard analgesics. I want to hold off a little while longer before trying opioids, so I have her on a new regime of Vitamin D3, K2, Magnesium and Strontium to try to build back some bone density. I've asked Ronnie to introduce her to Tai Chi as part of a new daily routine. I know Ronnie normally teaches yoga, but she has done Tai Chi in the past and I think the slow rhythmic movements would help Kitty build bone density".

"Are there any dietary requirements that could be put in place to help?" Hilary knew some of the others had benefited from nutritional changes.

"Good luck with that. She's a tough old bird, very set in her ways, I am not convinced she will go for it, but it's worth a try. I'll check on her later this week and update you if I need to".

Dr Arnot closed the last record on the computer and logged out of the system. Hilary reflected for a moment.

"Do you know that of all the residents here, Kitty is the one I know least about. Her record, or what there is of it, has huge gaps, where, I presume, she was working on top-secret missions. I know she has worked with Celia before, like most of the residents here now, but there's something strange in the way she reacted when I told her that Celia was coming here to live".

"I wouldn't worry about it, Hilary. If her file were that secret, then it would be eye's only; therefore, someone here would definitely know all about it. I guarantee, you would have all the gory details before the end of the week". He chuckled, picked up his satchel from the floor at the side of the desk, and took his leave. Hilary made a mental note to ask Beattie about her mysterious resident, she was the gossip go-to of all the residents. What Beattie didn't know about those living at Shady Fields wasn't worth knowing.

2. Malvern Hills. Worcestershire

Thursday 12th September 2002

Robert didn't understand how it had come to this. What a God damn mess! It was a very dangerous game to play, but he was going to set the record straight. The Prime Minister had just lied to Parliament and had set off a chain of events that history would find questionable at best. At worst, history may accuse the man of a war crime.

Speaking metaphorically, they had used him to make and fire the bullets. It was his reputation on the line, and he was not going to let them throw him under the bus. He had to clear his head. He pulled on his walking boots and his old wax jacket, then reached for

Nero's lead. On hearing the metal clasp jangle, the black Labrador magically appeared, looking up at his owner expectantly. Robert rubbed the dogs' ear, Nero sat, patiently waiting for his lead to be attached so that another scent-driven adventure could begin.

Nero didn't question a second walk in the day, he was just happy with his good fortune. He watched his master's every move, his muscles taut with anticipation. Robert selected a walking pole from the wicker basket filled with canes and umbrellas. Nero twitched with excitement; he began to hop from foot to foot. It was the stick he took when they walked the hills. The dog instinctively knew that when they got to the fork in the path they would turn left and up onto the slopes rather than right and down into the woods. The wood was his favourite place, where the exquisite smells of rabbit droppings, foxes and badger trails overwhelmed him. Instead, this time they would be climbing the paths and shaley hills in the gusting wind. It really didn't matter; he was going out with his master, and beggars can't be choosers.

Walking the Malvern Hills was Robert Crane's way of solving big problems. Out in the fresh air and away from the minutia of daily life, he could focus on the facts and logic of the problem he was wrestling with. His wife Abigail had warned him against doing anything rash. They had been married for twenty years and had two bright children, Sharon, and Colin. Their relationship had experienced a wobble a few years ago, all his fault, but they had repaired the damage enough to ensure their children had received a stable upbringing, felt secure, and were loved. She had not been the same towards him since, understandably, but he took her emotional outbursts and periodic hostility as his punishment. It was the least he could do. However, it did make him question whether her current concern was for him, the family, or the threat that his dismissal would pose to Abigail's very comfortable lifestyle.

There was no question that she made the most of being married to Professor Emeritus Robert Crane, OBE, the world renown expert on bioweapons and virology, with a particular knowledge of Orthopoxvirus (that's Smallpox and Monkeypox, for the lay person). They were invited to the best academic dinner parties, and it was just a matter of time before he was awarded a knighthood, and she would be Lady Abigail Crane. Maybe then she might be satisfied, he thought.

Officially he worked for the United Nations, leading inspection teams that monitored the research, development, and deployment of biological weapons across the world. Unofficially, he worked for the British Secret Service and had done so since his Cambridge University days and the prestige of his first appointment working at Porton Down. But despite his academic achievements and accolades, he'd had to acknowledge a lack of capability in his marital relationship, though he was on much safer ground as a father.

If he could have turned back the clock, he would have. He would have declined the offer from the security services and built his career on the reputation of his work alone, independent of their research grants. But he had accepted their shilling and had been obliged to toe the line. It hadn't been a problem until now. Everything he had done had been to protect the security and sovereignty of his country. What he was now struggling with was something entirely different. This was about furnishing politicians with a platform to justify acts of aggression based on a political agenda. As far as he could see, there was no threat to Britain, just an American President hell-bent on creating a legacy of fearless leader of the free world and cashing in on the 'special relationship' with the UK to achieve it.

It was difficult to know whom to trust. His political paymasters had hung him out to dry at the select committee hearing two days ago, on Tuesday. They had categorically stated that it was his report that had identified the development and deployment of biological weapons by Iraq. What they didn't say was how the political spin doctors had edited his report to raise red flags where none had existed before. It was only a word here and there that had been changed, they argued it was just semantics, but Robert knew it was more than that. Their version carried more inference than fact, it was the epitome of shroud waving. Someone had made sure he didn't see the final version until the Prime Minister had presented it to the House of Commons during the special debate. It was then that the world had gone mad.

He was obviously on autopilot today, as they had already reached the path that led high up into the hills. Nero suddenly stood still, looking off into the distance. A figure was approaching them down the slope. It was a woman in a navy trouser suit and crisp white shirt, with neat court shoes. Her head was down as she walked into the wind, and there was something familiar about the way she moved.

Having a dog meant that you got to know plenty of people locally, by sight. You hardly ever exchanged your names, but you recognised their dogs and knew them by name. It couldn't be that in this case because the woman was alone. No dog in sight.

As she drew closer, he realised who she was. Kitty Oliver! They had been part of the same team during their initial training at Chicksands in Bedfordshire. A peer group, but from very different backgrounds, all with brilliant minds, who had been singled out for recruitment into the service. They had completed some of their intelligence training and attended briefings together, but had never shared a mission. Their contact had been largely by letter and telephone calls, to check out minor details of something they had been working on at the time. Immediately he wondered why she was there; they hadn't spoken in more than eighteen months.

She was just yards away when she looked up and called to him.

"Fancy meeting you here, Robert, blowing the cobwebs away, are you?"

He had always liked Kitty, although it was fair to say that he didn't fully trust her. She was about 5'5" with golden blonde glossy hair and a distinctive port-wine birthmark on her left cheek that faded as it reached her neck. She was completely unselfconscious about it. She hardly ever covered it up and tolerated those who might stare. He thought it was brave to do that in a world where a woman's worth is often judged by her physical perfection. It had never held her back, in fact, one of Kitty's talents was honey trapping. She genuinely didn't care what others thought about her. When she wanted to, she could exude sex appeal and had used it to manipulate both men and women to give her what she wanted. She loved her job in a very unhealthy way.

"Hello Kitty, what are you doing here?"

She reached out to him, placing her hand lightly on his chest through the opening in his coat. She kissed him on the cheek in a familiar gesture.

"I saw the select committee recording and thought you might need a bit of moral support".

He breathed in her scent, warm and inviting, but he stiffened and pulled back from her.

"I'm fine, thanks. We are the result of our choices, Kitty, not the victims of our circumstances".

She slipped her arm through his and turned him back towards the way he came, Nero following his owner with this new human, of whom he was very unsure. He made a low grumble but made his way past them, seeking out the next new smell to track down.

Kitty was tucked into his side with a firm grip on his arm.

"I trust that you have considered the price of whistleblowing Robert. I know you are unlikely to take this lying down, but you need to understand the consequences of your actions, not just for you. You have a family; you need to consider them in all of this".

He stopped and pulled his arm free.

"Did they send you to find out what I am going to do?"

She looked hurt.

"Robert! It makes me sad that you would even think that. I'm here to offer you a bit of support. You have always taken the high moral ground, and at times you've been a thorn in their side, but this is different. The outcome of you sharing what really happened could be catastrophic for some. You could even bring the Government down and send reverberations across the pond, threatening our American allies too. They won't let you get away with it". They continued to walk along the path, deeper into the wood.

"I have friends in the media Kitty. I could do it in such a way that it wouldn't look like me, I could speak to them off the record, give them a starting point. They could do the digging and uncover what really went on for themselves. I would be caught up in the aftermath, but at least the truth would be out there. They wouldn't be able to put the genie back in the bottle. These politicians must be held to account; otherwise they will feel bold enough to do anything in the future. I can't take this lying down; you understand that, don't you?"

He felt much warmer now they were out of the wind and into the trees, he slipped his jacket off and folded it over his left arm. Dappled early autumn sunlight shone through the sparse canopy, and the rich golden carpet of early fallen leaves softened the noise they made as they walked.

"So, is it documents or emails Robert, what do you have that you could share?" she bent down to tug at the stick Nero had picked up. He dutifully let go and waited for her to throw it. She threw it into the trees, and he raced off in pursuit. She asked Robert again, "What have you got on them, Robert?"

He stopped and looked directly at her.

"It is safer for you if you don't know".

They walked on in silence, into the woods where the trees were now becoming thicker, and the path took sudden turns. She paced him and slipped her arm back through his, giving it a squeeze.

He felt a slight tug on the fabric of his shirt, then a scratch on his forearm. He was so deep in thought he didn't pay it any attention, revisiting the actions that were forming in his mind about what he was going to do to resolve this situation. He shrugged free of her, picking up the stick to throw for Nero again.

As they walked on, he felt his legs growing heavy and his head began to spin. His eyes couldn't focus, images swam in and out of clarity. He began to breathe heavily, he stopped on the path and reached out for Kitty to steady himself, but she stepped back away from him.

"What have you done, Kitty?"

He stumbled forward and dropped to his knees, the damp loam striking cold through the thin fabric of his trousers.

"I am truly sorry, Robert, but this is bigger than your conscience. Tell me where you have put the files, it really doesn't have to end like this".

She watched the colour drain from his face, he tried to speak, but the effects of the drug she had administered to him were taking effect. He tried to speak, but his vocal cords were paralysed, making him mute. The seizure began slowly, his body began to shudder, toppling him onto his side. As they intensified, he rolled onto his back, legs thrashing wildly about. White foam spewed out of his mouth and ran down his face and onto the ground.

Nero returned and dropped the stick at his master's feet. He could sense something was not right but thought it was some sort of new game. He made a play-bow to his owner, wagging his tail and waiting for the next move, but was met only with an uncanny stillness. Kitty bent down and picked up the stick. Throwing it for him again, the compulsion to retrieve got the better of the dog, and he set off after the wooden missile, into the thicket of trees.

She waited for a few moments until she was sure Robert had been completely immobilized. She put on a pair of latex gloves from her suit pocket, then set about dragging him to the side of the path. It was heavy work, but she was deceptively strong. She propped him awkwardly against a tree before retrieving his coat and rifling through the pockets. She found a well-used pocketknife, his mobile phone, some plastic bags for cleaning up after the dog and a few dog treats.

She roughly rolled up his shirt sleeves to expose his wrists. The dog was barking somewhere off in the woods, she didn't want to be here when he returned.

The pocketknife was quite blunt, and it took longer than she thought it would, to open up big enough wounds for the blood to begin to flow. The only previous experience she'd had of this sort of 'wet job' was the wife of a Russian diplomat who had worked for them for a while before betraying her handler. He had been captured and tortured to death by the KGB. When Kitty had staged her suicide, it had been in a comfortable hotel room with a candle, soft music, and a warm bath. Her blood had flowed easily, this seemed very different.

She could hear the dog rushing back through the undergrowth, and in the distance, the voices of walkers heading this way. The body could not be discovered before the other measures had been activated. She looked around for somewhere to hide it and caught sight of a fallen tree trunk covered in moss a little way off the path. With a Herculean effort, she dragged the body over to it, draped the torso over the tree trunk and swung the legs at a 90-degree angle. Then, with a neat trick of crossing the feet at the ankles, twisted the legs and let the momentum the movement created carry his body over the trunk and into the space behind it. She followed the body and crouched in the faded bracken just in time to hear the walkers pass by. That had been close!

She listened, and in the distance, heard the walkers discover the dog. They may well come back to find the owner, so she needed to leave now, the clean-up crew could stage the scene, her work here was almost done. She reached into her other pocket and drew out a folded note detailing why Robert had taken his own life. She tucked it into the right-hand pocket of his trousers and threw his jacket over him to cover the now bloodied shirt.

She stood, took one last look around before heading back towards the slope. It was a thirty-minute hike back to her car, but there was no rush. She pocketed the latex gloves and allowed herself a moment of regret. She had liked Robert; he was bright and passionate, but he was also ethical and honest. The latter were the two traits that were not congruent with their line of work and inevitably created problems. Luckily, his kids were both away at university now, they would deal with the fallout of their father's suicide and move on with their own lives. The clean-up crew would stage it, so there was no doubt in the suicide verdict. Pills and wrists, coupled with the note, there would be no doubt he had taken his own life whilst under enormous pressure and while the balance of his mind was disturbed.

She was breathing heavily when she got back to her car. She took her phone out and replied to the text that had told her Crane was leaving the house with the dog. Her message was short.

"It's done".

The car park was not deserted, there was a couple loading up their brand-new Ford Ka, it was a noisy and chaotic scene. The boot was open, and the man was juggling a small infant with red wellingtons under one arm, whilst trying to collapse the baby buggy with his other arm and right leg. His wife was trying to control a wet and over -excited spaniel dancing around them with a ball in its mouth. They were far too busy to notice her as she slid in behind the wheel of her car. She left as quietly as she had arrived.

3. Ingleby Derbyshire

Saturday 18th January 2020

It had been six months, and it was time to sort things out. Hilary had decided to sell her London flat and make the cottage her proper home, but that had been a hard decision. She wouldn't miss London at all; the dirt, the poor air quality, the congestion charges that extorted money from her for simply having a car. It was a garden flat, and her first home, and it had served a purpose when she had begun her career as a policy advisor in Whitehall. She had used it as a base but had visited the cottage in Derbyshire every holiday or long weekend she had taken. The draw wasn't the cottage or the location but the company. Ada had been her rock, her virtual guardian who had allowed her mother to build her own career without the inconvenience of looking after a young daughter.

As soon as she was able, Hilary's mother packed her off to the best boarding schools, and the holidays were spent with her aunt in Derbyshire. This suited everyone. Hilary and her mother had a difficult relationship, distant and without much warmth. Her mother's sister Ada had willingly taken on caring duties and had treated Hilary as the daughter she had never had.

Their times together had been filled with reading, learning, and laughing. What she really loved about Ada was that she never treated her as a child. She asked her for her opinion about things and when she gave it, she would challenge her thinking, making her explain her reasoning. What that resulted in was a woman driven by critical enquiry, and one who tracked down the solution to problems with a fierce logic and objectivity.

There were plenty of great memories but also the reminder of loss. Ada's papers and belongings needed sorting. Hilary had not been able to bring herself to tackle this task yet but knew it was overdue. As she moved from room to room in the cottage, she let the memories wash over her. The familiarity of her surroundings meant she could have done this blindfolded. Every scrape on the skirting board or wear on a doorknob was like an echo of times they had spent together, laughing, talking, debating, and growing closer.

She looked around Ada's bedroom, the subtle floral pattern on the quilt cover and the single framed photo standing on her dressing table, of the day they spent in Brighton, happy and smiling. These things made it just feminine enough, but not over sentimental. Ada disliked sentiments with a passion. She was a woman who dealt with practicalities and lived in the present. No lotions and potions, just a single pot of Nivea face cream had served her well. She was ninety-three when she passed and scarcely had a wrinkle in her velvety skin. Ada's voice echoed in her head, *"Stop this nonsense and get on with the job in hand!"*

Hilary walked over to the walnut armoire and opened the doors. Ada's familiar perfume wafted out. Penhaligans' Artemisia had been her signature fragrance, with its soft notes of vanilla and nectarine. The image that it conjured when Hilary smelt it was quite unnerving. She could see Ada sitting on the bed reading, so unerringly, that her heart pounded in her chest, she closed her eyes and shook her head to dislodge the image. When she opened them again, she was alone in the room. She broke the silence with a loud sigh,

"For God's sake, Hilary, get a grip. You'll never get this done if you carry on like this".

It was undoubtedly what Ada would have said, and was enough to bring her back to the reality of the moment.

Systematically she emptied the shelves and draws sorting things into piles; keep, charity shop, recycling. Her aunt was never extravagant, but she always bought the best quality she could afford, so there was very little in the recycle pile. There were a few pieces Hilary wanted to keep because they had strong memories attached to them. She would never wear them, but she couldn't bring herself to let them go either. After an hour, the armoire was empty and neatly labelled bags stood by the bedroom door.

Hilary was closing the cabinet doors when something caught her eye. At the bottom of the antique wardrobe was a drawer, just above the plinth that raised it off the floor, and Hilary could see a scrap of cloth or paper poking out, as if something was caught underneath. She'd not noticed it when she emptied the drawer and wondered if something had fallen out and become lodged. She carefully removed the drawer, expecting to see a solid bottom to the cabinet, but there was a hidden cavity and sitting inside was an old wooden box. It looked handmade with delicately crafted hinges, copper banding around the sides and across the lid and a small, engraved clasp on the front. She wondered where it had come from and what her aunt had kept in it. She lifted the box from its hiding place and carried it to the writing table by the window. It was beautiful, smooth, and satin-like to the touch. It was made from burr walnut and had the distinctive dark brown tracery of the natural wood grain. The lid was stiff as if it hadn't been opened in a long time, but with some effort, she popped it open. To her amazement, the bright, tinkling strains of a music box filled the room. She felt along the base of the box and, sure enough, there was the tell-tale key rotating slowly as the mechanism played. She recognised it as Fur Elise by Beethoven, and it drew another smile of remembrance. She had been in her late teens before she realised that the piece was not fleur-de-lis, as she had always thought.

Inside the box was a bundle of letters held together with a thin pale green ribbon. Love letters? Surely not, thought Hilary as she extracted them, before closing the box lid and returning the room to silence.

At first glance, there seemed to be about a dozen separate envelopes, all addressed to Ada at several different addresses, some abroad, some at a PO box and one here at Ingleby. The others looked old, by the style and condition of the stationery. The one, addressed here at the cottage, seemed the most recent.

Hilary hesitated, it felt wrong to read them, they were clearly important letters; otherwise she wouldn't have kept them. They were not official correspondence either, they were personal letters, and she guessed by the ribbon, also of an intimate nature. Ada was not one for frippery, so they were sent from someone she either held in high regard or had feelings for.

Hilary had always assumed that Ada had been a spinster all her life, no partners, lovers, or significant others. Her hand went to her neckline and her fingers traced the gold locket that Ada had given her along with a few other personal effects before she died last year.

Ada had received palliative care at Shady fields for the last weeks of her life, and until that point Hilary had no idea that she had worked for the security services and had even been decorated whilst in the service of her country. She had realised that this woman who had been her guardian, mother figure, confident and friend had aspects of her life that she had kept from Hilary, making her question whether she really knew her aunt at all.

In that last week, she had gleaned the details of her secret life from conversations with her and Daniel, who had worked with her when he first joined the service. This woman who had cared for her in the absence of her real mother, taught her things, fuelled her passions for reading, the arts, and a keen sense of right and wrong was in many ways an unknown quantity.

Hilary touched the small gold locket that she now wore permanently, and her mind went back to that conversation.

"I want you to have this, it was given to me by the only man I ever loved".

She remembered thinking at the time who the man might have been and why Ada had never mentioned him.

What this discovery meant, more importantly, was what had happened to him?

The answer was probably here in her hand. If these letters were from him, what else would she find out about Ada Hale?

4. Andalucía Spain

11th September 2002

Sharon was contemplating whether to skip the last week in Andalucía. The family she had been working for had decided to take their children on a late break before school started and had readied their yacht to sail down to the Canaries Islands. Ramon Navarez had been very generous, giving her an extra month's salary because of the change in plans. She had been employed as an au pair and tutor, keeping his children occupied during the national elections by teaching them English and French. When he had been elected, he felt his wife and the girls needed a treat, and their house in Tenerife beckoned. They came from old money and whilst his success had never really been in question, it was a relief. These were turbulent times, with talk of war in the Middle East and the US involved in ridiculous posturing, threatening to drag Europe into what seemed like a personal vendetta on the part of the current President.

Ramon had questioned Sharon on the role her father appeared to be playing in the unfolding drama, but of course, she could tell him nothing. She had only realised that he was part of the inspection team mission to discover Weapons of Mass Destruction (WMD), when footage of him arriving at Heathrow had appeared on the news a few weeks ago. She had been so absorbed in her romance with Nico, calls home had been with her mother. Her father was always 'away'. She promised herself that she would call today.

It was being reported that the select committee he had appeared at on Tuesday had not gone well for him, and the press were out for blood. She was certain, knowing her father and how important his integrity was, there was more to this situation than met the eye. Her father would never knowingly mislead or exaggerate a situation, as the tabloids were suggesting. He had always been there for her. Perhaps it was time for her to offer him some support. She had a strong feeling that this would not blow over for a while. She might even go home for a visit, but only if her father was at home. Her relationship with her mother had always been strained.

Her brother was clearly her favourite, probably because he was much easier to manipulate than she was, and her mother loved getting her own way. Having this extra week free with pay was a bonus. She wasn't due to be in Greece until the beginning of October, and she could arrange a flight home tomorrow for a long weekend.

Tall, willowy, and strikingly beautiful with long, glossy, dark brown hair, Sharon moved with an effortless grace that was elegant beyond her years. Her flashing eyes showed fierce intelligence that turned to stubbornness in a blink when she was pushed. She suddenly felt a strong urge to see her father, and the decision was made. She rang the home number and waited for it to be answered. After three rings, her father's voice sounded loud and clear.

"Hello, Crane speaking".

"Hi Dad, it's Sharon, how are you?"

"Hello Darling, what a lovely surprise. I am fine, thank you. How are things going, are you still enjoying your job?"

"Yes, everything is fine. I just wanted to check you were okay, the newspapers have been horrible".

"Yes, I'm fine. It is, what it is. Can't really say too much, but it will get sorted".

"The Navarez family have decided to take a break now the elections have finished, so they are sailing to the Canaries for a holiday. They don't need me. Señores Navarez has given me an extra month's salary and ended my contract early, so I'm at a loose end. I want to come home for a few days before starting in Greece, would that be okay?"

"Of course it will Sharon, you don't have to ask, although it will be a bit of a circus here. I could get called back to London at a minute's notice, but it will be good to have a bit of sanity around here for a few days. Your mother will be thrilled too".

"Yes, of course she will". Sharon said unconvincingly.

Her father laughed.

"She does miss you, darling, even though she may not show it. When will you get here?"

"My flight gets in on Friday morning, so I will see you for lunch, with any luck".

"Okay darling. Have a safe flight and I'll see you Friday". The line went dead.

Sharon felt so much better having spoken to her father. She was really looking forward to spending a couple of days with him walking Nero. He had sounded a tired and a bit preoccupied, which was understandable given his situation, so she was pleased she had taken the decision to visit. She turned and looked at the pile of clothes on her bed and decided she better start packing.

Her personal belongings were already packed in crates, which were being forwarded by air freight to Greece, so she just needed a carry-on bag for a few days. It would save endless waiting in the baggage hall. Her flight was uneventful and by the time she landed at the airport and passed through customs, it was 11.30 am. It would take a train and a taxi to get home, and that meant she wouldn't be there until at least 1 pm, but at least she would be in time for lunch. It was a good job she had a decent book with her. Faced with a choice at the airport of the latest Patricia Cornwall or James Patterson's 'Four Blind Mice' she had chosen 'Blowfly' because she loved the gritty heroine: Blonde, a sharp dresser, with a wardrobe of designer suits. Cornwall's creation, Kay Scarpetta was a perfectionist and workaholic. She loved to cook, particularly Italian food, and made everything from scratch, including pasta and bread. She had a beautiful home built to her specifications, including a restaurant kitchen. She drove a Mercedes, which she replaced often. Here was a woman that Sharon could identify with, she set her own rules and was no observer of the glass ceiling in a world clearly dominated by men. She competed with them on their ground and with their advantages, and still won every time. Not a bad role model, in fact.

Her father would smile and just shake his head, asking why she wasn't reading a proper book. She was lucky in that she could read whilst she travelled. It didn't matter whether she was in a car or train or taxi, she could read without adverse effects, unlike her mother who only had to look at a newspaper whilst she was in motion to be overcome with the worst biliousness that rendered her bedridden for two days when she returned home.

Malvern

Sitting in the back of the taxi, she slipped a bookmark between the pages of her book; she never turned the corner down; she was no psychopath! She slid it into her tote bag and readied herself to see her family. They were now just minutes from home, and as they turned into the lane, she saw flashing blue lights. Her heart came into her mouth, her anxiety level rocketed. Had something happened to her mother? The taxi driver drew up at the end of the drive and went to the boot to retrieve her bag. She fumbled in her purse and passed him two notes without waiting for change, then rushed down the drive and in through the open front door.

A uniformed officer standing in the hall put his arm out to stop her in her tracks.

"I am sorry you can't come in here miss, who are you?"

"I am Sharon Crane and I live here. What the hell is going on?"

"Please wait here, miss. I will ask the Inspector to have a word with you".

He disappeared into the living room, and Sharon followed directly behind him. There was total relief when she saw her mother sitting bolt upright on the sofa.

"Mum, what's going on?"

"Sharon darling, I am so glad you are here. It's your father; he's gone missing".

"What do you mean gone missing? I only spoke with him on Wednesday, gone missing where?"

Her mother looked a little vacant, Sharon grabbed both of her arms and gave her a little shake.

"Mother, what happened?"

Abigail Crane took a deep breath, she felt numb, she knew she needed to hold it together until they found him.

"He took Nero out for a walk yesterday afternoon and never came home. I got worried and sent Colin to look for him, but there was nothing, so we called the police at 9.0 pm last night. They came out to see me straight away, but by then it was dark, and they could not search properly. They came back with more officers and started to look for him at 8.0 am this morning. He took his walking pole. They have been searching the hills for him, but nothing yet. I'm worried that he might have fallen and couldn't call for help. Colin is out helping, and they called in a dog search unit earlier, so I'm sure they will find him. They are worried about his mental state of mind because of everything that's gone on recently".

Her mothers' hands began to shake, and Sharon rubbed at them, they were unnaturally cold.

"Let me put the kettle on, I'll make some tea, then you can tell me exactly what has been going on".

A tall man in a dark suit with short greying hair came into the lounge.

"Hello Miss Crane, I am Inspector Beech, I am leading the search for your father, I wonder if I could ask you a few questions?"

Sharon looked at him

"Hello, I have questions for you too, Inspector. My mother is in shock, she needs a cup of tea at once. When I have seen to her, then I will be happy to chat to you".

The Inspector smiled at her.

"I quite understand, but let my WPC make the tea, and we can chat in the meantime".

He led her by the arm across the hallway and into the deserted dining room. He called to the WPC to make tea for her mother, then feeling he had done what he needed to, turned to Sharon, gestured for her to sit at the polished oak dining table and closed the door behind them.

Before he could say anything, Sharon launched her attack.

"I want to know what the hell is going on — NOW! I arrive home to this… circus; my mother is obviously in great distress, no one is looking after her, my father can't be found, the doors are all open, apparently you have search dogs out looking for him. If you are in charge, then kindly tell me what the bloody hell is going on?"

The door opened and the WPC came in and put two hot mugs of tea on the table and left. Sharon lifted them up crossly, sliding a couple of coasters onto the polished tabletop, before setting them down again. The Inspector looked embarrassed.

"Sorry about that. So, when was the last time you spoke to your father, Sharon?"

Sharon huffed.

"I spoke with him on Wednesday to tell him I was coming for a visit because my contract had ended sooner than expected".

He took a notebook out and began to write stuff down.

"And how did he seem to you?"

"He was absolutely fine. He has not had a good couple of weeks with the enquiry, and he seemed a bit tired, but not overly stressed by it all".

The Inspector continued to write without looking up.

"So, you don't think he may do something to harm himself?"

Sharon felt a surge of anger begin swirling in the pit of her stomach and realised her face was beginning to flush.

"If that weren't such an offensive suggestion, I would laugh. My father is a highly intelligent and resourceful man. He comes from a generation where you face your difficulties head on. He wouldn't run away from them, and he certainly would not consider taking his own life, if that is what you are implying. He has probably had a fall and is lying somewhere, unable to call for help. You must find him". Her voice had a tremor in it.

He finally looked at her.

"We are doing our very best, Miss Crane; we have a dog unit up on the hills now, so it shouldn't be long. When you spoke to him on Wednesday, what did you talk about?"

"I called to tell him I was coming for a visit and gave him the details of my flight and how long I wanted to stay".

"Did he talk about the problems he was having at work, Miss Crane?"

"No, he never discusses his work with any of us, not even my mother. His work is highly sensitive and extremely technical. We wouldn't understand most of it anyway. I asked him how he felt about the public enquiry last week, but he dismissed it and told me not to worry about it. I knew it would have been difficult for him because they were questioning his integrity, but he would never rise to that. He was looking forward to me coming home".

The Inspector paused, clearly trying to phrase his next question carefully.

"Where does your father keep his papers, Miss Crane?"

"His office at work, I expect. He certainly doesn't keep anything here, if that is what you are implying.

Most of what he does is governed by the Official Secrets Act, he would not bring anything classified into our home. Now if there is nothing else, I need to be with my mother".

She stood to leave the room, then looked back at the Inspector

"Where's Nero?"

"The dog?"

"Yes, the bloody dog! If Dad had taken him out and had an accident, he would have sent Nero back home to get help. They have walked the woods and hills for years together, they know every path and track. If he were able, Nero would have raised the alarm".

She crossed the hall and went straight over to her mother. She sat down next to her on the sofa, reaching out for her hand. Her Mother stiffened as she took hold of her icy fingers.

"You are cold, Mum; can I get you anything?"

Her mother looked straight ahead, not even acknowledging that she had heard a word she'd just said.

"What's been happening, Mum?"

"Your father had been agitated since the hearing, he was worried about his job and the telephone ringing at all hours, people wanting to speak to him. The press has been hounding him too. One even turned up at the door the other morning, but he sent him packing. He needed to clear his head, so even though he had taken

Nero for a walk in the morning like normal, he decided to take him again yesterday afternoon. He had taken a call, the office I think, and he got really angry. He called for Nero, and they left the house at about 1.30 pm. When he hadn't come back at 4.30 pm, I began to worry. I sent Colin out to look for him but nothing, so at 9 pm when there was still no sign of him, I called the police again, and they sent someone around".

"You said you called the police again at 9 o'clock, what time did you call them first?"

"Colin called them at 5.30 pm, but they said it was too early to do anything".

"Where's Colin now?"

"When the dog search unit arrived, he went out with them to show them the normal routes they take when they go walking".

"How has Dad really been, Mum? Has he really been okay with what was going on at work?"

"You know your father, Sharon. He never discusses his work, but I do know he was anxious about something. He was preoccupied, obviously stressed, and he was drinking more heavily than normal. I have been really worried about him, about his frame of mind".

"Mother, you're not suggesting he might do something stupid, are you?" Sharon shook her head as if trying to dislodge the very idea.

"Dad would never do anything like that, he loves us too much for one thing, and he would never lose his perspective in that way. He would know that it wouldn't solve anything. It would make him look as if he were guilty of what they are suggesting, and he would never tolerate that".

Her mother turned on her.

"How would you know, you are never here, are you? That's typically of you, you always take his side. Like Bobbsey Twins, stick together like glue". Her mother looked accusingly at her.

"You think the sun shines out of him, but you don't know what it's been like for me. He's not been easy to live with, and God knows I have tried. He buries himself in work, then takes it out on me when it all goes wrong. I have put up with his philandering, his inflated sense of duty and his lack of ambition. He's not the saint you make him out to be, Sharon, and the sooner you realise that the better!" She rushed from the room and up the stairs, Sharon heard her sitting room door slam. She was stunned by her mother's outburst. The inspector popped his head around the door.

"Is everything okay, Miss Crane?"

"Yes, thanks, Mum's just having a bit of a meltdown, it's the worry. She'll be fine once you have done your job and found my father".

She walked to the window that looked out across the lawns and the hills rising from the lane that skirted the bottom of their garden. A man and a woman were talking to the police constable she had met on her arrival. They were dressed for a day in the office rather than a walk in the hills. Sharon guessed they must be something to do with the police, and yet something in their body language seemed off. They were speaking quickly and gesturing towards the path that led into the woods. Then, if her father had been there, he would have said 'the balloon went up!'

The constable ran into the house, calling for the Inspector. She noticed a figure coming along the path, and realised it was her brother Colin. His posture was hunched, his face was ashen, and he was clearly in shock. She ran outside to meet him.

"Colin, what's wrong? Have they found him?"

"Yes sis, they have, and he's dead".

With that short sentence, Sharon Cranes' world changed forever.

5. Undisclosed location - Somewhere in London

2020

In 2018, Vector 10 released the first batch of confidential government documents to the press about the existence of UK government surveillance programmes of other nations. The establishments were rightly incensed, but only because they had been found out.

It is precisely why the whole thing had started.

Vector 10 had embarked on a passionate mission to cause mayhem, motivated by an unquestioning enthusiasm for the protection and preservation of democracy. It was based on anger triggered by the blatant dishonesty and deceitful double-dealing of governments who had abused their power for decades. They had plumbed the depths of corruption whilst presenting the illusion of democracy and serving their self-interest. It was a direct threat to the accountability of parliament, and Vector 10 decided that serious action was needed.

There are two irrefutable indicators that tell you when democracy is under threat. Firstly, a clear lack of engagement in the political decision-making process, which weakens democracy when citizens feel that their elected representatives do not actually represent them and cannot be held to account for their actions. The longer it is allowed to go unchecked, the more blatant their MP's behaviour becomes.

Secondly, when technology is used to issue only a single viewpoint as fact, it polarizes the country, and its effects are felt across all sections of society. A population is much easier to control when it's divided, distracted, and fighting among itself.

According to many legal experts who were interviewed on mainstream media after the first batch of classified documents were released, Vector 10's actions had clearly violated the Official Secrets Act of 1911, making the action treasonable. The death penalty for treason was an urban myth, but if caught and found guilty, the sentence was life imprisonment. Despite this, Vector 10 felt a moral obligation to act, and there was also the money, of course.

Once the process to access the information had been established, it was simple to leak the documents into the public domain and watch the chaos that ensued. Unlawful acts had been committed by their government, in their name, which were shameful, yet it was not the policymakers and politicians who suffered the consequences, it was ordinary people. They had been dragged into false wars, their quality of life had been damaged by artificially created divides expertly manipulated and amplified by mainstream and social media. Less powerful nations were being exploited for their resources, just because they were unable to resist.

The point of no return came when Vector 10 realised that the government were deciding who was able to make money under their system and who stayed poor. Because of the fraudulent way they operated, they had breached their own and international laws and placed themselves beyond accountability. The effects of their actions were engineered to diminish and remove people's freedoms and liberties. It was not until the second batch of secret files were released that the government realised their security had been compromised, and they were being hacked.

Old government data files were routinely archived to a server at a secure location to minimise storage space on live systems. Vector 10 used a software RAT, a Remote Access Tool, to hack the legacy system, and embed an innocuous programme that piggybacked onto a maintenance file, whose job was to cleanse duplicate files from the system.

Sifting through batches of discarded data to see what merited being shared with the public was a job for a clever algorithm that targeted keywords and phrases. Taking screenshots of the data selected by the algorithm left no trace of the incursion into this secret world of lies and spin. It's what digital backdoors were made for, and there was no doubt that the information uncovered would cause maximum embarrassment and panic when it was released.

The second batch comprised intimate details of corruption and back-room dealings that incriminated public servants, politicians, industrialists, celebrities and even one of the lesser royals. By then, Vector 10 was casting the net wider, looking at all manner of corruption. No Government department was safe, HMRC, the National Archives, the Foreign and Commonwealth Office, they had all unwittingly opened their dirty secrets to this unwelcome visitor.

Vector 10 felt invigorated, a modern-day Nemesis, the avenger of crime and the punisher of hubris. How apt, then, that those who felt their birthright, position or fortune placed them above the law, were now facing exposure and subsequently, retribution. They could only do what they did and get away with it because of the smokescreen that rendered them invisible. Someone had to remove the protection of anonymity and bring their actions and deeds into the spotlight. Vector 10 was happy to accept that mantle.

Rufus Hurst, a journalist of legendary reputation who had broken some of the biggest stories in the last forty years using any means necessary, had been the recipient of this information. He was a one-off, detested by those he targeted. News editors found him a law unto himself, and fellow journalists admired and despised him in equal measure. By his own admission, the only qualities essential for real success in journalism were rat-like cunning, a plausible manner, a flawed moral compass, and a little literary ability thrown in for good measure. He made the perfect receiver for Vector 10, as he never questioned his source or the legality of what was being done. All he was concerned about was his own liberty, and that he stayed just on the right side of the law. Vector 10 had kept him supplied with information, so he never asked for more, ensuring that he was reporting information not procuring it.

6 Shady Fields

Saturday 18th January 2020

The Director General of British Security Services Daniel Grant breathed a sigh of relief as he ascended the main staircase of Shady Fields. This beautiful period property had a rich history imprinted in these walls, and they had been lucky to secure it for their project. In 2016, his boss Celia Browning had visited him in hospital after his last mission had gone horribly wrong. He had been shot and left for dead. The damage was so extensive that he knew he would never see active service again.

He hated the idea of a desk job, but she had turned up and offered him an exceptional project. She wanted him to create a residential home and safe house for former MI5 and MI6 agents who had reached retirement age, an achievement in its own right, but who carried in their heads, the details of missions that were still governed by the official secrets act. Celia's idea was to create Shady Fields as a haven for those who had given their whole life in service to protect our way of life. That was her project, and he was charged with making it happen. It was a complex and costly project, and he had delivered it, but, what he had not appreciated at the time was that Celia already knew that early onset Alzheimer's was her diagnosis and that one day soon, she would become a resident there herself.

He didn't realise it at the time, but he was her succession plan. She had prepared him to take over when she needed to step down. The difficulty was, that whilst he was wedded to the mission of the Security Services, he hated the politics of his role. He struggled to come to terms with politicians and civil servants who saw the world as a personal chessboard, and where their decisions had no lasting consequences. Someone had to keep the service honest, but that was much more difficult than he had realised.

Now here he was on the way to see if Celia was settling in. Daniel knocked softly on the door of apartment twenty-two and listened. He could hear someone moving about, so he knew she was at home. He waited a few seconds before knocking again, this time a little louder. The door opened and Celia stood in the doorway, looking blankly at him.

"Hi Celia, I thought I'd leave you for a day or two to get settled before I made a social call. How are you?"

"Hi Daniel, nice to see you. Kind of you to come and visit me".

He looked around the neat room, everything was in place like she'd been here a year. Interestingly, though, he noted that there was no personal object d'art at all. More like a hotel room than a home.

"Have you got everything you need?"

"Yes, thank you. Hilary has been very efficient, and I spoke to my children this morning, so everything is fine. They are still cross with me because they don't understand why I have chosen to come here rather than going to live with them, but it's my decision. The reality is that I don't really know them, and they certainly don't know me. It would be like living with strangers. I am much better here, left to my own devices and in a safe place as my condition deteriorates".

She said it with such detachment that Daniel just stared at her.

"Celia, it doesn't sound like you are talking about your life, surely their feelings need to be considered too. The last thing you need is to create a rift, given your circumstances. Your feelings may change as time goes by".

She blinked at him, and he really wasn't sure who this person was in front of him.

"Daniel, let's go for a walk in the garden".

She grabbed a cashmere cardigan, threw it around her shoulders and breezed past him towards the door. He closed the door and followed in her wake. They walked down the staircase, across the hall and out through the back of the house heading for the garden room.

Daniel had huge respect for Celia. She had given him a project just when his life needed purpose, then recommended him as her successor when she retired last year. She was a brilliant strategist and consummate politician, and used her time as Director General of the UK Secret Services to modernize and integrate systems to provide a much more comprehensive approach to intelligence gathering.

Modern terrorism is not fought toe-to-toe by secret agents in the field, as it once was. It was a digital cat and mouse game, where high-tech surveillance and control of big data ensured that any threat was discovered before it became an attack. Whilst covert human intelligence was still employed, electronic surveillance was now so sophisticated it had become virtually impossible to launch large-scale operations on a world power without being discovered in the planning stage.

Daniel was currently trying to understand the latest form of data-manipulation known as 'Deep Faking', which used Artificial Intelligence (AI), to manipulate images and video to the degree that it was almost impossible to tell false information from reality.

It wasn't new technology, it had been around for a couple of decades, but the new iterations were now so incredibly sophisticated, that it took mere seconds to damage the credibility of a world leader, a politician, or industrialist, to the point where they could effectively be 'cancelled' from society and rendered a non-person. Deep-Fake AI had the capability to remove a potential enemy or a perceived threat with just a few keystrokes.

It was becoming difficult to detect the real villains and counteract the effects that a 'fake news strike' could cause. Smoke and mirrors don't even begin to describe the nature of counter-intelligence in the modern world and no matter how fast the security services seemed to respond, technological innovation was always two steps ahead.

When Celia had prepared her handover to him, she had highlighted this as one of the coming challenges he would need to get to grips with.

"These are difficult times, Daniel, made all the more difficult by not always being able to trust what your eyes see, and your ears hear".

It was also becoming more difficult to recruit the very best university graduates to populate MI5, MI6 and technology support like they had done in the past. The rewards available in the private sector were much higher; better money, better benefits and organisations who realised that job enrichment was what they had to provide to keep their brightest and best on board.

Daniel was feeling decidedly pessimistic, and he knew it could only get worse. Millennials were the last generational group who felt a strong connection between their chosen profession and their sense of personal identity. They and future generations would expect a high degree of flexibility and balance in their work, with many demanding remote working options and four-day weeks. Work related mental health issues had become the hot topic. How can you recruit members of a generation who believe that their employer should do everything to provide a stress-free working environment, in a job where PTSD is seen as an occupational hazard? The services needed to recruit people who were both mentally and physical resilient, fit, fearless, and curious, and who possessed the ability to take risks where the outcomes were just not known. You couldn't get a description further away from that when you looked at the definitions of Generation Z.

He shook himself out of the flunk he was in. Celia had clearly wanted to speak to him privately, and he was intrigued. He was not sure if her subterfuge was necessary or imagined, but this was Celia. The fondness he felt for this woman who had helped shape his career surprised him. He was not a sentimentalist, but he had been deeply saddened by her Alzheimer's diagnosis, and he was determined not to let a medical label change their relationship.

They exited the building through the large French doors and stepped onto the paved terrace. She slipped her arms into the sleeves of the cardigan, pulling it tight around her slim frame, and tying the belt with some force. Then she trotted down the steps and onto the path that led into the grounds. Daniel had no choice but to follow.

When they reached the centre of the open lawns, Celia stopped and turned to look at Daniel.

"I am not going to beat around the bush, Daniel, I need your help. I have in my possession an insurance policy in the form of a series of documents from past missions that still have the potential to do damage on a national stage, if not a global one. Some are originals and some are copies, but all of them serve one of two purposes. There are those that I have kept purely for self-preservation. You will know by now that a Director General deals with the very best and the very worst of humanity, and sometimes the only way to distinguish the difference is by situation. The second purpose is to temper the ambitions of the megalomaniacs and power-hungry bullies we are sometimes forced to deal with that can still wreak havoc in the world. I need you to take possession of my insurance policy and keep it safe until I am no longer here. I cannot risk a traditional safe hold like a solicitor, which is not always the honourable profession it paints itself to be. I need you to hold it because only you will know when and if you need to use its contents. You are also the only one I trust not to destroy it".

Daniel shook his head.

"I am not the person you should be speaking to Celia; I am the current Director General, and it's my job to act on intelligence that comes my way because it's the right thing to do. Personal allegiances and friendships cannot be prioritized over the duty of my role. You know that. You were the one who gave it to me, for Gods' sake".

A smile played around her lips.

"Yes, I did, Daniel, and that is precisely why I am extracting this 'favour' from you. I would not be as crass as to suggest that you owe me, but you do. You were the best person for the job, but you also know how the system works. Our rules are 'flexible' for a reason. No one plays by the gentleman's agreement like they did fifty years ago. The world has been exposed to Al-Qaeda, Putin and Google. We are about to redefine our world and how it functions through Artificial Intelligence. The lines of engagement are being redrawn, and we need to stockpile any weapons we can get, to fight off the enemy. My insurance policy is one of those weapons".

Daniel tried a different tack.

"If I accept stewardship of this insurance policy, will it compromise me in my role if I read it?"

Her smile broadened.

"Of course it will, that is sort of the point".

He felt like he was standing on shifting sand.

"Why can't you entrust Peter King with it. He is the best analyst we have ever had. The man knows how to bury secrets, so they can never be found. Plus, I would trust him with my life".

"And that is your prerogative Daniel, I might trust him with your life, but not with mine. He is part of the insurance policy. There really is no alternative, so please get with the programme and consider how you will tackle this request. You do know that when you have retired and are facing an uncertain future, you will also have this conversation with your protégé because that is the way this game is played. World leaders, heads of secret services and diplomatic services across the world have similar arrangements. You can't expect to make a career out of mud-wrestling pigs without getting dirty, Daniel. The folder and USB stick that accompanies it are in my room now, please come back with me and take them away".

"I haven't agreed that I will yet". But it was said in such a half-hearted way that even Daniel was unconvinced.

"Daniel, this is tiresome. Of course, you will take it, just like I did before you and my predecessor did before me. Failure in this job at some time is inevitable but giving up is unforgivable. Some of it you already know anyway, and I fear that none of it will surprise you, that is also inevitable".

They walked back to the house in silence, both lost in their own thoughts. Daniel disliked being put on the spot like this, and he was aware that she was pushing their friendship to the limit by asking him to do this. He had wanted to change the culture of security services; it was why he had decided to take the job, and that meant doing things differently. Just because his predecessors had colluded with each other to keep shadier actions and decisions secret, it didn't mean that he would go along with it. Their job was secrecy and deception, but always in the defence of the nation, not to protect dubious actions or poor leadership.

When she handed him the folder, he took it reluctantly and went straight back to the office he used when he was in shady fields. It was Saturday, therefore quiet, and he would not be disturbed. He needed time to think and consider his next move carefully. The moment he read the file, there would be no going back. You could not un-know something, and certainly not something of that gravity.

It was a distraction he could do without, and yet now it was in his possession he felt an irresistible pull to read it. It lay on the desk, challenging him to open it. He buckled, and opened the faded manilla folder, selecting the first document in the pile. It was an email thread between the Prime Minister's office and the former Director General of Security Services, dated 2001. It described a clandestine agreement called the Tripartite Treaty. Its purpose was to reshape the geopolitical landscape of the Middle East by aligning Iran with the interests of the United States, the United Kingdom, and Russia.

The email exchange detailed what was at stake, if the treaty could exert influence over Iran's government, the treaty members could establish a dominant position in the region and counterbalance other powerful nations in the Middle East. The Tripartite Treaty was about the control of the Middle East. The fly in the ointment seemed to be the

Russians. It was clear that neither the US nor the UK had trusted the Russian regime since Putin took power. He was a loose cannon and notoriously fickle, and seemed hell-bent on restoring Mother Russia as a global power.

Daniel was shocked by the content of the emails, not because of the plotting, but that they had been arrogant enough to commit it to an electronic system with an audit trail. What he held in his hand was political dynamite and categoric proof of political collusion to usurp power from sovereign nations. If this was just one document, he was sure he didn't want to read the rest

7. The Crane Residence

Friday 13th September 2002

Sharon felt numb. She looked across at her brother, hoping he would say that it was all a mistake, but she knew by the look on his face that it was not about to happen. He was ashen, his cheeks sunken, dark circles had appeared under his eyes. He had obviously been crying. She had never seen Colin cry, even as a little kid he would clench his fists until his nails dug into his palms to stop him shedding a tear.

Their mother sat bolt upright in the fireside chair just staring into the distance, immobile and without any emotion on her face at all, just frozen. Sharon walked over to her brother and wrapped her arms around him, hugging him. She could feel him trembling. She pulled back from him and, looking him in the eyes, said.

"You need a drink. Let's go into the study".

She led him down the passage and into the quiet space that was her fathers' sanctuary. When things became tense between her parents, this was always the place he headed for. Her mother was more likely to storm out of the house and go for a drive to escape. Yet another example of how different they were.

She moved across to the bookshelf with the leaded glass doors and, reaching in, removed two cut glass tumblers and a bottle of Glenmorangie Single Malt whiskey. She poured them both a good measure and pushed his across the desk to where he sat in his father's old leather chair.

Sharon took a sip of the golden liquid. She loved the smell more than the taste but had persevered because it was her fathers' drink of choice. He would add a dribble of water to his, explaining that it helped to release the oils in the whiskey and soften the taste, but they had no water, so just for now it would have to be neat.

"What happened Col?" Her mother hated her shortening her brother's name, but she had never seen him as a Colin. He was an attractive young man, ash blond hair and grey eyes, with a playfulness about him that she envied. She was the one who had inherited her father's seriousness.

He swirled the drink around the glass, looking deep into the amber liquid as if at any moment it would produce an answer that explained what he had just seen.

"I had gone up to the hill path with Officer Priestley and his dog to see if he could pick up a scent. He wasn't very hopeful because of the weather conditions, but I showed him where Dad usually walks Nero. We had been searching for about an hour when he had a call on the radio to say they had found something. We'd already doubled back on ourselves by then, and I knew the spot they mentioned, so I took the track across the style and into the woods. Nero would never cross the style, but his German shepherd was better trained and went straight over. We met a couple coming out of the wood who said they had discovered a body, and the dog handler had asked them to come down to the house to give a statement. He was going to wait for help to arrive. As we walked further along the path, I could see a couple of other coppers, one had a spaniel on a lead and the other was trying to calm Nero down. He was going mad, barking at him. As I got closer, I could see that he was guarding Dad". He took a gulp of whiskey without tasting it, but the spirit hit had the desired effect. It shocked a bit of life into him, focusing his attention on what he had seen. He took a deep breath and continued.

"He was sprawled out, flat on his back, with his eyes open. I knew he was dead. His shirt was splattered with blood. When I looked at his arms, I realised ….. He had cut his wrists, Sharon".

Colin broke down and began to sob like a baby. Sharon rushed to his side, sitting on the arm of his chair, pulling him close to her to offer comfort, but his words had a terrible effect on her too. Emotions ran riot through her, questions tumbled through her mind, tangled together, not making any sense at all. Before she knew what was happening, they had both sunk to the floor, clinging to each other and sobbing… uncontrollably.

Minutes passed, or was it just a few seconds? Colin's breathing steadied and began to regain some control. He pulled away from her and wiped his face on his jumper.

"I need to go to Mum, just to see how she is doing".

He got to his feet and picked up the now empty glass, placing it back on the desk. It must have fallen to the floor when he slipped from the chair. He left the room searching for their mother, and Sharon also stood; she needed some fresh air to clear her head. She made her way to the back of the house and into the boot room to find her jacket. It hung next to where her father's coat would normally have hung. She felt another surge of emotion welling up, so she grabbed her coat and burst out of the door. Pulling her wax jacket around her, she became aware of the musty smell it had acquired from lack of use. She wasn't the only thing that needed some fresh air to blow the cobwebs away. She strode off purposely through the garden and down towards the orchard.

The effects of the brisk walk and being outdoors began to have the desired effect. Her breathing became more focused, and her heart rate steadied. By the time she reached the orchard gate, she felt that she was back in control once again. She was struggling to believe that she would never see him again, never chat or laugh or argue with him once more. That couldn't be right. They had so much unfinished business between them, he needed to help with career decisions, tell her which boyfriends were no match for her, he needed to walk her down the aisle and love his future grandchildren. He needed to come back right now! She hadn't finished learning from him yet. Sharon felt a hard lump grow in her throat, it physically hurt, and the only relief was to let the tears flow again, but this time in a quieter way that she found strangely soothing. She felt tension leave her chest and allowed memories of him to flood into her mind.

The first thing that popped into her head that she could grab onto was the day she had learned how to use a memory palace to store important information. She didn't realise what it was at the time; she would be a teenager before she realised the value of such a technique. She had been about seven years old; it was the big summer holiday break, and she was pestering him to play with her.

"Sharon, how would you like to play a new game?" She jumped at the chance.

"Do you know what a memory palace is?" She shook her head in awe, her eyes opening wide.

"It's an easy way of remembering many important things. Would you like to create one in your head so that you can store your memories and important facts in it?"

Sharon nodded eagerly.

When people use a memory palace, they often create an imaginary location to store their mnemonic images, the pictures of the important things or people or events that they love or need to remember. Sharon decided to use her favourite place, her father's study because that was where she loved spending time and that's where he taught her how to use it. The bookshelves gave her plenty of space and reference points to link names and things to.

Her father had walked her around the room with a bag of her favourite soft toys and asked her to place them in specific spots. Then, he sat her in his leather chair, placed a light blindfold around her eyes and asked her to tell him what to retrieve and from where. She remembered the feeling of anticipation as he retrieved the toys according to her instructions, hoping she had remembered correctly. She had squealed with delight when he revealed every one of the toys back in the bag. They played the game regularly throughout that holiday, but she didn't really need to. She had picked up the concept immediately, and as she grew up, began to realise that it was the secret of her success with exams. She ace'd any exam she sat by adopting the memory palace approach to her studies. She had once asked him where his memory palace was, and he had replied,

"A Sultans' palace in Dhofar".

She remembered how grand and mysterious it had sounded.

"Why a palace in a faraway place, Daddy?"

He had just smiled at her and replied.

"It needs to be a place where your heart feels at home, and you remember every stick of furniture, every room and passage without any effort".

That was also why Sharon had chosen his study for her memory palace.

She breathed deeply and headed across to the bench in the corner of the orchard, sheltered by the tall hedge that ran along the bottom boundary. She sat on the hard wooden slats and pulled her coat around her slim frame. There was something niggling away at her that she couldn't put her finger on. It didn't make sense that her father would commit suicide. That was not who he was! He would face down his problems, not run away from them. He loved them all too much to leave them in this way. When she last spoke to him to tell him she was coming home, there was no hint that he was depressed or suicidal. He was angry, yes, but not suicidal.

If he was that desperate and had taken himself off to do this terrible deed, then why had he taken Nero? He doted on the dog and certainly wouldn't have done that with the dog in tow. She could not let this go, she would find the Inspector and tell him what she thought. She couldn't have people think the wrong things about her father. Someone had done this to him, and they should be searching for the culprit.

She heard footsteps in the lane on the other side of the hedge and lowered voices. Whoever it was didn't know that she was there. The Inspector spoke first,

"We haven't found anything yet, but we are still searching. The wife isn't much use, still in shock." A woman's voice replied.

"I called him yesterday, but he was very evasive, all he said was evidence that he had that he refused to hand over. He was very angry."

The inspector spoke again, but the voices became quieter as they moved away, back towards the house. "Will the wife comply with the verdict, do you think?" The woman again "she will not want to rock the boat, his reputation and pensions remain intact as long as ……" They faded away".

When Sharon was sure they had gone, she made her way back to the house. People were milling around, and there was a steady stream of police officers coming out of the house with some of her father's belongings in large polythene bags. She pushed past them and into the kitchen, where the Inspector was standing, deep in conversation with a woman. She was mid-height, slim build, with brown hair cut in a precise bob. They stopped talking and looked at her when she entered the room.

"And this is Professor Cravens' daughter, Sharon, Ma'am". The Inspector said a little too loudly.

The woman took a few steps towards her

"Hello Miss Crane, Celia Browning, I am so sorry for your loss. I am with the Foreign office, and I have been sent to see if there is anything your family needs at such a difficult time?"

She looked intently at Sharon, waiting for an answer, but Sharon didn't know how to respond to that.

"Where is my mother?"

The woman was observing Sharon closely, looking for involuntary micro-expressions.

"The Police doctor is with her, he has given her a sedative. She is understandably distressed by today's events. He felt it was best for her to rest a while, particularly while the search takes place".

"What search? Why are you taking my father's things?"

The Inspector intervened.

"In a case like this with your father's position and recent events, we need to check that there is no sensitive material he may have left behind. It's a matter of National Security, and we need to be sure that he has not been compromised as a result of the parliamentary dossier that he wrote".

The woman rolled her eyes and quickly interjected.

"What the Inspector means is we have to be sure that any sensitive material he has been working on recently is returned to secure storage. Your father's work was critical, and we need to know that proper measures have been taken to ensure there are no classified documents left in the house. I know it's difficult, but if we do this now, we can leave you and your family in peace to deal with this awful situation. Is there anyone we can call to be with you; a family friend or relative to support you all?"

The woman's words were right, but there was no care or emotion in them, it was clear she was just following some protocol that she had trotted out before to some other bereaved family. Sharon pulled a chair out and sat at the kitchen table.

"He never bought work home, and certainly not classified papers. You would know that if you worked with him. He always said that he would not put us at risk in that way, so you are wasting your time. You would be far better trying to find out who did this to him because one thing is for sure, my father was murdered. There is no way he committed suicide".

There was no drama in the way she said it, just a level and factual statement. As the two officials looked at each other, something silently passed between them, although Sharon could not tell what it was.

"I know you are upset, but our SOCO team are quite sure that your father did take his own life. There was a note found in his pocket. If you consider the pressure he was under recently, it is understandable".

The woman feigned sympathy with her head on one side, but Sharon was not taken in.

"You don't know him. He would never do such a thing. And it just doesn't add up".

"What do you mean, what doesn't add up? The woman's eyes narrowed".

Sharon scanned the room trying to put her suspicions into words but came up with nothing. After a short pause, she blurted out

"What about Nero, have you bought him back yet?"

The Inspector came forward.

"Yes, he's with your mother and brother, he was guarding your father's body".

"I am telling you that my father loved Nero like a child and there is no way that if he was going to do what you are suggesting, he would have taken Nero with him. The idea is as absurd as suggesting he would have taken me along. Something else is going on here, and I intend to find out what".

"I understand how hard this is for you to accept, but as I said, your father left a note explaining his reasons".

Sharon stuck her chin out in defiance.

"I want to see it. I want to see what he said to us when he decided to abandon us".

Celia Browning gave her a stare that was devoid of emotion.

"I am sorry, but that is not possible. It is evidence for the coroner".

She turned and left the room.

8. The Swiss Lounge, Geneva

6th January 2020

They had to be careful about meeting in public places because someone always recognised them. Adam Hunt's security detail was a dead giveaway, but he also had one of the most famous faces in the world. An ex-Prime Minister of the UK meant he had lived a decade of his life being visible to the world 24/7. His ex-Chief of Staff Stewart Pearson was equally familiar, but that was more to do with the scandal that ended their association rather than anything else. He had publicly fallen on his sword so that Adam could walk away relatively unscathed, yet there was no doubt that the clean image, good-guy in politics-for-all-the-right-reasons, building a new way forward, fixing a broken system had been tarnished.

They were still a pair with very close associations, but there was nothing that could formally link them any more. That would make things too complicated. When they met it was either in passing or by chance at an event and onlookers might say they greeted each other, occasionally shared a lunch then parted, but it was no more than that.

What people didn't realise was that this was an inner circle of such power and influence, that there were few world leaders who would refuse to take a call or grant a meeting to the self-styled Diplomatic Envoy that was Lord Adam Hunt, a Life Peer. A perk of the job that every ex-Prime Minister received for his service.

Consequently, this meeting was taking place at The Swiss Lounge in the Palais de Nations in Geneva. High above the drone of conversation, three large frescoes peered down from three windowless walls. These masterpieces were created by the Swiss artist Karl Otto Hügin, they depicted scenes from Swiss history combined with moral and religious themes. The biblical figures of the Good Samaritan, the Good Shepherd, St. George and St. Martin were particularly striking. For those privileged few who could gain access to this prestigious venue, they would find themselves rubbing shoulders with key movers and shakers from the worlds of global politics, human rights and peace keeping.

The two men were deep in conversation in a discrete alcove at the far end of the room. A security guard stood with his back to the men, scanning for anything that could be interpreted as a threat. A second guard stood by the door in the same watchful pose. Nothing was getting in or out of that room without their permission.

Pearson was an anathema. He saw himself as the sacrificial lamb to Hunts' 'Man of the People' persona, like many politicians of his day. Hunt had convinced himself that he was one of the good guys. The ethical champion that did the right thing and was all about trying to deliver a new sort of politics that levelled up, so that ordinary people could better themselves and their families. Promises of more inclusive education and better jobs had won him his first election as party leader, but no one understood what it had taken to get him to that position better than Stewart. He also knew the extent of his dealings and the laws he had broken to get to this stage. He would not allow himself to be thrown under any more buses.

Deals had been done, money and promises of honours had been traded to get him over the line as leader. It hadn't really been his turn. Several other candidates were viewed as a far better choice, a more traditional choice, but the party hierarchy had been won over with the promise of an electoral landslide in their favour and Pearson had delivered. It was what made him the most powerful political strategist of his day, but like so many of his species, his fall from grace had been utter and complete. The party he'd delivered victory after victory for had thrown him to the wolves as soon as it suited them. Only Hunt had remained supportive of him, although not publicly, and he had appreciated that show of friendship.

Hunt dropped a folder onto the table between them and let his hand rest on the top of it.

"These are the selection papers signed by the Deputy General Secretary, it's safe to say my appointment is in the bag and the announcement will be made next week at the summit. It has been a long time coming, but we've finally got it! It wouldn't have happened without you Stewart and I just wanted to say thank you. It's time to bring you back into the fold, how does Head of Communications sound, Chief of Staff sounds so old hat?"

Pearson smiled

"That sounds great, *Your Excellency*". He made a curt bow of his head.

Hunt sat back in his chair and stretched his legs in front of him.

"I want you to prepare the press releases and let me see the drafts, this must set the right tone from the outset. Then let's draw up a list of the Saudi Royal families and the weak links in all of them, strike while the iron is hot".

Pearson nodded, picking up the folder.

"Already done. I will email them across for you to see. There's just one minor thing, it's hardly worth a mention, but I think you should know. Vector 10 has released another batch of classified documents onto the internet, about a thousand of them, and there's a mention of Jon Dowie-Brown in a few of them. I've got someone on it, and we have a plan B if it turns out to be true, but I did just want to make you aware. It will be a minor inconvenience at worst, but forewarned is forearmed".

"Bugger" said Hunt under his breath. "It can't do any real harm after all this time, but I don't want to put a dampener on the announcement. Except for you and I, everyone involved is either dead or gaga by now, surely?"

"Like I said, it's a minor issue, and I've got people on it, but I don't want anything to blind side you. As soon as I know what it is that's been released, I'll do a damage limitation release if it's needed. We have got this".

Hunt looked at his from hooded eyes.

"You better have, we've come too far to be scuppered by a piece of history I paid to have dealt with at the time, Stewart. Keep a watching brief and let me know the minute you have any news".

Pearson's flight back to London was uneventful, so he had time to reflect on the enigma that was Vector 10. No one knew who he was or where he came from, but he had terrified and inspired people in equal measure. The world's great hackers normally left a fingerprint somewhere, but Vector 10 was a shadow. He had picked up where Julian Assange had left off. In

2010, in partnership with five newspapers, Assange's organisation Wikileaks published a series of secret documents provided by a US Army Intelligence analyst which damaged US credibility and created severe diplomatic tensions. A manhunt was conducted that saw him escape and seek sanctuary at the Ecuadorian Embassy in the UK. That had outraged the US, as their calls for him to be forcibly removed from the embassy had been met with a stony silence. The British refused to breach the sacrosanct protection of diplomatic immunity and sanctuary, and he had stayed there for months. Everything that Assange had done, had been done very publicly because he wanted maximum exposure. The Americans had egg on their faces, and they didn't like it one bit.

Vector 10, on the other hand, was secretive to the nth degree. The first batch of secret documents were released in 2018, and it was clear that the information came from multiple sources, stolen from some of the most secure servers in the world. The material was selected with care, and on several occasions had embarrassed the document owners, who were not even aware that they had been hacked until they found themselves on the internet or explaining their breach to the media. Vector 10 knew from contacts in the security services that they were desperately trying to discover how their systems had been hacked and by whom.

This latest batch of documents released seemed to be from the eighties and nineties, which left Stewart feeling slightly anxious, as this period covered Hunts' time as Prime Minister. The mention of the cartographer Dowie-Brown also rang warning bells, so Stewart put one of his most trusted researchers on the case. He needed to be sure that this was an insignificant file and not one capable of derailing their current project.

His Uber deposited him outside Portland House, just before 4 pm, and he entered the building, nodding at the uniformed guard on reception. He pressed his security card against the glass panel and waited for the lift doors to open. Their offices were at the back of the building, with no real view to talk about. They were small and eye-wateringly expensive, but the address made it worthwhile. To attract investors, you needed to be seen as a player, and that required a prestigious address.

Ally, his researcher, was waiting for him by his office door. She looked concerned and was holding a folder close to her chest.

"Good trip?"

He nodded.

"Not bad, but I am hoping you have good news for me".

She shook her head.

"Sorry, but I think you may have a problem. Checking the files that have been released, I used the dates and key-word searches and came across three documents that may pose a problem. The first is a paper by a political intern serving at party headquarters during the Iran-Iraq war. It explored the claims that the war was orchestrated by foreign powers to create a prolonged conflict with various proxy groups, militias, and factions within Iran itself. It clearly suggests that these groups could be manipulated and armed by something they referred to as the *Tripartite Treaty* to further destabilize the region and maintain the chaos of war. That would allow them to exploit the situation to their advantage. It predicted that they would carve up the contracts to rebuild infrastructure once the conflict had ended. It cites the US as the main beneficiary of those contracts".

Stewart felt a little ripple of unease. If that was the worst, then that was containable.

"What else then?"

Ally tapped the folder.

"The other two are related documents. A report from the cartographer Jon Dowie-Brown, who worked for the MOD during the early nineties. As part of the cease-fire agreement with the UN, Iraq had been prohibited from producing or possessing chemical, biological, and nuclear weapons. Numerous sanctions were used to get the Country's regime to comply, causing severe disruption to the economy. Saddam's continued refusal to cooperate with UN arms inspectors led to a four-day air strike by the United States and Great Britain in late 1998 (Operation Desert Fox). Jon Dowie-Brown had been charged with mapping the sites in Iraq that could be used to manufacture weaponized biomaterial in sufficient quantities to pose a significant threat to the West. These maps were used by the Inspection team tasked with finding WMD".

At this point, Stewart became decidedly more uncomfortable. He had met Dowie-Brown at a briefing at number 10 and found him to be an awkward and argumentative man who was idealistic and not able to think strategically at all.

"And the third document?"

She laid the folder on his desk, slowly and deliberately pushing it towards him.

"It's an email thread between Dowie-Brown and Emeritus Professor Robert Crane, the head of the UN Inspections team. The exchange directly questioned the weapons sites mentioned in the parliamentary briefing that took the UK and the US into the Iraqi war. It categorically states that not only did the sites in that report not exist, but that the claims made about the capability that Iraq had to manufacture WDM are simply not true. Dowie-Brown challenges Professor Crane and the authors of the briefing to cite their source for the claims because he wants to go on record that the information did not come from him. He states that, in his view, it was a complete work of fiction and that the advisor who helped to author the briefing would have known that the information was false".

Stewart rallied.

"Well, that might have been his opinion, but it's difficult with time pressures and so many people inputting to a briefing like that, to say where information came from and who would have had the final say about the wording".

The woman cast her eyes down towards the floor.

"They have saved the Coup-de-grâce for last, Stewart. In the email reply, Crane claims to have a final draft of the report that is timestamped and has your signature and your notations on it. He claims that it clearly shows that you were the one that altered the report for the briefing".

9. Shady Fields

Friday 17th January 2020

Dowie-Brown's stubbornness was the personality trait responsible for making his career a chequered one. First, in Military intelligence, which he had always thought an oxymoron if ever there was one, and later as a special advisor to MI6. He had been lucky to leave with his distinguished career intact, choosing to go before he was dismissed. The private sector had welcomed him with open arms.

Had the choice been his to make, he would have led a life governed by his own rules, but his employers didn't work like that. In the performance reviews he had been subjected to by his bosses, he was described as perverse by the civil service. In the private sector, he was revered as a creative and a pain in the arse. A label he liked and wore as a badge of honour. It was one of the things he had in common with his friend Robert Crane. They were both highly principled and intelligent men who questioned incompetence and stupidity when they saw it and earned enemies because of it.

Dowie-Brown had watched one of those enemies arrive yesterday. She had got out of the car and straightened the skirt of her designer suit. Immaculate, never a hair out of place, the vision of what a civil servant should look like. He knew different, however. This woman was steely in her determination to complete her orders, regardless of the casualties. It was one of the characteristics that had guaranteed her meteoric rise through the services. He felt it was the reason Celia Browning had reached the lofty heights of Director General, and she hadn't done that without getting some blood on her hands.

Jon never thought it idealistic to believe that the security services were there to protect the nation from people that wanted to do serious harm. It was what they had come into existence to do, but in the last forty years the levels of political interference had become too pervasive. The service was meant to be objective, independent, and certainly not in the pay of political parties. It seemed to be a malaise that affected the whole of science. It was unadulterated confirmation bias. You looked for and used only the science and evidence that supported your standpoint, and everything else was labelled misinformation. The price you paid was your professional integrity.

When Security Services work involved political expediency, then Jon had a problem with that. He and Robert had operated as specialist advisors and their teams had been responsible for identifying any site in Iraq that was capable of producing and launching weapons of mass destruction, particularly, bio weaponry. Jon had been the one who created the maps that identified manufacturing, production, and testing sites. Robert had the much more dangerous job of entering those hostile research facilities and conducting full inspections of their equipment, their research programmes, and their ability to weaponise biomaterials. Jon had the easy job.

Unbeknown to them, their findings had challenged the preconceived notions and agenda of powerful individuals within the government of the day. Jon had been in regular communication with Robert throughout the whole process, and as their report neared completion, Robert Crane found himself in a precarious position. The original intelligence had come directly from the CIA, which was unusual as they were not known to play well with others and hardly ever shared. There was mounting pressure to manipulate the report's conclusions to align with the desired narrative and political agenda.

Jon's contribution had been scrutinized, but it was Robert who was being pressurized to present the report with a particular slant. Their task had been to conduct a comprehensive analysis, and present an unbiased report on the threat Saddam Hussein posed with his intention to deploy bioweapons against the west, in particular the UK and USA. With their reputations on the line, they diligently conducted their research, collected the data, and engaged in discussions with all the senior scientists working in Iraq. Virtually none of the CIA intel was factual. There were a couple of locations of research facilities that were correct, but not much else that was.

As the investigation progressed, it became clear that both governments wanted them to find something that simply wasn't there. The uncomfortable truth and inconvenient reality was that there were no stockpiles of WMD or even the raw materials to make them in the foreseeable future. And even if they had the materials, they would be in no position to weaponise them in significant quantities, and even less chance to create a delivery system capable of threatening Western Countries. They had rock solid evidence that challenged the government's narrative. He had shared his findings with Celia Browning, a senior officer coordinating the intelligence for the report. She had done nothing. Her only advice was semantics, she'd said to him, *'Isn't it possible to suggest that the risks that the government feared are authentic, without falsifying the information?'*

Robert's revelation posed two main risks, according to Celia. Firstly, the whole team faced a potential backlash from powerful individuals who were unwilling to accept any outcome other than the one that supported their strategic objectives. Secondly, she had observed that their professional reputations and careers were coming under scrutiny. Their independence and integrity were being questioned by their peers in the face of mounting pressure.

Jon exchanged email with Robert shortly before he submitted the final draft of the report, and it became clear that he had ignored Celia's advice. The conclusions did not align with the expectations of the government department, and the Prime Minister's Chief of Staff Stewart Pearson seemed intent on manipulating the report's findings to reflect their desired narrative.

Robert had refused point-blank to comply, but the pressure increased, and during a conversation with Jon a week before his death he suggested that they were using personal threats to up the ante. They warned that his reputation could be irreparably damaged, his whole body of work called into question, and he could be removed from the project entirely, citing professional incompetence.

Jon was deeply disturbed by the conversation. To treat scientific advisors in this way threatened not only national security but, on a more fundamental level, the very principle of freedom of speech and academic rigour. Jon wondered where it would all end if those in power were able to write an alternative 'truth' that would be accepted by parliament, mainstream media and the population without question or scrutiny. It was a way of controlling the whole population through contrivance of fear.

The only thing they had as academic scientists was their reputations, and a misinformation campaign, character assassination, or attempt to undermine their credibility would be the end to their existence. If the goal was to bring Robert to breaking point, where he succumbed to the pressure and changed the report to fit the desired narrative, then he would compromise his integrity in the process. As the pressure intensified, Jon knew that Robert felt torn between his commitment to the truth and the mounting risks he faced. It was the single biggest ethical dilemma of his career. Jon clearly recalled their last conversation; he was in no doubt that the pressure was taking its toll on his professional and personal life, and something would have to give.

When the Prime Minister read the sensational summary to a packed House of Commons, Jon had that sinking feeling. He knew what they had done. They had bought about such overwhelming pressure that Robert had buckled and produced the report they had asked him to. Jon felt gutted. He understood why Robert had done it, but wasn't sure he could forgive the ethical and intellectual betrayal. He had tried to contact his friend to discuss it, but he was unable to reach him. The man was clearly under siege from all quarters. The weeks went by and there were rumblings in the media, that questioned the validity of the report the Prime Minister had presented. They kept the pressure up, forced a public enquiry into the now famous sexed-up dossier. The next thing Jon heard was that Robert had gone missing and within hours, his body had been discovered in the woods near his home. He had committed suicide.

Jon had felt anger that surprised him in its intensity. They had forced him to a point of no return. His family must have been devastated, bewildered that their mild-mannered scientist husband and father had taken his own life. There is no way he would have shared the real story; he would have been too ashamed.

Jon's last conversation with Celia had been difficult. He had shared his knowledge about Robert's concerns and the obvious pressure that had been placed on him to falsify the dossier. She wanted to know if Robert had confided in anyone else and detailed the danger that it could put them in. The whole thing had left him feeling sick to his stomach.

After that conversation, Jon had taken the decision to withdraw from MI6 as a special advisor. Some venture capitalists had approached him to help them design software that could map the earth in 3D based on satellite images, so he had taken his knowledge into the private sector. That project had been an early forerunner of Google Earth, and although he had not seen it through to the global success it had become, he did very nicely from it financially. He had spent some of it travelling, he had wisely invested some of it, but there was a small pot that he had set aside for a specific purpose. He chose to come to Shady field because he knew she was coming here. One of the few places you can't keep a secret is inside the service. People had been shocked by Celia's diagnosis, and Jon was still not sure that he believed she was as bad as people said. He knew that if he wanted to confront her, this would be the ideal place, so he had a retired consultant friend write him a letter explaining the need for convalescence after a serious bout of pneumonia. The idea was to spend six weeks here, but of course, if he concluded business early, he would make a miraculous recovery. A little subterfuge was worth it. He had not exactly decided on how he would get justice for his long dead friend, but he was nothing if not resourceful.

10. The Crane Residence

Tuesday 14th January 2020

Almost twenty years after her fathers' death, her mother Abigail passed away in 2019 following a short illness, and it fell to Sharon to clear out the family home. Colin was living in Australia, running a '*Mussel Boys'* franchise on Bondi Beach. It was a fast-food restaurant that served only green lipped and local mussels thirty-four different ways, and he had no intention of returning to the UK. It had taken him more than forty years, but he had finally escaped from his mother's overbearing control. Sharon knew that her mother was difficult to live with, and she was amazed that he had endured her for so long.

Abigail Crane had remained angry with her husband and, by default, with Sharon, until the day she died. She was angry because he'd had an affair, angry that he had chosen to stay with them, and angry because for the remaining years they lived together, he had loved someone else. She was angry with Sharon because of the bond she had with her father and the fact that they were so alike. But her deepest anger was reserved for the fact that he had committed suicide and left, rather than face the storm. Sharon looked around the house and shivered, it was too long for anyone to be angry and hold a grudge. Sharon felt it was the equivalent of drinking poison but expecting someone else to die.

Every moment they had spent under the same roof, her mother's disappointment hung around the house like a layer of dry ice, thick and silent. She knew she had to live her life away from her mother's hostility, but Colin hadn't been that lucky. She had left just three weeks after her father's funeral, but Colin had remained to care for their mother. He had always been her favourite anyway, so the situation suited him. He never had to be responsible for his actions or earn an independent living. In the early days, she had indulged and supported him, but as the years passed, she had also suffocated him with the endless demands for his attention. She had lived a half-life since then. Thirty-five years is a long time to be angry.

Sharon had taken the decision to go out into the world and free herself from her mothers' controlling behaviour. She was surprised at the residual guilt she felt but pushed it away when it threatened to raise its ugly head. She had never regretted her decision, but had lived her life missing the years she should have had her father.

When she was twenty-nine, Sharon had married Nico Louca. He was an adorable and passionate Greek man in his thirties. He had dark curly hair and kind eyes and could make her laugh better than anyone she knew. His family welcomed her with open arms and loved her unconditionally. They married in his hometown of Porto Germeno, with the restored ancient Greek fortress of Aigosthena forming a stunning backdrop to the proceedings. As expected, her mother didn't attend the wedding. Colin stepped up to the plate and gave her away in a traditional ceremony at a whitewashed chapel with a sky-blue roof. Four hundred guests partied around the clock. Nico's family was huge, they were loud, they argued and hugged each other in equal measure, and they loved and supported her in whatever endeavour she chose. Compared to her experience of family, it was an overwhelming experience. She didn't know family could be like that.

Sharon was surprised by how many echoes of her father there still were around the family home. There were his pictures, awards, books, and antiquities from his travels abroad, but the biggest shock was when she tried his study door, it was locked. After ten minutes of hunting for the key, she unlocked the door and was astounded to find that the room had remained completely undisturbed. Her mother had mothballed her memories of him by closing that room off from everyone after the circus that was the inquiry into his suicide had left town. No one had entered it since, Sharon had not expected that.

A thick layer of dust had settled on every flat surface, and the wooden shutters were firmly closed. She opened them, they were stiff and complained loudly as she moved them on their dry runners. His chair was still pushed against the wall like he could just come back at any minute with his morning coffee, so he could carry on working. She traced her fingers along the wooden surface of his desk and left tracks in the dust. Cables had been left trailing down onto the floor where the police had removed his computer as part of their investigations. The bookshelves were lined with his eclectic choice of reading, autobiographies, a full set of Ian Fleming novels next to a leather-bound first edition of Hemingway's 'The sun also rises'. His very essence was here, like an echo of him. His smell, his memory, it almost felt like she could reach out and touch him.

This is where she wanted to start the clearing process. Colin had wanted to engage a company to take the lot away, but Sharon said no. Colin wasn't a reader and didn't want any of his father's books, but she found herself wanting to do this task. She secretly hoped it would bring her closer to her father, or his memory. So she set about sorting and boxing her father's collections. The books she wanted to keep she placed on the largest bookcase and would ship them home with the other things she was taking. The books that she had identified for sale, some of the finer volumes, would go to Brindlehursts Auctioneers.

She booted up her laptop and opened a spreadsheet she had already created. This suited her logical mind, and she felt strangely comforted by the process of cataloguing everything. It would not be a quick task, but it would be a satisfying one. By late afternoon, she had listed about two thirds of the books. Coffee had sustained her, but now she felt the gnawing of hunger pangs and headed to the kitchen to see what she could find. She found pasta and a tomato stir-in sauce in the cupboard, hardly appetizing, but it would give her the energy boost she needed to finish the book inventory today. She ate at the breakfast bar in the kitchen, washed up the pots and plate she'd used and topped her coffee mug up before returning to the study for round two.

Looking around the office, she was quite surprised by how much she had already completed. There were packing cases on the far side of the study that were filled with paperbacks for the local charity shop. She had also begun to fill a document crate with personal papers; Insurance policies, plans for the house extension her father had commissioned but were never realised, even her parents' marriage certificate.

The final shelves she needed to clear were her father's treasured books. These were not all first editions, and some were not very valuable, but these were the volumes he would read again and again. Some because he loved their stories, others because they were useful references for his academic work. Tucked away at the end of one of the shelves was an old hardback with a cream dust cover, as she took it from the shelf, she realised it was hers. Her father had given her this copy of '*Emil and the Detectives*' when she was eight and had contracted chickenpox. She had been quite poorly, so he read to her every day until she was better. She often wondered what had happened to it and assumed her mother had got rid of it in one of her clear outs. She opened it, flicking through the pages, looking at the classic pen and ink illustrations she loved so much.

Memories of her childhood days began to fill her mind, and her attention to the book began to wander. As she absent-mindedly flicked the pages, she caught her thumb on the dust cover and the book fell to the floor. The dust jacket was still in her hand, and she saw that there was a sheet of pale blue paper lining it. She sat down at his desk and carefully separated it from the cover to have a closer look. It was a letter written on tissue-like airmail paper, it was thin and crackled with age.

It was a set of instructions for a treasure hunt, written in her father's distinctive hand. Her pulse quickened, and a little thrill fizzed through her body. Her father was reaching out to her from long ago, stirring her interest. It was obviously a game that he had set for her to discover during one of the school holidays and had been long forgotten. She knew she would not be able to resist following it to its conclusion. She was suddenly transported back to her childhood, she, and her father against the rest of the world. The familiar excitement of having a puzzle to solve begin to rise in her.

She gently laid the blue tissue paper on the desk, smoothing it out so that she could read the pencil notes on it.

'In this room where knowledge hides, seek the book with the serpent guide. Beneath the symbol of the oath, lives or dies, unveil the truth, to where the treasure lies'.

Sharon read it through a couple of times to see if the words triggered anything in her memory. As she was in the study, it made sense for the clue to refer to something in the room. She looked around the room filled with books and knowledge and at the partially cleared shelves. What if the clue referred to a book that she had already packed away. Her mind went back to that first memory palace game. The mention of serpent guide suggested to her one of her father's medical textbooks with the caduceus, the Staff and serpent on the cover. It was where Sharon had hidden the soft toy snake for her father to find. She had not packed it away yet and took the book down from the shelf to carefully examine it. The spine was faded and slightly lumpy, and holding the book at eye level, she looked down inside the spine and spotted a small scroll of paper. She shook the open book over the desk, and it slid out. Unravelling the scroll, she could see some feint text. Her father always kept a strong magnifying glass in the top drawer of his desk. She opened the drawer, yes it was still there. She took it out and looked at the faded writing.   The first line was a four-digit code (1-8-9-8) and a phrase,

'Beneath the gaze of a watchful eye,
the next riddle waits to defy.
Decipher the enigma, follow its trail,
to a place where hidden secrets prevail'.

Again, she looked around the room, hoping it would trigger another memory. On the only wall that was not covered with bookshelves was arranged a selection of paintings and pictures, now darkened with age. Sharon was drawn to her favourite painting in the study. One she had earmarked to pack and take home with her. It was a little kitsch by modern standards, but she had always loved it. It was a small oil painting by Viggo Pederson dated 1898 of a baby boy in his crib being rocked by his dark-haired sister in a pale blue smock. 1-8-9-8! The painting sat in a heavy, gold plaster frame that was too big for the small picture. She looked closely and saw a tiny plaque on the bottom, which she hadn't noticed before. She took a tissue from her pocket, dabbed it on her tongue then gently rubbed at the little plaque, surprised at how much of the dirt came off. Using the magnifying glass again, she read the fine writing and gave a sharp intake of breath, it read "*A watchful eye*".   She examined the painting closely, but years of dirt and faded varnish had diminished a lot of the detail. She made a mental note to have it cleaned and noticed that just visible was a small, embroidered footstool that the little girl was standing on. It was just like the one her father had under his desk. She moved his chair out of the way and crouched down, pulling the dusty footstool out from beneath the desk. It was well-used, and the wool tapestry that had seemed so bright and cheerful in this shadowy study when she was small, now looked dusty and faded. The centre had sunk from years of use. She turned it over and looked underneath, but there was nothing. Tracing the trim along the base of the stool, she noticed some of the upholstery pins were missing. Not strange though given the age and condition of the thing, but she tugged at the fabric and felt in the opening the touch of paper. Carefully, she pulled out another note. This did seem a little elaborate, even for her father. The times they had played together were special memories for her. They had been a bone of contention with Colin, though, as her father had told him he was too little to play. That had made her feel special and definitely closer to him.

She unfolded the small note and looked at the same faded text again.

'Trust not Beyond the Realms of Death,
behind the bars, a secret prevails.
Turn the hands of time, embrace the past,
and behold the secrets that will outlast'.

She was surprised at the strength of emotion that this clue evoked. She recognised the reference immediately; it was one of her father's favourite heavy metal tracks, called *'Beyond the Realms of Death'* by *Judas Priest*. Heavy metal rock was one of her father's guilty pleasures, much to her mothers' distaste. The song is about a man who is awaiting death and alludes to his suicide, she ran the lyrics through her head.

> *"Keep the world with all its sin*
> *It's not fit for living in*
> *Beyond the realms of death."*

Sharon felt as if all the air had been sucked out of the room. She was suddenly back there on the day his body was found, with all those unanswered questions banging at the door of her subconscious, demanding to be heard. Was this really a message from him? Was he trying to tell her that he had taken his own life? Why would he do that! Why would he have telegraphed his intention to her, and it was to her because the language he was speaking to her in was their language? One that only they shared. She looked back at the clue and read it again. What it actually said was TRUST NOT the realms of death, behind the bars... the bars of the music maybe? A secret prevails. Then it hit her like a truck!

He was not confessing his intention to commit suicide; he was telling her the exact opposite. He was telling her that if he died unexpectedly, it would not be suicide, and suddenly, everything fell into place. He knew he was going to die, but how was that possible? He had got involved in something that was so important, so shocking, so dangerous that someone was willing to kill him for it. She never believed the suicide story, even when the evidence seemed overwhelming. There were questions about the events leading up to his disappearance, questions about his involvement in the report that had triggered the invasion and its accuracy.

At that moment, she knew with certainty that her father had been murdered. It wasn't too much of a stretch to link it with the last thing he worked on, some sort of cover-up? He must have known something that would compromise someone, or could compromise the Government.

Don't be ridiculous, she scolded herself. You sound like some mad conspiracy theorist. She looked at the clue again. The next part of the phrase read,

"Turn the hands of time, embrace the past, and behold the secrets that will outlast".

This was now ridiculously easy. On the mantelshelf there was an ornate clock on a heavy marble base that harboured a secret of its own. She knew that when the hands were turned backwards a small slit opened in the base, just enough to slide another clue inside.

She followed the instructions, and sure enough, the slit opened, but instead of another pale blue note she could see a small brown envelope. The slit was too small to reach inside. She rushed from the room and into the kitchen, where her handbag lay on the kitchen counter. Rummaging inside, she pulled out her manicure set and took out the tweezers. Back in her father's study, she carefully extracted the small envelope. Trembling with anticipation as she opened it and pulled out an A6 microfiche and a final brief note, all it said was,

"Ask Ada Hale for help".

There was a telephone number on the back of the paper.

She knew that whatever was on the microfiche it was the reason her father was killed, and it was possible that it was still dangerous information to possess. She had no idea who Ada Hale was or if she would help. Actually, that was not strictly true, she did have an idea who she might be. Sharon had a decision to make, she could destroy it and walk away, or she could find out exactly why her father had been killed and by whom.

In that instance, she knew why he had left her the message. He knew exactly which option she would choose..

11. Ingleby Derbyshire

Saturday 18th January 2020. Late afternoon

Hilary had read the letters. They shone an altogether different light on the life her aunt had lived. The confirmed spinster that she had taken at face value had engaged in a passionate love affair.

The letters detailed a brief, but intense relationship with a man called Robert Crane that only lasted for about six months. They had worked together on an assignment in Dhofar, but he was married, with a young family, and it had been decided to stop things before they went too far. He had gone back to his family, and Ada had remained in her role with MI5, but it was clear that the affair had made a huge impact on them both. The letters were not graphic or sentimental in the way that some love letters are. These were written in ordinary language but contained such deep and honest emotions they bought Hilary to tears. It was obvious that he was ready to leave his family and begin a new life with Ada, and yet the penultimate letter made it clear that it was she that had put an end to the relationship. It was the only one in Ada's own hand, and it had been returned to her with a simple note that read,

I know you are right, but my heart is broken. R

My Dearest Robert,

As I sit here, writing this final letter, my heart aches with the weight of a decision I never wanted to make. Our time together has been filled with moments of passion and shared intimacy that I will forever hold dear. However, I have come to realise that the path we have been walking is one that can only lead to destruction and heartbreak.

I have spent countless hours thinking about the consequences of our affair, and the toll it would take on your family. The guilt that gnaws at me has become unbearable, for I never intended to be the cause of any pain or upheaval in your life. My intentions were never to disrupt the delicate balance of your family, but I fear that is the destination of the road we are currently travelling.

Love is a complicated thing, capable of bringing immense joy and happiness, but also capable of inflicting indescribable pain. It is with a sad and heavy heart that I realise I must step away, for the good of all involved. Your family, your children, and your

commitment to them deserve nothing less than your full dedication and devotion. I will never make you choose.

I know that this decision may bring about a sense of loss, sadness, and perhaps even anger. Please understand that it is not a reflection of my feelings for you, but rather a reflection of my respect and consideration for the lives we could potentially shatter. You deserve happiness, but it should come from a place of authenticity and integrity, one that does not compromise the bonds that tie your family together.

In the coming days, I will do my best to mend the pieces of my heart, to move forward and allow time to heal the wounds that this separation will undoubtedly leave behind. I implore you to do the same. Robert, please know that I will always love you, and you are irreplaceable for me. Cherish the love you have within your family, nurture it, and let it be the guiding light that illuminates your path.

Know that I will always cherish the memories we shared, the stolen moments of passion and connection. They will forever remain etched in the depths of my soul. But now, it is time for us to part ways, to find solace in the lives we had before our paths crossed.

Goodbye, my love. May life bestow upon you and your family an abundance of happiness and peace. Remember, there is beauty in the everyday moments, in the love that surrounds you. Embrace it with open arms, and let it heal the wounds that time cannot erase.

With all the love and strength I possess,

Ada x

The tears coursed down Hilary's face, and snippets of conversations they had shared in her last few weeks flitted in and out of her mind. Ada had purposefully sacrificed the chance of happiness to protect him and his family. No wonder that she had been so keen for Hilary to consider her own direction of travel and her personal life. She had not realised that Ada had turned away from what was clearly the love of her life. There had been one more letter from Robert Crane that was postmarked seventeen years later and with a very different tone.

This one was of a much more cryptic nature. The essence of it was that he had been drawn into a situation that could result in the loss of his reputation and livelihood. He was unsure of the outcome, but if one of his family reached out to her for help, then he wanted her to give it. It was signed simply '*Your Robert'*.

Hilary was unsure what to do with that. She wondered if anything had ever come of this request, and if a family member had sought Ada out. She had never said so if they had. She wondered whether Daniel knew anything about this side of Ada's life. It was possible. They had worked together at various times in their careers, and he might also know Robert Crane. She would ask him when she got back to Shady Fields.

She retraced her steps down to the kitchen to pick up her bag before setting off. The phone rang, the unexpected noise made her jump. No one knew she was there, so it wouldn't be for her, and it never rang for Ada, so it must have been a sales call. She let it ring. It stopped. Hilary thought no more about it and gathered her bag, keys, and phone and headed for the door. The phone began to ring again. Hilary decided to answer it, if it was a sales call, they needed to take the number off their database.

"Hello, who is this, please?" Hilary's voice was monotone.

"Hello, could I speak with Ada Hale please?"

"Ms. Hale is not available, who is this, please?"

"My name is Sharon Louca and I wanted to speak with Ada Hale because I wanted to ask her about my father. I believe she may have worked with him some years ago".

"I'm sorry, but Ada passed away six months ago. May I ask you what your father's name is?"

The line went quiet, but Hilary knew that she was still there.

"My father's name was Robert Crane, he passed away in 2002". There was a hesitation, "I know this is going to sound odd, but I've just found some documents of his, and he left instructions to contact her if I needed help. Obviously, that boat has sailed now. Sorry to have troubled you".

Hilary had a split second to decide.

"Wait Sharon. Let's meet. This is going to sound weird, but I also found some information today whilst clearing my aunt's belongings, and your father's name was mentioned".

"Really?" there was surprise in Sharon's voice. "Where are you?"

"I'm in Derbyshire, how about you?"

"I'm not that far away; I'm in Worcestershire. Did you know that they knew each other?"

Hilary was a little unsure of how much Sharon knew, but she was intrigued by this turn of events and decided she was keen to know more.

"No, but I'm staying overnight in Birmingham, then travelling back to London tomorrow. I don't suppose you would like to have some dinner tonight; I'm staying at the Albany in the town centre. It's close to the train station. Can you join me?"

There was no hesitation this time.

"Yes, is 7 pm okay?"

Hilary felt unexpectedly nervous as she waited. The restaurant was quiet at this time in the evening. She positioned herself with her back to the wall so that she could look out on the other diners and have a clear view of the entrance. She was casually browsing the menu when movement caught her eye. A tall dark-haired woman in a figure skimming dress and elegant heels hovered by the waiter's station. She scanned the tables, but before she could do anything she was professionally shepherded towards Hilary by an observant head waiter.

Hilary stood and offered a seat to the woman.

"Hello Sharon? I am Hilary. Please have a seat".

They ordered drinks and made small talk, each ordering something light from the menu and when the waiter left the table, there was an awkward silence. Sharon was the first to speak.

"I don't know how to start this conversation, but I have come into the possession of some information from my father, and he mentioned that if I needed help, I was to contact Ada. It was clear that he had feelings for her and trusted her deeply. Just my luck that I am too late".

Hilary had a gut feeling about this woman and couldn't deny how intrigued her own revelations had left her.

"Your timing is indeed very strange, Sharon. I only recently found letters from your father to my aunt from their time in Dhofar. I understand that they may have worked together for a short time".

"I agree, it is a bit of a coincidence. How close to your aunt were you, if I may ask?"

"We were very close actually; she was like a mother to me. Her death has left a real gap for me".

"So, can I ask a delicate question?" Hilary nodded.

"Was she the "other woman" in my fathers' life?"

She added quickly before Hilary could answer.

"I am sorry to blurt that out. I always knew there had been someone else, but he had decided to stay with us. With hindsight, I could understand him, my mother was not an easy woman to live with, or even to like at times. He stayed because of us, my brother and me, and my mother never let a day go by where she didn't remind or punish him".

Hilary was still coming to terms with this new knowledge. It felt strange talking about such an intimate part of Ada's life, but she had come to her to find out more, and that is what she intended to do.

"I do know that they had an affair and that my aunt ended it".

She took the letter from her bag and passed it across the table for Sharon to read.

Sharon opened it tentatively and read it through. Hilary had left Robert's response attached and watched as the recognition of her father's handwriting passed across her face. The waiter delivered their food, and they ate in silence. When their meal was finished, and they sat with filled coffee cups, Sharon spoke.

"Your aunt was a remarkable woman".

Hilary smiled at the thought.

"Yes, she was. Your father wrote to her one more time, asking her to help if you ever came to her. I think the letter must have been written shortly before he died, but I know that if you had come to her, she would have

helped if she could. That was who she was. So, what would you have asked from her?"

123

"Before I answer that, Hilary, may I ask you what you do for a living?"

"I run a private retirement home for civil servants. Why?"

"What I'm about to tell you is going to sound fantastical, but I need to share it with someone to see if I am being logical or completely mad".

Sharon took a sip of coffee and began.

"From 1998 to 2002, my father headed up an inspection team in Iraq to look for biological weapons. They didn't find any, but the report that his team produced was falsified to say that they did exist. That was because they needed to create a reason for a pre-emptive strike, we ended up supporting the Americans and invading the country. I also believe that my father was going to blow the whistle and release the original report, but he was murdered before he could. It was made to look like suicide. The official cause of death was suicide, but I never believed it. I said so at the time, but I was in my mid-twenties, no one listened to me. Then recently, as I was clearing my father's study, I came across a microfiche with files on it, and it clearly states the report that he submitted was tampered with. If he had released it to the press, not only could it have bought the government down, but the Americans would have been implicated too. There are so many anomalies in the investigation into his death that it would not take much to get some sort of re-investigation going, but I am wary of starting something that may have severe repercussions".

She breathed a deep sigh of relief now that she had unburdened herself. Her hand trembled as she took a long drink from her water glass.

Hilary was intrigued by the woman's story. She didn't look like a conspiracy theorist. If she'd heard this just a few years ago, she would have discounted it as a flight of fancy, a woman having never got over the loss of her father. But the last two years had been a steep learning curve and Hilary was well aware of the steps' government, the civil service and other official bodies would go to, to protect their secrets and not wash their dirty linen in public.

"Is the information you have genuine, Sharon? I mean is it official and could it be verified?"

She thought for a moment before answering.

"Yes, I believe it is".

"So, what did you want from Ada? She wouldn't have been able to help".

"I think you are wrong. They met while working in Dhofar. Your aunt was either a scientist, a diplomat or working for a government department. I may not know the detail of my father's missions, but I know that he worked for the Secret Service in some capacity. His work was far too sensitive for any other explanation to fit. It makes sense that he directed me to her because he thought she would be in a position to help. I'm only sad that it took me so long to discover the information he left. If I had got to it earlier, then perhaps we would have stood a chance to put right this terrible wrong".

Sharon broke down. All the tension and loss came out in a huge wave of emotion. Hilary passed her a tissue

from her bag.

"If you would trust me with the information, let me take it to my boss, and see what he thinks".

Sharon sniffed and dabbed at her eyes.

"I don't want to seem ungrateful, but you manage a residential home, what good will he be?"

Hilary gave a furtive glance around the room.

"Well, Shady Fields is not the run-of-the-mill retirement home, our residents were all active MI5 and MI6 agents in their working life. Ada was a training officer and also operated in the field as an intelligence gatherer, and it is my guess that's how they met. My boss happens to be the Director General of security services, Daniel Grant".

Sharon seemed unsure.

"But surely if there was a cover-up, then it wouldn't be in his interests to go raking it all up after all this time. Wouldn't he be in favour of letting sleeping dogs lie?"

Sharon smiled.

"If you knew Daniel, then you would know that it's not how he works. He will know what to do and how to proceed. Let me have a word with him?"

"Okay, I printed his files, but the documents I have with me are just copies. I have the originals in a safe place".

"I would not expect anything less".

"Good, take them and see what he thinks, but I want to be kept informed". "Not a problem," said Hilary.

She took the envelope from Sharon and watched as the woman left the restaurant. If what she said was true, then this was a heap of pain to be bought down on someone's head. Daniel never backed away from a fight, but there were some things so big that even he may struggle to find answers. As she travelled up in the lift to her room, Ada occupied her thoughts. She must have been a quite brilliant agent; she had fooled Hilary all her life. There was still that familiar sadness that loss creates, but Hilary felt that she was also developing an enormous sense of pride in this woman she had called her aunt.

12. Thames House

Thursday 17th September 2020

Daniel once again found himself in the bowels of Thames House. The lift deposited him into a grey corridor with dull khaki painted, steel doors running down both sides. No carpets meant that footsteps echoed loudly, just to add to the feeling of apprehension when you were working here late at night.

He had pulled many an all-nighter in this place. The smell of the artificially cleaned air was distinctive and mildly depressing. He walked past his old office door to the one marked 'Peter King', knocked and entered without being invited.

"Well, you are either here to sack me or you want something under the radar......again. I'm surprised you found your way down here without a road map". Peter gave him a grin.

"Hello Peter. I did offer to bring you up to the fifth floor with the rest of intelligence gathering, but you turned me down flat".

Daniel walked over to the bank of screens Peter was facing. They cast a ghostly blue light that made his grey hair look even paler. Yes, it was true, Peter could have had Daniels' office on the top floor if he had asked him for it. He was one of the most trusted and respected agents Daniel had worked with.

Peter continued to stare at his screens, he had no use for a view over the Thames or even natural light, they were both overrated as far as he was concerned. Peace and quiet, being left alone with his tech' and all this information was all he wanted. Others thought that what he did was boring and tedious, but Peter loved it!

Daniel prized this mans' skills and knowledge because he also knew that what happened in this place enabled every other agent to do the work they did with a degree of safety. Peter King's contribution to protecting the safety of the nation could not be underestimated.

When Daniel had become Director General, he had tried to promote him, he wanted him to leave the archive and lead the digital data gathering unit, but he had remained adamant, he wanted to stay where he was.

'Archives' wasn't at the sharp end of things, there were no clandestine meetings, or subterfuge to set the pulse racing, but he was the grease on the organisation's gears.

Daniel was constantly amazed by his abilities; he could remember things after the briefest glance, he called it a 'natural gift'. He could also spot patterns and trends in information that were invisible to others. His personality and mental processing had been identified early on in his training, and he had proven himself invaluable on numerous occasions. He was one of the rarest and most strategically capable people Daniel knew, and he wanted him as part of his top team.

Peter, on the other hand, was very self-effacing about his talents. He'd always demonstrated a natural thirst for knowledge in his early life and was nicknamed "*the bookworm*" by his peers at school. He never saw it as an insulting fact, he was proud of it. At university, he enjoyed his studious reputation. He was never the first choice of the sports captains, but was always top of the list for debating teams and general knowledge competitions. He made being a nerd cool. As he matured, his insightful observations and formidable logic enabled him to focus with laser-like precision on important facts and discard the red herrings. It bought him to the attention of Secret Service recruiters at Cambridge, and he was thrilled to be invited into the covert world of espionage, data analysis and secrets.

Peter had worked with, or for, Daniel in some guise or another for many years. He liked and respected him, which wasn't always easy in the service. There have been many empire builders, thieves, and downright scoundrels that patronized Thames House. Daniel Grant had integrity; it was as simple as that. Peter was not an idealist, but he was a man with strong ideals. He had told Daniel straight when he had offered him the last promotion,

"Why would I want to swap all of this just to rub shoulders with the elite? I'm much happier being one of the 'hoi polloi' thank you very much".

Daniel had laughed.

"Peter, the last thing you could ever be is one of the masses".

Daniel walked over to him, trying to make sense of the scrolling code on his main monitor.

"As usual, you are correct, Peter; I need something under the radar. I'm not sure even you can help, but I need you to track down some official files that will be heavily redacted and then try to un-redact them".

Peter smiled, straightened up in his chair and read from an imaginary sheet of paper held up in one hand.

"Welcome to the arcane, secretive subculture of redaction, which is the practice of removing or concealing portions of documents before publication. It's a phenomenon that most ordinary people are unfamiliar with, but governments, barristers, journalists, and historical researchers are accustomed to blacked-out spaces on documents that come across their desks. It is a consequence of dealing with sensitive subjects. Redacting is now widely recognised as part of government-imposed secrecy across the globe".

He rolled the imaginary document up into a scroll and threw it over his shoulder.

"Peter, this is serious!"

"It must be if the Director General is requesting it. Surely, you know how to get hold of this stuff through official channels. You ARE National Security, so in theory no one can refuse you".

Daniel had come this far, but now he was asking for Peters' help, and he knew that he needed to give him a bone to gnaw on.

"We are looking for documents concerning things that happened some years ago that may deal with a possible government cover-up. I don't know what we are going to find when we turn these rocks over, but I have a feeling that it's serious. I can't risk anything getting out until I'm sure of exactly what we may be dealing with. And I have no idea how far up the ladder this goes, who's involved, or the repercussions if this does resurface. It's imperative that I see the full picture, so I can make the right decision about what to do".

Peter knew extremely well the duplicitous world they lived in and how one person's truth was someone else's conspiracy theory.

"What is it you are looking for, and I'll see what I can do?"

Daniel took a breath.

"Right. I need a few things; anything you can trace about something called the Tripartite Treaty from 1994 to 2002. Everything you can find out about the public enquiry into the dossier that took us into the Iraqi war, and anything about the lead witness, Professor Robert Crane. Will you be able to check if your search raises any flags along the way too?"

Peter was making notes as Daniel spoke, when he suddenly stopped.

"You do know that Vector 10's latest release through 'Rufus the hack' contained some stuff relating to this, don't you? And something called the Tripartite Treaty. Is there a link?"

Daniel was surprised. He knew that there had been another release of secret files, and he had a team working on it, but he was positive nothing had come across his desk about this. And yet, the timing of this leak seemed too much of a coincidence.

"What documents? I've only heard whispers about this Tripartite Treaty before, but not in any great detail. I need to know the who, the what, the where and the when, and I need to know now".

Peter began making swift keyboard strokes and in seconds his screen began opening document icons until it was filled with text. He selected the one he was looking for and began to read.

"An intelligence report from MI6, title: Resource Control of the Tripartite Treaty, April 1994. The intelligence received suggest that this group was working to gain control over Iran's rich oil reserves. The group was working behind the scenes to secure long-term access to their resources by destabilizing Iran's government and installing a more favourable regime".

Peter puffed his cheeks out,

"That would suggest some heavy government involvement, or at the very least influence. That's the only way the group could gain that sort of economic advantage. This sounds like a group of serious power brokers, Daniel".

Daniel had heard rumours of such a group, but it had been inference, nothing more. He certainly didn't know they had a name and had appeared in intelligence briefings decades ago. It would suggest that it was a threat of its time and that something had happened to remove that threat.

"Can you find out what happened to them, Peter? Did this stuff lead anywhere?"

"We know that there are shady power brokers at work now. They are rich, secretive, and feared. Every intelligence service is aware of factions like these but finding anything on them is like plating fog. They are very influential and have links to global finance, oil-exporting nations, Asian central banks, hedge funds, and private-equity firms. They know how to cover their tracks, Daniel. They hide beneath layers of bureaucracy and the red tape of shell companies and offshore trusts. The reason they make us uneasy is that we don't know who they are or who the money is behind them. We know their resources seem unlimited, and they can shape global financial markets by orchestrating conflicts. It's estimated that their combined assets are around $18 trillion. That is equivalent to forty percent of the wealth held by global pension funds. Add to that the tripling of world oil prices, it's my guess that there must be some Petro-investors at the heart of this. It's not a difficult leap in understanding where the roots of the Tripartite Treaty might go".

"How do you do that? This is a secretive group; how can you possibly know this stuff?"

Peter just grinned at his boss,

"It's a gift and a curse".

Daniel was beginning to feel a sense of urgency in running some of this to ground.

"Do we need a financial specialist that can help you track it all down?"

There were too many questions and not enough answers for Daniel's taste.

Peter returned to his screen, speaking over his shoulder,

"There is one thing in our favour, Daniel. If this stuff goes back to the noughties, then there is a chance we can retrieve the information. Early digital redaction wasn't always foolproof. You can sometimes view redacted text in documents by copying and pasting them into a Word document. If you had a lazy civil servant or agent who just used formatting with a black highlighter to block out the offending text and didn't merge it with the original document, then it's retrievable. Leave this with me, but it won't be quick".

Daniel nodded.

"Do what you can and remember strictly 'ears only'. Don't create any paper trail with this until we know where the breadcrumbs lead".

13. City of London

Monday 14th September 2020

Stewart was reading the report that Ally had just completed, and she had been correct in her assumptions, this was not looking good. The documents that Vector 10 had released were not all politically sensitive, but some were, and those were truly incriminating for some very high-profile politicians. It was as if it were designed to do the most damage to specific individuals' reputations. In some ways, that was worse. Top secret stuff caused international ripples and the equivalent of 'handbags at dawn' diplomatically. This stuff was much more targeted and could damage a reputation so badly that it would have the effect of cancelling them out of the current geopolitical landscape. No one would touch them with a barge pole. Lucrative positions and figurehead board positions would disappear like snowflakes on a hot plate.

He had primed Ally to look for specific events, associations, and relationships, and if she could find them, any journalist worth their salt could too. His days of having influence over the mainstream media had gone. In fact, it was worse than that. He had made enemies of the major publications while he was head of communications at Number 10. Those bastards had long memories and never passed up an opportunity to settle old scores. His arch nemesis Rufus Hurst would take enormous pleasure in doing so. He had never forgiven Stewart for banning him from a ministerial briefing because he'd asked Prime Minister Hunt too many awkward questions. There would be a queue a mile long if some of the editors got wind of a possible scandal they could use to discredit him or Hunt. He needed a plan of action to neutralise this threat, otherwise his old friend and partner in crime wouldn't hesitate to throw him under the bus of public opinion if the whole story got out.

He checked himself. For God's sake, calm down Stewart, no one knows the extent of what happened back then. Very few of those involved are still alive, and those that are, are probably gaga by now.

The problem was the internet; the gift that keeps on giving. Back in the days when he was operating out of 10 Downing Street, they used the internet for research, but the majority of Joe Public didn't bother with it that much. It was the mainstream media that ruled the airwaves, the BBC, other broadcasters, and the newspapers. They all wanted to get the inside track and he held the key. He enjoyed the power his position afforded him, they had to play ball, or he would favour more cooperative journalists who would be rewarded with better access to ministerial briefings and interviews.

Prime Minister Adam Hunt and his team had been unchallenged for such a long time that many of them accepted their position as the overpaid agents of wealthy individuals and global corporations. They had become disconnected from the concerns and problems of average working people.

As his power grew, rumours of a corruptible system of politics and governance dominated by a handful of billionaires with well-financed special interests, also grew. He couldn't pinpoint the specific time when it became the government's role to decide to broker access to lucrative deals, but from his perspective, that was certainly the trajectory that they were on. Political parties and ideologies used to matter, but that was becoming less important the more it became a political game. What was most surprising was that it really didn't matter who won elections or created policies. The overriding effect was that the game they were playing was the important thing. Point scoring, shifting blame and taking credit for things they had no real part in was the icing on the cake.

It was Hunt's government that had started that particular hare running, but it was much worse now. In less than a generation, the political system was there for the taking if you had enough money. It is true that we get the politicians we deserve, the only redeeming point was that at least we were not the USA. They were even worse.

His influence had grown along with the duration of their being in power, and he had taken the opportunity to cultivate a few important contacts inside the security services. Nothing too high up, but enough to be useful on the inside from time to time. His phone pinged, he looked at the screen. It was a message from one of those contacts, he opened it and read the single sentence.

'Need to meet to discuss the Tripartite Treaty, bring plenty of 'Alan Turing' with you'.

The reference to £50 notes was telling.

Stewart muttered.

"Cheeky bastard! Trying to extort money from me is a dangerous game to play".

That hubris quickly deserted him, and he felt his heart make a bid for escape up his chest and out of his mouth. Not only was this career threatening, but he knew it was going to be very, very expensive.

14. Shady Fields

20th January 2020

Kitty Oliver noticed that a word that people often used about her was reckless. Her parents had said it about her throughout her adolescence, tutors and professors had said it about her throughout her school and university days, and even her bosses said it when she joined the Secret Service. That last one surprised her because she thought her daredevil spirit was best suited for espionage work. She joined the service for the excitement because she knew she was not cut out for the mundane. She had always had a rebellious nature. If anyone told her, she shouldn't do something, it was a good reason to do it.

She was certainly not a classic beauty by any stretch of the imagination. Her square face had a small button nose and steely grey eyes, and a hard line to her mouth that left you feeling that this woman could be quite ruthless. Her hair was golden blonde and glossy, and she had a pale port-wine birthmark on her left cheek that faded down onto her neck. She was ordinary, most of the time.

The astounding thing about Kitty was that she had an internal switch that, when flicked, turned her into a formidable femme fatale. That was why her Secret Service bosses tolerated the recklessness because it was widely known that she was the best in the business.

She was always the first choice for honey trap missions, and the number of foreign agents she had turned or bled dry for information was almost legendary. She took risks that other agents wouldn't consider, and even she was not sure whether it was because she felt invincible or had a total disregard for her own safety.

Kitty was proud of her reputation, but was prone to being over-confident because of it. Her favourite boss had been Celia Browning, who knew how to handle her. No micromanagement or cautious approach from Celia. She would hand Kitty the jobs no one else wanted, knowing she would deliver a positive result. When she had made mistakes, Celia had forgiven her, and it had not hampered her career one bit. In fact, Kitty felt that her boss was more lenient and gave her more leeway than any other agent in their department. She secretly believed that this was because no other agent took the chances she did to get a job done. It wasn't like she was impervious to fear, she just couldn't remember ever feeling it. She felt anxiety, or sometimes worried about getting a job done, but never fear. Perhaps that was what an adrenalin junkie was, someone who loves the rush but does it because the barrier of fear that keeps most people safe from harm, does not exist for them.

She had applied to join the service when she was twenty-six, after a big fight with her father, who was worried that she was becoming a wastrel. When he threatened to cut off her allowance unless she found gainful employment, she began to consider a career that might suit her talents. She passed the civil service entrance exam with flying colours, reinforcing her conviction that she was clever, resourceful, and suited to a job that was unusual and that carried with it the promise of adventure. She was born to be a secret agent!

Her training as a field agent was challenging for a number of reasons. She didn't find it beyond her intellectual capability, but the mundane trade craft was too boring. She could tail someone for miles in busy environments without losing them or being 'made'. Dead drops were easy, and she was already an accomplished pick pocket with her masterful powers of distraction and misdirection.

She also had an ear for languages, and had taught herself to speak Arabic and Russian, but Kitty didn't warm to her chosen career until she attended the weaponry course. It was there she discovered that this was something she could really excel at. She found the sessions on the use of blades, poisons, and hand-to-hand combat particularly exhilarating, but her eagerness was not without controversy when she injured another candidate and one of the instructors through her overenthusiastic participation. It progressed to the point where her training had to be on a one-to-one basis because none of her intake were prepared to risk their health and safety.

By the time she was given her first solo mission, she was already regarded as a specialist for assignments that called for sexual entrapment and for her emotionless ability to kill to survive.

Her main claim to fame was that in over thirty missions carried out in hostile environments, she had never once been captured or interrogated. This was something of a service record and quickly earned her the sort of notoriety that she revelled in. Towards the end of her career, she had been offered the opportunity to instruct new recruits, but she realised that the role of tutor would offer no challenge, so she resigned from the service. Her reputation was such that she was always in demand for private contract work, but she was very selective and only undertook 'wet' jobs.

There is an unspoken upper age limit for international assassins, which is driven by practicality. She knew her time was almost at an end, when she discovered that climbing up a drainpipe and exiting out of a 3rd floor window was much more difficult when your occupationally acquired arthritis reared its ugly head. The truth was that Kitty was a 61-year-old borderline sociopath, who, despite her polished, polite, and entertaining personality, was a consummate and convincing liar who cheated and manipulated others without guilt or remorse.

Kitty fitted into life at Shady Fields with some difficulty. She had settled in but was struggling to settle down. She was surrounded by people whom she, rudely referred to as 'missing in action' and accepting this reality as her future, made her feel like she had given up. Her physical condition, not her mental state, was the primary reason for moving into Shady Fields. The 'sawbones', Dr. Arnot was definitely delaying giving her the medication that would reduce the pain and discomfort she was experiencing. 'Take up tai-chi' he had told her. Knowing that you can kill someone with a drinking straw, but having the dexterity and strength to do it, are not the same thing. She'd decided to give Arnot a little more time before she would have to have a serious conversation with him.

When she heard on the internal house grapevine the news that Celia Browning was coming to live here too, she was shocked. Kitty understood the need to be in control of your life for as long as possible, but it saddened her to think of her old boss and mentor losing her mental capacity. Kitty wondered if there was anything worse than that. Her physical body was failing her, but that was no surprise given the life she had put it through. The arthritis, the hypertension, and type 2 diabetes meant that her physical health was deteriorating. Dr Arnot had been very graphic with his diagnosis at her last medical, six weeks ago.

"Many think that thin people can't get diabetes, but given your history Kitty, it really was inevitable. You have had almost constantly raised cortisol levels linked to your fight or flight mechanism, and high alcohol intake too. That is a recipe for diabetes, and you will need to stick to a planned diet and knock off the vodka too".

Kitty sighed,

"What's the point of still being around if you can't do the things you love any more?"

Dr Arnot had rolled the pressure cuff around the machine and popped it back into his medical bag.

"Don't be so melodramatic, Kitty. It could be worse, you still have your faculties, no signs of dementia, also common with people in your occupation. I am not saying you can never have those things again, just to be sensible and take them in moderation. It's about learning a new way to live your life without so many bad habits. You are never too old to learn new things, Kitty,"

Her face betrayed a slight smile.

"I have learnt plenty of things in my life, Doctor. Like the way to a man's heart is between his fourth and fifth rib with a stiletto and when you are an agent working undercover, never lick the spoon, but I don't fancy turning into a crusty old woman with hairs on her chin who looks forward to a repeat of

Midsummer Murders as the highlight of her week. I don't want to be dependent with people pitying me".

As he stood to leave, he gave her a look of censure.

"You can choose to make the best of your life here, knowing that your medical conditions will get worse and need support, or you can spend your time howling at the moon, your choice. The reality is, you can't ignore that you are ageing and not with good health. There are counsellors and therapists here that can help you make the adjustment. That has to be better than becoming angry and bitter about the hand you have been dealt, doesn't it?"

"If you say so". She said begrudgingly.

She would have a friend that she could speak to once Celia was settled in, it might not be that bad after all. There were also a few of the others that could be coaxed into a bit of harmless fun to spice things up a bit. Perhaps Arnot was right, maybe her sense of adventure was precisely what Shady Fields needed. She might start with Bill and Ben, the dynamite men. If Bills' reputation was to be believed, he was a rule bender and an explosives expert to boot. There must be an hour or two of fun right there.

15. The Basement Thames House

Tuesday 21st January 2020

One of the benefits of having an eidetic memory is that you store huge quantities of history in your head. It would have made him a very popular choice as a member of a pub quiz team, that was if he'd had any mates to go to the pub with.

Peter was quite the authority on modern Russia, Perestroika and the emergence of Putin, and he was keen to understand if they featured in the Tripartite Treaty. If it was such a big deal globally back then, he knew there was bound to be some sort of connection, but the Soviet Union was going through one of the most turbulent times in modern history during the eighties and nineties. Finding the link to how and where the Russians fitted would not be obvious because so much was going on around that time. There was the war in Chechnya and the catastrophic domestic economic crisis. This was a fascinating hare Daniel had set running, and he would definitely chase it down. In fact, it would be his pleasure.

Peter knew that during the 1980s, Mikhail Gorbachev launched a number of domestic and military reforms that helped bring an end to the Cold War between the West and the Soviet Union. He held nuclear disarmament talks with President Ronald Regan, heralding a new détente, Perestroika. The West hailed him as a visionary, a modern leader who bought down the Iron Curtain, but closer to home, critics of Gorbachev believed his actions had orchestrated the collapse of the Soviet Union. When they ousted him, Boris Yeltsin took his place. The West saw him as a modernizer, but he became known in Russian inner circles as a drunken buffoon.

With the Russian situation so precariously balanced, destructive infighting pitted high-ranking officers against each other. Modernizers against traditionalists, there had to be casualties. Vladimir Gorski was the Minister of the Interior at that time, a mountain of a man with an extensive history of murders and a substantial collection of turned agents under his belt. Before he went into politics, he was a KGB Chief, a contemporary and namesake of his favourite and best KGB agent, Vladimir Putin. The thin veneer of respectability he presented wasn't sufficient to disguise what he was capable of. Many who fell afoul of him described him as having a reputation for being completely ruthless and totally untrustworthy. At least, those who survived him did.

Using this historical context, Peter discovered a series of dispatches relating to trade negotiations between the three superpowers, where Gorski's name kept appearing. That didn't track. He was the Minister of the interior, and international trade was not in his portfolio. There were only two possible reasons for his involvement; firstly, he was on the take, cutting himself a slice of that lucrative cake, or secondly, he was a back channel for the leadership, with an active role at the negotiating table.

Peter considered the scenarios, the most likely conclusion was that the traditionalists were so fearful of how far Russia might fall, they had taken the decision to be on the inside of this venture. That was probably based on the premise of keeping your friends close, but your enemies closer. Yes, when Peter thought about it, it was obvious, Gorski had taken it on himself to enter into the Treaty, supported by factions who wanted to be rid of Yeltsin to safeguard Mother Russia's interests. The Soviets had spent many years becoming a major oil and energy producer. If there was a pact to emasculate an oil producing nation, Gorski would want to be in on that game.

Peter's hypothesis made absolute sense, but proving it would not be easy. This was information so sensitive that there would be nothing in writing that could be traced back to the group. The very idea that the three Superpowers of the day would work together to destabilize another sovereign nations' energy business was unthinkable. It went against every convention and broke every rule over the way global economics was handled.

Peter decided to make a call he had been putting off for eighteen months. He picked up the phone and selected a number from his speed dial list. It rang twice before the familiar, sultry voice of Dr. Evelyn Anderton, answered with,

"Well, hello Peter, and what can I help you with today?"

She was a brilliant academic specialising in international energy politics. He could picture her sitting in her cluttered office at the Georgetown Institute for Global Affairs.

"Hello Eve, how are you?"

He wasn't sure of his welcome after their last encounter. Eve responded,

"If you are wondering whether I am still speaking to you after the events in Oslo, then the answer is yes. My pride hurt for a few days, but hey, life's too short to stuff a mushroom. I wondered if you would ever call me again".

He could hear the warmth in her voice and relaxed a little.

"Sorry, Eve, time just never seemed to be on my side. I'm pleased you are still speaking to me; it would have made my request more difficult if you were still mad at me".

"So, this is not a personal call, you just want to pick my brains again?"

"Yes, I am afraid so, and it's a bit obscure".

"Oh Peter…. All right, what do you want to know?"

"What can you tell me about the Tripartite Treaty, it would have been back in the eighties or nineties?"

Peter hoped she had something that could set him on the right trail. She sounded surprised,

"Well, I wasn't expecting that! I can only give you conjecture because there is precious little evidence, but if it existed, it was an agreement between three major economies to undermine an energy deal between three major oil producing countries: Iran, Iraq, and Saudi Arabia. The stakes were high because if a deal of that magnitude were brokered, it could have reshaped global energy dynamics. The East could have held the West to ransom by restricting access to energy or controlling world prices. It would have been massive. If it did exist, it came to nothing because it was around the time of the Iraqi War and the conflict changed the relationships and the stakes. Everyone became focused on Saddam Hussain, and the rest is Geography, as they say".

She waited for a response.

"Is that it?" Peter sounded a little disappointed. She continued,

"There were suggestions that oil reserves had been exaggerated, casting doubt on the integrity of the energy deal. People questioned the authenticity of the story but given how volatile the world was at that time, I can believe Western powers would still be very nervous about a scenario that could hold them to ransom in that way. I did do some digging at the time, but as I say, it all went away when the US and UK invaded Iraq". She paused. "What's this all about Peter, it was all a long time ago, what's your interest?"

Peter became guarded but tried to sound casual.

"I'm working on something unrelated, and I came across the name and wanted to fill in the blanks. Probably nothing, but you know me, I like to be thorough".

"Not in all things, darling, just your work!" The barbed comment hit home.

"Would you believe it was just the wrong time and place, Eve?"

"That is the story of my life, Peter, timing was never my strong point".

Peter grinned, feeling that a burned bridge had just been repaired.

"Could be worse, like having a heart attack when you are playing charades!"

Eve laughed.

"Don't leave it so long next time, take care Peter, I mean it, don't be a stranger". She hung up.

He felt strangely uplifted. He had huge respect for this woman; her intellect and her friendship, it was just sad that he couldn't reciprocate her feelings for him. She was incredibly well-informed, and her strategic thinking was razor sharp. Their discussions had been long and detailed, and it had been a long time since anyone had challenged his intellect in the way that she did. Unfortunately, that was it, no physical spark or attraction on his part. He had thought their relationship was lost, but the call had salvaged it. If he'd realised that was all it would take, he would have contacted her earlier.

His reflected on what she had just said. He knew exactly where to look next. He pulled up the search box for their immense database, entering a few keywords that would call up the Middle East oil production reports for the period. There were three sources he wanted to examine: the countries internal reports, the impact on supplies after the Kuwait invasion and OPEC reports for that time. In seconds, his screen was full of data. Tables, lists, graphs, and bar charts showing him production quotas, exports, prices and much, much more. Immediately, his inherent ability to recognise almost imperceptible trends in data told him that there was a pattern to the discrepancies. The evidence strongly implied that a deliberate attempt to manipulate energy production and distribution markets was in play. Scrutiny was not strong at that time, but in the intervening years, data analysis had become much more sophisticated. This level of misinformation would be picked up by a year ten schoolboy today, but back then it would have been far easier for this scheme to slide under the radar. If the Russians had seen these figures and believed them, they would have entered into any agreement that would diminish the hold the Middle East would have had over them. Oil was one of the few things they could still use as a bargaining chip on the world stage, and to have it 'traded down' would have been disastrous. They would have done a deal with the devil if they had to. Peter was satisfied, he was onto something.

If Gorski was part of the Tripartite Treaty, and had knowledge of the Middle East energy negotiations, it would put him right in the centre of the game and give the Russians enough clout to sabotage any deal on the table that was not in their own best interest.

Peter was faced with two simple questions; what was the involvement of the Tripartite Treaty in making sure that the deal did not go through, and what lengths did they go to, to achieve that goal?

16. Shady Fields

Tuesday 21st January 2020

The day room in the west wing of Shady Fields was rather grand, with high stucco ceilings, pale green linen covered walls, highly polished parquet floors and a selection of large comfortable chairs and settees. A number of occasional tables with chairs set around them were laid out with boardgames. The table framed by a large bay window was set with a small chess set. Jon Dowie-Brown sat at the table; arms folded in a defiant gesture.

"I want to use my set".

Ben Faulkner smiled,

"Well, you can't!"

"Then I won't play" Dowie-Brown's lips set firmly.

Ben shook his head slowly from side to side,

"Don't be ridiculous, it doesn't matter, does it?"

Dowie-Brown looked directly at him.

"Yes, it does matter, it matters very much to me".

Ben tried again.

"Why are you making such a fuss? It's just a quick game".

Dowie-Brown sat upright in the chair.

"I am making a fuss, as you put it, because at my age, taking a stand is all I have left. I have dodgy lungs, a clicky hip and acid reflux that I have affectionately nicknamed Vesuvius. I can no longer go anywhere until I have confirmed the vicinity of a bathroom, and I wear invisible hearing aids that are set so high I get feedback when Beattie walks past in her nylon cardigan". He gestured over his shoulder at an old lady who had just settled down with the remote control of the large TV in the corner of the room. He continued.

"Picking my hand-carved ivory chess set over this cheap plastic one is one of the few things about my day that I can control. Now be a sport, and please fetch it from my room".

Ben relented,

"OK, give me the key, where is it?"

"It is in the decorated wooden box on the table by the side window".

He handed his key over, and Ben took it reluctantly. He left the room to make his way up the stairs. A thin smile played around the old man's lips. These small victories held too much significance for Dowie-Brown's liking. The quicker he was out of here the better.

Celia wandered into the library, taking in the décor, the furniture and the extensive wooden bookcases that lined three sides of the room. It was empty, and yet there was a crackling log fire in the grate that had only recently been lit. Celia thought it seemed pointless if no one was here to feel the benefit, and it made the room warmer than it needed to be. She circled the rooms' perimeter, looking at the extensive range of noteworthy and thought-provoking books that filled the shelves. There were many volumes that, on another day, would have demanded her attention, but today she was not interested enough to select anything to read.

She slid into a well-padded chesterfield-style armchair chair set close to the white marble fireplace, completely at a loss about what to do next. She was not settling in well. The upheaval had been greater than she'd anticipated, and Daniel was being very pious about the request she had made of him. She wanted her health problems to go away, to be able to function like she used to. She had always been in a position of seniority and was comfortable giving the orders. Having to accept that she could no longer function in that way was challenging and problematic. She credited herself with being a good leader, adept at spotting talent and giving people ample opportunities for advancement in their careers. She felt that it was the least she could do in her line of work. Pay rises were fine, but you had to be alive to spend them, and in the old days that was not something which could be taken for granted. Her logic then was simple, if you paid them a decent salary, they were less likely to become double agents solely for the money. The people she worried about were the ones who did the work purely for the adrenaline rush. They were unlikely to make old bones because of the unnecessary risks they took. She had lost a few good people along the way, although not as many as her predecessors. Overall, she believed her stewardship of the worlds' greatest security service had been relatively uneventful to the casual observer. Of course, it had not been without crisis or scandal, but one of her major strengths had been her ability to control the message and keep the truth well and truly hidden.

Jon Dowie-Brown interrupted her musings by appearing in the doorway.

"Hello Celia, may I ask how you are settling in?"

She watched him close the door behind him and move elegantly across the room to take the chair facing hers. He continued,

"It has been quite a while, hasn't it? We lost touch after I left the service, or should I say, was manoeuvred out of the service".

There it was Celia noted; that sense of victim that Dowie-Brown did so well.

"Hello Dowie, water under the bridge by now I would have thought. It didn't seem to hamper your impressive results in the private sector, in fact, just the opposite. I must confess to watching you climb the ladder of success with some interest. You know you would never have reached those dizzying heights with us. Patriotism isn't as lucrative as self-interest, is it?"

Dowie-Brown's cheeks flushed as instantly as if she had slapped him.

"You sanctimonious bitch" he spat out. "What would you know about patriotism? The service has not been about patriotism for fifty years or more. It's about political expediency and serving the interests of the government. As far as the service is concerned, the real patriots are disposable. They are collateral damage in a deadly board game that you people play for fun".

"For an intelligent man, you can be monumental in your naivety. Patriotism is about ensuring we come out on top, regardless of the 'colour' of our government. We navigate policy changes to ensure we limit the damage politicians do to our country and its interests".

"Does that include the destruction of our own because they threaten to share the inconvenient truths of the day?"

His eyes flashed with anger, bordering on hatred.

"Oh, please, save me the righteous indignation of hindsight. Like I said, it's water under the bridge. We make decisions that are necessary given the circumstances and the information available at the time. Of course, with the benefit of hindsight, some of those decisions turn out to be flawed, but we learn from them, and we get better at the game. What happened to Robert, and I assume you ARE referring to Robert Crane, was regrettable, but at the time the threat he represented seemed very real and the safety of this country was in genuine peril".

He scoffed.

"Just listen to yourself will you, the country was in peril! This is not 'Biggles goes to war', you participated in a cover-up so vile and insidious that words fail me. You allowed a man whose shoes you were not fit to clean, to be hounded by civil servants and kingmakers. A man whose whole life had been given in the genuine service of keeping the world a safer place, and you threw him to. the wolves. You took his reputation as a scientist and an expert, and you left it in tatters. You compromised his integrity and his values so that the only course of action left to him was to take his own life. We know now that it was poor leadership and politics that created that God-awful situation, and that with time, Robert Crane would have been vindicated, but it all came too late, the damage was done. Celia, I honestly don't know how you can sleep at night".

She had listened to his outburst calmly, her hands resting lightly in her lap, back straight, though no longer relaxing in the chair.

"I gave him every opportunity to change his mind and play along. I spoke to him just before he left the house on the day he died. It didn't need to end like it did, it was his choice. It is what it is, I can't turn the clock back, what was done can't be undone. It was a regrettable situation, but we got the result we needed at the time. There really was no alternative Dowie, and if I am honest, I can't see why you're still so angry about it all, it was a blip in history that no one else was really bothered about".

Her final statement was the one that lit the blue touchpaper, in an instant, Dowie-Brown shot out of his chair and rushed at the woman opposite. Three seconds later, he had his hands around her throat, squeezing. He wasn't sure how much time had passed, but when his white-hot rage dissipated, Dowie-Brown was left hovering over the small figure slumped in the corner of the chair, angry red welts appearing around her neck. He stepped away, turned, and quickly left the room without looking back at the prone body of Celia.

He needed to get away from here. His blood was pulsating though his veins, and the pounding in his ears was almost deafening. He rushed through the house and into the garden room at the rear. The large French doors to the terrace were closed at this time of year, but he threw open the middle set and burst out into the cold air, hurrying across the lawns and into the grounds beyond. It was some time before he had calmed down enough to be aware of his surroundings. He found himself standing on the old painted wooden jetty that overlooked the ornamental pond. The vegetation at the water's edge was brown and bedraggled, and the surface of the water broken only by the odd ripple of fish hunting for scarce food. He could not recollect ever losing control of himself like this before. The ferocity of his anger scared him. He clung to the handrail trying to regain control of his breathing, slow deep breaths in through the nose and slower controlled exhalation out through his mouth. His head began to clear, and his heart rate slowed, he considered his next steps. He didn't know if he had actually killed Celia, he hadn't stopped to check for a pulse or to see if she was still breathing. It was quite possible that he had just committed murder. The strength of his hatred frightened him. He always blamed her for what had happened to Robert. She was the one who had pressured him into remaining quiet about what he'd discovered. There was no doubt in his mind that she was also behind the thinly veiled threats issued to himself and his family, threats that would become much more than mere threats if he went public with what he knew.

Initially, he'd blamed Robert for yielding to the pressure and committing the cowardly act, but then saw that Celia was the main protagonist in the whole sordid affair. Knowing Robert as he did, it would have taken something significant to thwart his whistleblowing intentions of exposing the government's cover-up. Dowie-Brown had experienced the same pressure at first hand when two of Celia's departmental 'heavies' visited his home to deliver an ultimatum. They explained the cost and the consequences of going public in clear and precise terms. Loss of reputation, loss of livelihood, and if he continued, possibly loss of liberty. His nerve abandoned him. He had acquiesced and gradually resumed a life that had served him very well over the years. And yet lately, the guilt he harboured over Robert's death began to sting. He analysed it, over-thought it, played numerous scenarios over and over in his head, and reasoned that he needed to make amends in some way. He would bring those guilty for his friend's anguish and subsequent actions to justice. As he gradually regained control of his emotions and his senses, the consequences of his recent actions began to dawn on him. He knew his options were limited, but he realised that he must go back and accept responsibility for what he had just done.

Ben Faulkner came downstairs with the ornately decorated wooden box under his arm. He entered the day room expecting to find Dowie-Brown waiting for him to begin their game, but he wasn't there. Beattie was sitting in one of the armchairs, absent-mindedly knitting and watching an old rerun of Dads Army, chuckling away to herself at the on-screen antics of

Mainwaring and Co. It was at times like this Ben knew he didn't belong here. He should have been climbing one of the famous Scottish Munros or sunning himself on an exotic beach in the Maldives, but his lifelong friend and partner-in-crime, Bill Tandy, did need to be here. So, for now, he just had to accept his fate, even though deep down, it felt like giving in to ageing.

"Hi Beattie, have you seen Dowie?"

She looked up from the shapeless powder-pink 'thing' that hung from her metal needles.

"Yes, he wandered off in the direction of the library about ten minutes ago, just after you left him".

Ben went to look for him so they could start their game. As he entered the hallway, he felt a distinct draft coming from the back of the house. That was unusual. He felt Shady Fields was always a little too warm, particularly in the winter months, but given the age and health of some of the residents, better too warm than too cold. He opened the door to the library and immediately saw Celia Browning slumped in the fireside chair. She looked very pale. He rushed to her and felt her carotid artery, looking for a pulse. He noticed the livid blue line around her neck. Yes, there it was, a pulse, feint, but present, however she was not breathing. He pulled her unceremoniously onto the floor, roller her onto her back and administered artificial respiration. Between cycles, he called out for help. A passing care assistant raised the alarm. People came running from all directions, including Hilary, who was coming down the staircase from her office.

Ben continued to resuscitate her and after a few minutes, with Hilary on the floor at her side, Celia's eyelids began to flutter and she regained consciousness. She coughed and tried to sit up, but Hilary gently restrained her.

"Stay where you are, Celia, an ambulance is on the way".

She turned to Ben,

"The marks on her neck?"

He looked serious and nodded.

"I think someone tried to kill her, Hilary. If I hadn't found her when I did, she may not have made it".

Hilary felt her stomach tighten. That could only mean one thing, someone here wanted Celia dead, and if they didn't find out who it was, they may well try again.

The raucous siren created a cacophony that preceded the ambulance as it raced up the drive, skidding to a halt at the front of the building. Celia was now sitting in a chair, the colour slowly returning to her face, and adamant that she was not going with them to hospital. A quick telephone call resulted in Dr. Arnot's appearance and Hilary cleared the library of all onlookers, leaving a tense negotiation taking place about whether the ambulance crew could insist on taking Celia against her will. In the end, she was taken up to her room and put to bed.

Ben took Hilary to one side and mentioned that he had not seen Dowie-Brown in all the commotion.

"He may have seen what happened and given chase to an assailant, he may have been injured himself. We need to find him, Hilary".

"Yes, you are right, let's send……"

She stopped in mid-sentence as a dishevelled Dowie-Brown appeared in the entrance hall. The suave and sophisticated man had been replaced by someone who looked every year of his age and scared, really scared.

"Dowie, are you all right? You look terrible, what's happened?"

She rushed over to him, guiding him onto one of the leather settees.

"Ben, please fetch him some water, Layla can look after Celia".

Ben was back in a blink with a large glass of water for Dowie-Brown and a smaller one of what Hilary suspected was malt whiskey for himself. She offered him the water and noticed how his hand shook as he raised the glass to his lips.

"What happened Dowie?"

The man was clearly going into shock, she could feel his whole-body trembling.

"Did I kill her, is Celia dead?" The tremor in his voice gave it a weedy quality that was totally uncharacteristic.

"Are you saying that you attacked Celia, Dowie? Why would you do that?" It made no sense to her; he was not a violent man.

"I lost my temper. I wanted to know about Robert, why she betrayed him, but she just didn't care. She made him take his own life, and she just didn't care. Something in me snapped and I went for her. Is she dead?"

Ben crouched down so that he was at eye level with Dowie-Brown.

"She's not dead, but it was a bloody close call Dowie, what the hell were you thinking?"

Tears began to well up in the man's eyes.

"He was my best friend, and they hounded him to his death. She was in charge, and she stood by and let it happen. When I asked her about it, she just shrugged and mentioned collateral damage. He was brilliant and principled, and they made his last few weeks' hell". He broke down.

Hilary gently covered his hand with hers

"What was his name, Dowie?"

He lowered his head,

"Robert Crane". It was clear she would get little else out of him for quite a while.

Hilary snapped into leader mode.

"Ben, take Dowie-Brown up to his room and stay with him. Dr Arnot will come up to check him over. I will stay with Celia until the ambulance leaves. Once I'm satisfied that she is okay, I will speak with Daniel. He needs to know what has happened".

Dr Arnot was in the entrance hall with the paramedics.

"I will take full responsibility for her; we have the best facilities here, and she is in no danger. You know the situation now, and I will speak with your control room to confirm that Ms. Browning will remain here".

They looked confused, but he spoke with such authority they shrugged, picked up their bags and left.

Later, when Celia was resting in her room on Doctor Arnot's orders, she began to think about that whole sorry episode. Her neck felt damaged and tender, and her voice was croaky. Celia had been shocked by Dowie's reaction; she had clearly underestimated the strength of the friendship that had existed between Dowie-Brown and Robert Crane. Crane had always been a thorn in their side, he was stubborn and opinionated. When she made that last phone call, he had categorically refused to see reason, and he was not willing to compromise his principles for anyone. The arrogance of the man. How could he think that his clear conscience was more important than the Government?

From that moment on she knew that Crane would not 'go quietly', in fact, the opposite was true. He would become a whistle-blower. There is something unnerving about that breed of person. Crane saw himself as a sort of martyr, holding the government accountable for the truth. His actions would have been regarded as traitorous and could have put the country at great risk of damaging their strategic relationships with world powers, just when Russia was starting to see reason and give Western capitalism a whirl. Stubbornness has a lot to answer for, Crane deliberately refused to accept the consequences of his actions by insisting on going public with what he knew. It didn't seem to matter what they threatened him with, he was adamant that the truth must come out.

Kitty Oliver was her last resort, she became Celia's solution. Crane had worked with Kitty a number of times in the past, but even so, she was never one to let sentiment get in the way of a job. Celia closed her eyes and recalled the events that unfolded in her office that early September evening like it was only yesterday.

Kitty and Celia sat in her office enjoying a single malt. Celia explained that this was a 'special' job. She had used Kitty on black and wet ops' several times before, so she was familiar with the drill. Go to the office, out of hours, on the pretext of a simple catch up. On the desk there would be a folder that you were expected to read whilst the boss prattled on about nothing in particular. Everything had to be committed to memory, then the folder would be slid back into a desk draw. No mention of the target or the job. Plausible deniability was the thing. Celia did not want to know the where, when, or how. The only instruction was,

"It cannot be traced back to us, be creative".

Celia watched as a sly smile slid across Kitty's face.

"Any thug can commit a murder, but it takes a true artist to commit a suicide". She drained her glass and left.

Three days later, Celia received the notification that Robert Crane had been reported missing by his wife, and the rest, as they say, was history. They managed the media fallout and the subsequent public enquiry, but her experience had taught her that this was one case that would come back to bite her one day. The clean-up crew had botched their job, the local plod had not grasped the serious nature of the situation and made errors, and she hadn't been convinced that his family wouldn't start asking questions. Despite her best efforts, there could be a breadcrumb trail to follow. She was grateful that it had not begun to unravel under her watch.

However, Dowie's attack had bought a new urgency with it. This historic and sordid affair was the case in the file that she had passed to Daniel, and if she was honest, the one about which she was most worried. If Dowie-Brown had been hell-bent on revenge, and he discovered that Kitty had been responsible for Crane's death, then he would be gunning for her too.

Daniel hadn't helped matters with his attitude to the files. What the hell did he think would happen? Every DG had a file of dirty laundry, and he was being idealistic if he believed that he wouldn't have one by the time he needed a successor. In any case, Daniel needed to take immediate action to stop this situation getting out of control. It could be worse thought Celia, at least no one is sniffing around questioning the 'suicide'

17. Shady Fields

Tuesday 21st January 2020

In the calm sanctuary of her office, Hilary had slumped into her executive leather chair. That had been a close call. To nearly lose a high-profile resident when she'd barely had time to unpack was a massive failure on her part. What had she missed? She could only read the unredacted parts of Celia's file, which basically left only her gender, her old address, and her date of birth. She had no idea that Dowie-Brown and Celia had a history, and that there was also a connection to Robert Crane.

She couldn't put it off any longer, she really needed to speak with her boss to keep him in the picture. Her phone rang and she picked it up.

"Daniel, thanks for calling back, I know how busy you are, but I need to keep you up to date with a situation we have here".

Hilary wasn't quite sure where to start, so she plunged in with the burning question that was on her mind.

"Have you heard of a Professor Robert Crane?"

There was a short silence and Daniel replied cautiously.

"Well, that's an odd question. Why do you want to know about someone who has been dead for decades? What's going on, Hilary?"

"Jon Dowie-Brown attacked and tried to strangle Celia Browning today".

She let that land before throwing another curveball.

"His excuse was revenge for the death of his lifelong friend Professor Robert Crane, who committed suicide whilst on a mission that Celia was heading up in the nineties. I know the service is an incestuous place and that paths cross all the time, but is it a coincidence that their paths should cross here? I am not buying it, Daniel. Then, if that wasn't strange enough, I was contacted three days ago by a woman called Sharon Louca who wanted to ask my aunt for her help. When I explained that she'd recently passed away, she told me her father had left her a message telling her to find Ada and ask for her help in proving that he was murdered. Her father was…. Wait for it…. Professor Robert Crane. It turns out that he and Ada had an affair years ago. He trusted her implicitly because she was the love of his life. I know this because I discovered their love letters when I was clearing out her things at the cottage. Now Daniel, you know I'm a level-headed woman, but honestly this feels like the universe is trying to tell me something".

Daniel took a long breath.

"Okay, we probably need to talk, I'm coming down there tomorrow, but there's stuff going on that is bigger than all of this. Is Celia alright?"

"She is, but it was more luck than judgement. She isn't saying anything about the attack and refuses to take it any further. Dowie-Browns' reasoning doesn't make sense, but it's clear he can't stay here. I'm not prepared to take the risk that he could try again. Why do I get the feeling that there is a perfect storm brewing?"

Daniel hesitated,

"I'm not happy having this discussion over the phone, I'll be with you tomorrow right after my ministerial briefing. I know I don't have to say this but keep them separated. Can you post a guard on Dowie-Brown overnight, just in case?"

Hilary was concerned, Daniel clearly knew more than he could say at the moment, but she also knew that he would never put a resident at risk.

"Ben Faulkner has agreed to chaperone him, he was the one who discovered Celia, to be honest, Daniel, he probably saved her life. He will make sure Dowie-Brown isn't left alone. Dr Arnot has already prescribed a sedative; Dowie was in shock when he turned up in the hall, which makes me think it was an argument that escalated rather than a premeditated attack".

"Okay, I'll see you tomorrow Hilary, and be careful, we need to keep a lid on this"

Wednesday 22nd January 2020

Hilary got very little sleep that night. The room she used when she stayed over at Shady Fields was small and quite basic. It wasn't furnished to the same standard as the residents' rooms, it just needed to be functional. Over the last few years, it had come in useful when 'incidents' had happened. Spare clothes were always hanging in the wardrobe and basic toiletries in the bathroom cabinet. She pulled up the blind to let watery, winter sunlight wash in through the sash window. She quickly showered, dressed, and went along to her office, where Layla had already switched the coffee machine on and left the incident reports from yesterday on her desk.

Her priority was an update on Celia, so she fired off a quick text to Dr Arnot, asking for the status of both patients. He replied immediately. '*Celia will not be talking much today because of the soft tissue damage to her throat, and Dowie-Brown will probably feel quite groggy for a couple of days due to the after-effects of the medication I prescribed.*' She breathed a sigh of relief and silently thanked the good news fairy.

She opened the folder Sharon had left for her and decided to spend the next thirty minutes reading through the contents. She found herself looking at two copies of the same report. It was the ministerial briefing that Prime Minister Adam Hunt had delivered to the House of Commons, which justified the support the UK gave the US over their decision to invade Iraq. They appeared at first glance to be the same report, but there were slight alterations in the text of the second copy, which was also covered in pencil scribblings across the pages and in the margins. On closer inspection, it revealed that the author of the original report felt that the second version was seriously flawed. Subtle semantics had changed the meaning and intent of the report, and an unaware reader would draw very different conclusions to those described in the original document.

Essentially, the first report confirmed that after rigorous investigation, there was absolutely no evidence to support the belief that Iraq had the capability and the infrastructure to manufacture and deploy biological weapons of mass destruction. Eleven sites had been identified as potential high-risk locations across the country, yet on further inspection no physical evidence of manufacturing capability was discovered at any of them. The biomaterials that had been found were medical-grade and typical of research facilities across the world. The report's author had gone further by stipulating that there would need to be sophisticated processes and equipment in place if their intention had been to weaponize them, yet neither of these deductions were present either. The unequivocal conclusion was that Iraq posed no significant threat at that time.

After reading the second report, Hilary had identified three main differences. Firstly, there was the warning that materials had already been purchased and hidden in secret locations to ensure that the inspectors could not find and confiscate them. These locations were very different to the first report, and the maps showing the locations had been altered.

Secondly, the weapons they had made, were ready to deploy, and could easily reach the West, probably within hours of a strike being ordered. They would most likely use a dirty bomb to ensure the widest level of contamination, killing thousands, maybe hundreds of thousands. Compared to the first report, this read like a work of fiction.

Thirdly, all the critical information in the second report had apparently been confirmed by an informant working with the CIA. He was an Iraqi government driver who said he had overheard a conversation between a local man and the Iraqi head of military services. He claimed to have heard them confirm the existence of biological weapons and an intention to launch them into Europe to create 'as much damage as possible'. The two versions of the same report epitomized bias and how a slight change in perspective could change the tone and the intent of a document significantly.

A third document in the folder was a copy of an email thread between Robert Crane and someone called Pearson, a ministerial aide to the then Prime Minster Adam Hunt. In it, Crane underlined the discrepancies and warned of the consequences if this

179

misleading information was presented to Parliament. Celia Browning had been cc'd into the digital conversation. This was a clear indicator which showed that whatever was happening, Celia was fully aware of what was unfolding.

Hilary had been young at the time, but could still remember the sensationalized headlines of the House of Commons debate and the fateful outcome. She now realised which version of the report they had presented.

"What the hell?"

Hilary couldn't quite believe what she was holding in her hands. If these papers were genuine, then they were evidence of a government conspiracy to mislead parliament to guarantee the result of the vote supported the invasion of another sovereign nation; to commit an act of war based on a falsehood.

Hillary was shaken, not just by the revelations revealed, but by the extent to which the 'powers that be' had gone to, to keep the original document out of the public eye. Her hand began to tremble, she needed to clear her head. She closed the folder and locked it in a draw in her desk. There was just time to do her normal rounds before Daniel arrived, and she craved a bit of normality after what she had just read.

She started her inspection up on the second floor, where some of the more advance dementia cases were cared for. The main difference between this floor and the others was scale. The public rooms were smaller, the open spaces had no access to other floors, and there were code locks on all doors that lead to exits. The only other difference was that there were visibly more staff on this floor. Because these residents were at a later stage of dementia, their behaviour was more unpredictable and for some, that included significant mood swings, confusion about their location or time of day, even hallucinations for an unfortunate few.

She walked into the day room and saw that Charlie Bingham had now been transferred to this section. Charlie was their longest serving resident, having moved to Shady Fields the first week it opened. He was a lovely gentleman who wore old Saville Row suits with handmade shirts that had seen better days. At nearly 90 years of age, he was trapped in a world that no longer existed, and Hilary was not sure if it was his dementia that kept him locked in the past or whether it was personal choice. His granddaughter Lyndsey was a regular visitor, and they were often to be found enjoying afternoon tea in the garden room. He would regale her with stories of fast cars, first class travel and lunches in Monte Carlo with the jet set. When Hilary first met him, she had assumed he was a teller of tall tales until the day she went to his apartment and saw his collection of framed photographs. He called it his rogues' gallery. Here was the evidence of a noteworthy life that included the likes of Desmond Tutu, Graham Hill, David Niven, and Nelson Mandela as friends. His family was monied aristocracy, but a scandal in his younger days had threatened the family name, so they shipped him off to South Africa on a diplomatic posting that involved occasional work for the Secret Service.

He had made amends through his service for any indiscretions and here he was, now in the autumn of his years, with just those memories and visible signs of vascular dementia. He greeted her warmly.

"How lovely of you to come and see me Helen, it is Helen, isn't it?"

She smiled warmly at him.

"Hello Charlie, how good to see you again, it's Hilary".

He gave her the full benefit of his diplomatic training.

"Of course, it is how silly of me. And how is that dashing husband of yours? Has Bill decided to run for President again?"

Hilary didn't miss a beat.

"No, Charlie, he thinks two terms is enough".

"Quite right, my dear, you need time to enjoy life a little after all that hullabaloo".

A short thin woman, who was at least eighty, with a shock of unkempt white hair suddenly appeared through the archway. She saw Hilary and gestured to her.

"Come quick, this is urgent, and bring a big banana!" she turned around and went back the way she came.

"Well Charlie, I have to get on, I have a busy schedule today".

"I quite understand and give my best wishes to the President".

Hillary decided not to pursue the old woman, Sylvia James, who was a long-term resident because she knew that whatever the pressing need for a big banana was, when Hillary caught up with her, the bizarre request would almost certainly have been forgotten about.

As she made her way back down the stairs, she realised that this was exactly the thing that kept her days normal. They cared for people who saw the world through a different lens. Some of them had done extraordinary things in their lives, had quite unique skill sets, and all of them had sacrificed elements of their personal life to serve their country. That touch of reality made Hilary feel like she was making a difference every day by being here. Plus, they did make you laugh.

She finished her tour of the ground floor, had her regular update with Layla Strong, the general manager, then went back to her office. She brewed a fresh pot of coffee, poured herself a cup, and sat down at her desk to reflect on the revelations contained in the files. With a single knock on the door, Daniel breezed in. Every time she saw him, she felt that little frisson of excitement. Her logical brain told her that it was because he was the best boss she'd ever had and the feeling she experienced was loyalty. However, her emotional brain told her it was something else; so she did what she'd always done, she buried those feelings deep inside and changed the subject.

"Morning Hilary, are you okay? You look a bit flushed".

Daniel pulled out the chair opposite and sat down. Hilary retrieved the documents she had read earlier from her desk drawer.

"I wasn't sure what to think about all of this, I thought Sharon may have been seeing things that were not there. It's easy to do when you lose someone unexpectedly, but then I read these".

She opened the folder and handed him the reports. He took them and slipped them back inside the folder.

"Aren't you even going to look at them?"

He looked away.

"I don't need to; I know what they say".

Hilary shook her head in disbelief.

"Are you telling me these are real, that we had a government that knowingly lied to parliament and committed an act of war based on false information?"

"Have you heard of Vector 10?"

Daniel was still attempting to put the pieces of the puzzle together, but he didn't have a clue what the picture on the lid looked like.

"Yes, of course. He's our equivalent of Edward Snowden. He has released three batches of classified documents to date, no one knows who he is, where he's getting his information from or why he's doing it. The last release seemed to target high-profile figures and celebrities. But what has Vector 10 got to do with this?"

Daniel shrugged.

"I'm not sure, but I think the perfect storm you mentioned is about to make landfall. The last time I was here, I called in to see Celia, and she gave me some documents and email threads related to this case. The papers revealed that an agreement to support the US and their invasion of Iraq was deemed essential, but also indicated that some key figures in the government realised that the country may not support that action unless we were directly threatened. It appears that the information presented to the house was significantly exaggerated in order to win the vote. Not everyone believed it, and the vote just scraped through.

As the cost in lives mounted and the reality of the war began to hit home, many people questioned the decision to go to war. The mainstream media applied pressure on Ministers by asking very difficult questions, eventually they forced a public enquiry. Typical of most public enquiries, though it was heavily skewed away from the agreement and the decision-making process, focusing solely on the reports themselves".

"The inspector who authored the report was Professor Robert Crane, and halfway through giving his testimony he committed suicide. It was deemed that the error was his; and because of the circumstances of his death, and out of respect to his family, it all went away. The outcome was that no blame was attributed to any serving Minister, it was put down to stress and pressure of the job, human error, poor interpretation of the facts, blah blah…"

Hilary shook her head, the frustration seeping out.

"This world renown expert was thrown under the bus in order for some duplicitous politicians to walk away with a clean slate?"

"That's what it looks like. The documents in the latest release from Vector 10 seem to be targeting those senior figures who might have been involved in such a cover-up. They also suggest some sort of collaboration of powers actively engaged in manipulating the oil and energy markets. This is serious Hilary, the repercussions for us and the Americans if this were proven, could set off another conflict".

"So, what do we do, Daniel? We can't un-know this stuff. Robert's daughter Sharon is stubborn, she has the bit between her teeth and won't let it go. And if I am honest, I can't say I blame her. This suggests that someone assassinated one of our own on our soil and got away with it. That's as bad as it gets, Daniel, the Americans are supposed to be our allies!"

"Not quite, it could be worse, what if we orchestrated the whole thing?"

He looked very grave.

"It would mean that we assassinated one of our own, on home ground!"

18. Shady Fields

Tuesday 21st January 2020

Daniel knew he had to question Celia, but he wasn't sure how helpful she would be. She could only give him what she remembered, and with her condition deteriorating, that window was slowly closing. He would speak to her today before returning to London. Once again, he found himself knocking on her door. She opened it and smiled brightly.

"What a lovely surprise Daniel, it's been a long time, come in, come in. Do you have time for tea?"

She ushered him in and closed the door onto a room that was very untidy. Clothes draped across furniture, pictures skewed on the walls and draws open with contents spilling out, it looked like the place had been ransacked.

"Celia, what happened here?" He asked.

"Just doing a little spring-cleaning" she said, blinking.

Daniel hesitated when he saw the state of the room, but decided to press on with his questions.

"Celia, we need to talk. I've been looking at the documents you gave me relating to the Tripartite Treaty. Something highly irregular was going on. Meetings took place with the Prime Minister's personal staff, without Government Ministers or even their under-secretaries present. That's not how decision-making takes place. If I didn't know better, I would say that MI6 was following a partisan agenda, meeting the needs of the Government rather than being the impartial protector of UK security".

She had turned away from him and gazed blankly out of the window into the far distance.

"I remember recruiting you, Daniel. You were at Cambridge, still wet behind the ears, and we lured you in with tales of spies and intrigue".

"That wasn't me Celia, I was recruited when I served in the army, we didn't meet until I'd been in the service for a year or more".

Daniel realised that she was experiencing an Alzheimer's episode. There was a glazed look in her eyes, the slowing of her mental processing and her faltering speech.

She turned and blinked vacantly at him.

"What documents are you talking about?"

"Your insurance policy folder. You handed it to me a couple of days ago".

"I haven't given you a folder, what are you talking about?"

The difficulty with the disease was that it didn't just take old memories, for some, it stopped them making new ones. He wondered if she was aware of that and had used one of her more coherent moments to hand the file over. He had known Celia for a long time and knew what an intelligent woman she was. It wouldn't surprise him if somewhere in her belongings she kept a notebook or an aide-mémoire with a list of things she had to do, systematically ticking them off, until she lost her ability to do even that. He knew that some of her memories of her involvement with the Robert Crane incident were intact, and he had nothing to lose. He began to speak slowly and carefully.

"Celia, do you remember Professor Robert Crane, he was a scientist who headed up our inspection teams in Libya, Kuwait and Iraq?"

She looked at him and a spark of recognition registered on her face.

"Yes, yes, I remember him. He was a very troublesome and stubborn man".

Her eyes scanned the ceiling as if searching for something hidden there, her gaze returned to Daniel, this time a little sharper.

"Robert Crane was so pedantic, and he didn't always think about the practicality of things. I remember he was a brilliant academic, but not very realistic. Why are you asking about him?"

Daniel continued to follow the thin breadcrumb trail that her folder had set in motion. The document that had triggered his enquiry was a copy of a memo to Stewart Pearson, Chief of Staff at number 10 at the time, talking about the problems they were having with Robert Crane and how Celia was struggling to keep him in line.

"Yes, I imagine he was a real handful. What exactly was he being stubborn about Celia?"

Again, her gaze swept upwards, scouring the dark corners of her room for the answers he needed. Her face registered delight. She turned back to Daniel; the spark of awareness burning brightly in her eyes, and began to narrate the history he so desperately needed.

"Do you remember that odious little man, Pearson? He was working out of the Prime Minister's office at the time. He was always pushing his own agenda. Well, he wanted Crane to ignore the final edit of the document. Yes, that was it, he just had to keep his mouth shut and not contest the report's finding. But he wouldn't do it. We tried everything to get him to see reason, at first, we thought he would go along with it, but when the journalist contacted him, he saw an opportunity to blow the whistle. Quite how he thought he would get away with it is beyond me. Pearson was furious. He said Crane was jeopardizing everything, our relationship with the Americans, undermining our government, even creating an anti-west uprising in the Middle East."

She paused, furrowing her eyebrows slightly. A deep frown appeared around her eyes.

"Kitty Oliver had been our CIA liaison at the time, and she said that they were very nervous about trusting Crane to remain silent.

She looked away from Daniel.

"I liked Kitty. You always knew where you stood with her. So I got her to pay him a visit. She was one of my most solid agents, she'd done this sort of thing many times before, and I knew I could trust her. She did what was asked of her, but the others were very sloppy and left loose ends. We contained the worst of it, but it was touch and go for a while. Every time someone started asking questions it raised a flag, and we stonewalled them with the usual stuff. Closing ranks always works, don't you find, Daniel?"

He nodded and smiled at her.

"Thanks for your time, Celia. It's been most enlightening". He turned to leave.

"Are you sure you won't stay for tea?"

She blinked at him again, but this time he got the feeling that Celia was fully back in the room.

"Thank you, but no, I have things to do".

As he made his way back to Hilary's office, he realised that he had just seen a side to his mentor that he'd not seen before. She revealed that she was capable of great ruthlessness and duplicity, and he knew that whilst her condition could exaggerate certain traits, it was unlikely to create ones that were not present in the first place. Maybe he had never really known Celia as well as he thought he had.

19. The Crane Family Home

Wednesday 22nd January 2020

As she wandered around the family home, moving from room to room, Sharon was feeling frustrated. She knew there were protocols and procedures that had to be observed if she was going to get to the truth, but patience had never been her strong suit. So far, Hilary had been good to her word, and had taken what they'd discovered to her boss, but if she was being honest, she couldn't see why he would want to help them with the investigation, when the outcome might mean damaging the service he ran.

She'd toyed with the idea of taking what they already had to the press, but she reasoned that if she did that, she could be burning her bridges and running the risk that Mr. Grant would not give them the help they so desperately needed.

Her phone rang. She rooted it out of her bag and swiped right to answer,

"Hello, Sharon speaking".

"Hi Sharon, it's Hilary here. Where are you at the moment?"

"I decided to stay at the house. I still haven't finished clearing it out, and it makes a reasonable base for me to work from. There's a lot of this stuff that's apparently quite collectable, so the estate agent suggested I do a complete inventory. What can I do for you?"

Sharon absent-mindedly fiddled with the fringe on the table lamp.

"Is your computer working?"

"Yes, it's fine, why?"

"Good, I've managed to get copies of the coroner's report and the Special Branch scene of crime report, and they make for interesting reading. I'll message them across to you now".

"How on earth did you manage that? I've been asking for years with no luck".

Sharon was keen to see what additional information they would contain; set against the sketchy picture of events she had constructed over the years. Her laptop on the coffee table pinged as the message arrived. She flicked through her messages,

"Got it. Allow me some time to read them and I'll call you back". She ended the call and turned to the laptop.

The Special Branch scene of crime report was lengthy. It recorded everything, who was present, what their role was, what actions they took, the evidence they recorded and even some of the images they'd taken on the day.

The coroner's report was more concise, and contained a lot of medical terminology that Sharon didn't recognise. Thank heavens for Google, she thought, pulling a foolscap pad towards her. She began reading and making notes as she went along. Two hours later, she put down her pen and let out a long breath. There were several pages of scribbled notes, punctuated with question marks, arrows and underlining, but the top page comprised a list of questions she had formulated as she read. She dialled Hilary's number; it was answered after the first ring.

"Hilary, Sharon, I don't quite know where to start. I've been through both reports and all I can say is that I know for certain that someone killed him, and it was staged to look like a suicide. Anyone reading the report can see some glaring anomalies that suggest it was orchestrated by someone high up and with real connections".

Hilary was at her desk with the reports in front of her.

"Sharon, I've put our call on speakerphone. I have someone here with me who can help us with the technical details. Dr Marina Kinskey has a medical degree and considerable expertise in autopsy and forensic pathology. Why don't you talk me through what you think, then we can compare lists"?

Sharon turned to the notes she had produced and began to read.

"First, the body. It had to have been moved. The photos show him propped up against a tree, yet when my brother first saw him, he was lying on his back. If he'd bled to death, as the report suggests, there's not a sufficient quantity of blood on him or on the ground around him. That would suggest he was killed elsewhere and moved. Plus, where he was found is on a path that is regularly used by walkers. He couldn't have been there from Thursday afternoon until Friday afternoon without being discovered. Then there's Nero. If he'd been on that path, Nero would have come home, it's only about ten minutes away from the house, so he would have made his way back when he was hungry. Nero's priority was always his mealtimes. Then there are the vomit trails and the lividity mentioned in the coroner's report. I've done some research and lividity can't occur in the case of people who bleed to death because there isn't enough blood left to pool, to cause the markings.

"Next; the tablets. There were two blister packs of Temazepam found by his body, and they say he took fourteen tablets. Dad wouldn't even take an aspirin for a headache. He hated taking tablets, but when there was no other option, he took them with lots of water because he used to complain that they got stuck. The bottle of water they found was unopened. No way would he have taken tablets dry"? Also, if they thought he had taken something, why were there no blood test results?"

"Then there's his coat; It was a blustery, chilly September day, and he went out in his Barbour jacket. He must have because we never found it at the house. He was found wearing just a shirt and trousers, no coat. That also means no dog treats or dog lead and no poo-bags. All the things he took with him when he walked Nero. He had to take treats for Nero because his recall in the woods was so awful, so Dad had to bribe him to get him to come back. He would never have walked him without the means to clean up after him, and he needed the dog lead to help navigate the style going into the woods. Nero was too heavy to lift, so he guided him over with the lead".

"Was there anything else you noticed?"

"Yes" Sharon paused for dramatic effect.

"I've left the best till last. It's the first time I've seen a picture of the suicide note that was found in his pocket, and I am one-hundred percent certain that it's not Dad's handwriting. It has similarities, but it's not his". Sharon sounded triumphant and continued.

"There are lots of small details that don't make sense either, like the water was found by his left hand, but Dad was right-handed. The other bizarre thing is that there were no fingerprints found on anything; the pill packets, the penknife, the water bottle, and Dad had no gloves with him".

She turned a page and scanned the notes again.

"The trousers are a mystery too. The knees of his trousers were damp and dirty like he had spent time on the ground, but I can't understand why, if he'd propped himself against a tree. I think that's all".

The intensity of her revelations had left her slightly out of breath.

Hilary waited until Sharon had regained her composure.

"We both agree with all of that, Sharon, the only other thing Marina wanted to add was about the vomit trails from the corners of his mouth. She thinks the only way that could have happened was if he was lying on his back for some time. That would also explain the lividity, but he couldn't have moved himself to a seated position after death, so someone else was definitely involved".

Sharon suddenly felt deflated.

"But if all of this is so obvious, Hilary, how could it have been missed? There's enough here to warrant an autopsy at the very least, if not a full inquest".

Marina decided to cut into the conversation.

"Hi Sharon, Marina here. I agree with everything you've identified, and the conclusion I would draw is that either these details were wilfully ignored, or this is an example of some of the worst incompetence I have ever come across".

"I agree", said Hilary. We need to present our findings to Daniel and get his advice on what we do next. I'll call him to arrange a meeting".

Sharon again felt a mix of emotions. She was excited that she'd been right all along. She knew her father would not have left them in that way, he was too strong, too principled for that. Someone had made it look like a suicide, but if the evidence had been investigated thoroughly, they would have realised that whoever did it had not made a very good job of it. What she couldn't shake was the growing anger of the alternative. Someone had decided to kill her father because of what he knew, and more to the point, what he was going to do about it. She was also worried that they would not see how important this was to her and her brother. They had ruined her father's reputation and left a stain on his character, simply because he wanted to do the right thing.

Now she knew what she had to do. She would go to Shady Fields and appeal to Mr. Grant to get to the truth and get justice for her father. She would leave first thing in the morning.

20. Thames House

Thursday 22nd January 2020

It was only 4.00 p.m. yet it was already dark. The cold steel windows of Daniels' London office framed a velvet picture, bejewelled with blinking lights from the traffic below and the flashing advertising hoardings that barked out their corporate messages. Daniel was oblivious to the view. He was far more concerned about the current situation. The carefully orchestrated cover-up was slowly unravelling, and Daniel was particularly worried about the unpredictability of it all. He had little or no control over much in this whole sorry episode, and had no idea what further revelations might be uncovered. He needed to take decisive action.

He called Mitch Bennett and Marina Kinskey into HQ to try to make sense of it all. He had known Mitch for a long time and had a huge respect for him. He had saved Daniel's life on two occasions. The last time, Mitch had dragged him out of a building that was under enemy fire, suffering from a gunshot wound that would have killed a less fit man. Daniel was so badly injured that it forced his retirement from active service. Celia had sent Mitch to find Daniel, and he had risked his own life to rescue him.

A knock on the door heralded their arrival.

"Come in".

Mitch filled the doorway, he was forty-one, tall and powerfully built. He had wide-set blue eyes, a nose that had been broken more than once, a strong mouth and a scar that ran across his chin, giving him a horizontal dimple. His bulk could be intimidating too. Daniel had appointed him as head of MI5 because of his unerring common sense and integrity. His colleague, Dr Marina Kinskey was also tall, just a shade shorter than Bennett. She was slim and angular with a shock of curly hair the colour of a rusty bucket. She had vivid green eyes, magnified by a large pair of tortoiseshell spectacles. It did occur to Daniel that the best agents were supposed to be the ones who could be invisible in a room full of people. That would never happen with these two, and yet they were among the best he had in his team. He was aware that in the last few months they had become an item. He was pragmatic about stuff like this, officially, personal relationships were discouraged, but he felt that these two were professional and mature enough to make it work without causing problems.

They sat at the end of the meeting table facing the display screen on the wall. Marina fired up her laptop and a multi-page file opened up for them to view.

"It has taken nearly four months of investigation for our techies to come up with absolutely nothing that we can link to Vector 10. They did, however, find and expel a couple of Russian hackers from our network. The Russian government denied any involvement, of course, but the more we looked into what happened, the more it became clear they were trying to orchestrate a far-reaching spying campaign. None of the areas where their activity was identified correlates with anything that Vector 10 has released, so we have concluded that they are not working together, and our system has been under attack from two discrete sources".

She took a sip of water from the glass that Mitch had placed in front of her. Daniel looked at the screen.

"So, the Russians broke into peripheral areas of our network where there were fewer security protocols?"

"Yes, they were probably hoping that once they were in, they could progress to more valuable targets, but that didn't happen. We also discovered that there were a couple of attempts made on MI5 and MI6 security files that have all the signature hallmarks of the Chinese, but again they came to nothing. It's becoming a real problem Daniel, this incident has forced us to review all our security protocols, and we have to face facts, the most powerful asset we have, namely confidentiality via secure channels of communication, can no longer be guaranteed. Not only are we vulnerable to cyberattacks, but we have also been actively targeted by more than one superpower".

Daniel thumped the table.

"What the hell has the cybersecurity team been doing? They have been given more than their fair share of resources to deal with this sort of attack, and it sounds to me like they wouldn't have even known about this had we not been looking for something else! We must look like a bunch of sodding amateurs to the hackers. I'll get Peter to put together a taskforce to look at what we need to do to strengthen our security protocols". He paused.

"On another note, I want you to tackle something else that's looming on the horizon that might be a significant problem".

Marina broke the connection with the wall screen and began to take notes. Daniel continued.

"There have been some murmurs in the system about something called the Tripartite Treaty. It was a partnership that began back in the nineties, and references to it have appeared in the latest document spill from Vector 10. There seems to be some connections between Adam Hunt, our ex-PM, who now runs his global foundation, focused on third-world development, sustainability, and global domination",

Mitch and Marina looked up at him quizzically.

"I added that last one, it's my personal opinion. He is also tipped to take the role of Diplomatic Envoy for the Middle East".

He waited for a response, but none was forthcoming.

"We suspected that power brokers from the Americans, us and the Russians were trying to work together in a bid to weaken the bargaining power of the OPEC countries, but there was nothing concrete".

Mitch looked at Marina.

"Long before your time".

Daniel was displaying irritation by drumming his fingers on the tabletop.

"I've had Peter King looking into it to see what he can uncover, and what's really telling is that virtually nothing has been committed in writing. At a time before the internet became all pervasive, you would have expected there to be records of meetings, sightings, documents of some sort, but we have virtually nothing. Peter believes that although the focus of the plan seems to be about manipulating energy markets, he thinks there may also have been another agenda at play. He thinks that the Tripartite Treaty may have been related to Iran's nuclear programme".

Marina was struggling to keep up with this train of conversation, she glanced at Daniel to see if he could add some context. He obliged.

"The Iraqi conflict and the inspection regime that followed could have provided an unparalleled opportunity to accurately assess their nuclear facilities, gain valuable intelligence and ultimately prevent Iraq and maybe Iran too from developing nuclear weapons. By doing that, any party involved would be able to safeguard their own interests and maintain a balance of power. Because of the political fallout around how that conflict started, the Tripartite Treaty receded into the shadows, but there are signs to suggest that they may still be operating and could be responsible for the current energy prices and supply fluctuations that are playing havoc with the economy at the moment".

Mitch rubbed at the horizontal scar across his chin.

"But what is there to go on, Daniel? If they were careful enough that they left no trace at the time, where do you want us to start?"

Daniel nodded.

"Peter contacted a colleague he'd previously worked with, and they came up with a name, Vladimir Gorski. They think he may have been the Russian link. He popped up in places where he shouldn't have been as a Minister for the Interior. It's possible that Gorski, along with someone senior from our government at the time, may have been working with a counterpart, probably from the CIA, as the main partners of the Tripartite Treaty. I want you to use your connections and contacts and see what you can find. I've got some files from the documents released by Vector 10 for you to read, as well as some email threads from those we think were involved at our end. Do what you can, I want a full report in five days. And I want everything shredded after you've read it, and nothing committed to digital files. This is an ear's only operation, so not a word to anyone other than me. Oh, and I don't want any digital trail between you two either".

"No problem, Daniel, I will just delete the notes I was making".

Marina pushed the enormous tortoiseshell frames back up her nose, magnifying her clear, green eyes. Daniel directed his next comment at Mitch.

"Are you still having your apartment regularly swept for bugs, Mitch, particularly now, with Marina there".

Mitch looked shocked.

"How long have you known?"

"Since the aftermath of Ragair, you went through quite an ordeal, Marina, so I get it. As long as you maintain professional boundaries, I've no problem with the two of you, but I need you both to be vigilant. It's a potential weakness that others would be happy to exploit".

Marina looked unabashed.

"That does sound a little paranoid, Daniel".

"In my long career, Marina, I have learned one thing, only the paranoid survives in this game".

21. Shady Fields

Friday 23rd January 2020

Sharon hadn't had much sleep; she'd been too on edge. Early that morning, she had followed Hillary's travel directions to get to Shady Fields for a face-to-face conversation with Hilary and hopefully convince Mr. Grant to take direct action. She had already established that there were enough unexplained discrepancies in the reports to call for an inquest. As a family member, she could make that request, but there was no way of knowing what the consequences of doing so might be. She didn't want to make things worse and send everyone who knew something running for cover. However, she felt that they were dragging their heels, so she decided that her response would be to dig hers in harder.

A staff member admitted her into the elegant entrance hall and asked her to wait while she informed Hilary that she was here. A few minutes later, Hilary appeared at the top of the broad staircase, at the same time as Jon Dowie-Brown, accompanied by Ben, happened to walk across the hall towards the library.

Sharon recognised him immediately.

"Uncle Jon?"

Dowie-Brown stood in front of her scrutinizing her face for clues, after a few seconds, recognition burst across his features.

"Sharon? Sharon Crane, my goodness me, as I live and breathe".

He flung his arms around her in a warm embrace.

"What on earth are you doing here?"

"I'm looking into Dad's death Uncle Jon, he didn't commit suicide, he was killed".

Hilary couldn't move down the staircase quickly enough, and reflected later that it was like watching a train crash in slow motion.

Dowie-Brown pounced on her words.

"What do you mean, killed?"

"I mean, we think he was murdered either because of what he knew or what he was about to go public with. Hilary Geddes is helping me".

Sharon looked very young and vulnerable at that moment. There was a naivety about her that made Hilary wonder if she'd done the right thing by agreeing to help her. She interrupted.

"Sharon, why don't you come up to the office, and we can talk about what our next steps should be?"

Hilary was desperate to split these two up before things could get any worse, but Dowie-Brown was not about to let this opportunity go to waste.

"You do know that the woman who was involved in this sorry episode lives here, don't you? Celia Browning was involved in the inspection visits your father was leading at the time of his death. If you want to know what happened to him, you need to start with her, she knows more than she's letting on".

Dowie-Brown looked triumphant at delivering his coup de gráce. Sharon was startled by this news.

"She was the woman who came to the house on the day his body was discovered. She told me she was there to take Dads' papers away for safe keeping".

Dowie-Brown scoffed.

"More likely, she was there to cover up what had happened. She had been threatening him with all kinds of sanctions during that week. I know because she intimidated me in the same way. Your Dad was stronger than me. I caved in, but he didn't. I thought she must have threatened him to such a degree that he took his own life".

"But he didn't Uncle Jon. They covered it all up, they made it look like he'd done that, but the official account of what happened reads like a work of fiction. None of it adds up, and there are clear signals that someone killed him, it was covered up".

Hilary had to act now before this went any further. She took Sharon's arm and attempted to guide her towards the staircase, but she pulled away. She stared at Hillary.

"Did you know that this woman was linked to my father's death?" She threw the accusation squarely at her.

Hilary repositioned herself at Sharon's side and became a little more assertive.

"I'm willing to talk about recent developments but not here, in a general thoroughfare. Please come up to my office and I can tell you what we have learned".

Sharon took a couple of seconds to weigh up her options, and decided she needed to know far more than just making a point, so she allowed Hilary to guide her up the staircase, along the corridor and into her office. She called over her shoulder.

"I'll come and find you later, Uncle Jon".

Sharon paced the floor in Hilary's office.

"I need to speak with her. What harm could it do if I had a chat with he? I remember her, she was in the house at the time, I spoke to her on the day they found him. For God's sake, she went through his things at our house, and he was barely cold. Celia Browning must know something, and I want to know what".

Hilary was very annoyed that a chance meeting with Dowie-Brown had escalated the situation so quickly. "It's not that easy, Sharon; she's here for a reason. Her medical condition means we need to ensure that she's protected from unnecessary stress and pressure. I am not prepared to let you interrogate her while she's under our care".

Sharon's eyes flashed, and her body language shouted confrontation.

"She will have answers about what really happened, I just know it".

There was a short pause and a knowing look crept across her face.

"You know she knows, and you're trying to keep it quiet. How could I have been so stupid to believe that you wanted to help? You're trying to keep a lid on it. You are all in it together, trying to cover it up all over again".

Her eyes flashed real anger.

Hilary took a deep breath and said in a quiet voice.

"I am going to put your comments down to understandable frustration. I know this is difficult for you, and you have been on a roller-coaster of a journey for the last few weeks, but ask yourself if I was part of a cover-up, would we have got this far? I certainly would not have shared the information that I have with you. I would have stonewalled you, and you would be none the wiser".

As she was talking, she poured Sharon a cup of coffee and set it on the desk in front of her.

"Outbursts like this don't help. If we're to get to the bottom of this, we need to work together. Now sit, and I can bring you up to date with where we currently are. We can decide on our next course of action".

Her calm, almost hypnotic voice had the desired effect and Sharon visibly relaxed, sat down in the chair and reached for the coffee. Hilary continued.

"What I will do is have a word with Daniel and see if we can organise an informal discussion with Celia to see what she remembers. That's the best I can do. I know how difficult this is for you, but there are issues of National Security at stake, and all the people involved in this, except you, are governed by the official secrets act. With hindsight, I'm certain we should not have involved you to the degree that we have, but we genuinely want to find the truth about your Father's death too. However, I am not prepared to do that to the detriment of the wellbeing of someone under my care. Someone with a serious medical condition. Let me do my job properly, Sharon, that way we stand a greater chance of getting the answers you want".

To Hilary's surprise, tears began to trickle down Sharon's cheeks. She sobbed, almost silently at first, but the sobbing became more intense and then came the gut-wrenching moans. Sharon let go of decades of hurt and grief in the safety of Hillary's office. Hilary moved towards her and when the sobs began to subside, gently laid a hand on her shoulder.

"Would you like something stronger than coffee?"

Sharon nodded her head, Hilary poured a small shot of malt whiskey into a neat tumbler and held it out for her. She took it, downed it in one, and shuddered violently.

"I hate whiskey". She said, smiling weakly.

"I used to drink it with my dad, but I never really liked the taste. It was just another thing we could share".

She took a mirrored compact and pad from her bag and set about repairing her once immaculate makeup. She reviewed her efforts in the compacts' small mirror, satisfied, she returned the compact to her bag and sat back in the chair. She spoke directly to Hilary.

"I'm sorry about that. I don't think I realised how long I've been carrying all of this around with me. I never believed he would take his own life, but when so many told me he had, I was forced to accept it. But if someone did murder my father, then I have a right to know, and I have to clear his name and reputation. It is the least I can do for him". Hilary nodded,

"I fully understand, and it's why I agreed to help you, but I have to be honest Sharon, we may discover who was ultimately responsible for your father's death, but you may not be able to make that knowledge public because of who was involved. I don't want to give you false hope, we have no idea where this paperchase will lead, but you may not get the result you are hoping for. I don't want to add to your disappointment after what you've already been through".

"I appreciate that Hilary and I do understand, but we've come this far, I don't think I can stop now. I've booked a room at the Bull's Head in the village. I want to be nearby in case there are any further developments. If it means that I get to know what really happened to him, then that may have to be enough, but I have to try".

Hilary reverted to her project manner persona, took a note pad from her desk draw, and began to write a list.

"I suggest we prepare the questions we want answers to, then enlist Daniel to find the best way of getting those answers".

22. Peter Kings Home

Sunday 25th January 2020

The phone rang, and at first, he thought it was in his dream. A far away bell was dragging him into a cold, dark place, and he wanted to stay where he was. The ringing became incessant, and he began to feel the physical sensations of being woken from a deep sleep. The ringing continued. He opened one eye and looked at the clock. For Christ's Sake, he'd only been in bed for three hours. He almost wondered who would be ringing him at 6 am on a Sunday morning, but he already knew. He picked up the phone and answered the call.

"Daniel, is this important or do you have a death wish?"

"I'm really sorry, Peter, but I wouldn't ask if it wasn't really urgent".

"Well, unless there has been an attempted kidnapping of the Queen or Raheem Stirling has been sold to Real Madrid, SOD OFF!"

"Vector 10 has just released a video onto the internet. It's quite grainy, but it appears to show Robert Crane being interviewed in a pub by a prominent journalist. Crane confesses to falsifying his reports and misleading Government departments to gain some notoriety".

"And how does that constitute an emergency, it happened decades ago?"

"Well Peter, that's the interesting thing, experts that have seen it are stating categorically that it's a deep fake. The technology was in its infancy back then, and whilst it might have fooled people at the time, by today's standard it is amateurish".

"Still not hearing an emergency!"

"Why would Vector 10 release a video that suggests a conspiracy to implicate Robert Crane now? More to the point, that video was never released before. Where has it been, and who does it belong to? It clearly wasn't needed because he was found dead, allegedly having committed suicide".

"I am going back to sleep now".

"Peter, Vector 10 is feeding us information that's leading to something significant. He has an agenda and I think it might be linked to Adam Hunt. He was the Prime Minister at the time, and it may yet prove that he took us into an illegal war. Vector 10 has also released unrelated documents; they are linked to the Tripartite Treaty, and I think it may be the link he wants us to find. He is sending us a puzzle to solve, and the timing is no coincidence".

"Okay, mildly interesting and possibly important but still no emergency!"

"Stay with me, Peter. What if his timing is no coincidence? Word on the street says that Adam Hunt is lined up for the Diplomatic Peace Envoy for the Middle East. That would give him unrivalled access to the Saudi Royal Family and other key players in the Middle East. What if the Tripartite Treaty is still in operation? What if the appointment is somehow critical to the next stage of their plans? My gut tells me that they are behind the current volatility in the oil markets and that they are trying to trigger a conflict. If we don't find the underlying cause of this, it could escalate and with the state of relations in the Middle East, that may involve nuclear deterrents".

Peter was now wide awake.

"Okay, you finally got there, that is an emergency. So, what are you looking for?"

"I need you to find the link between Hunt and the tripartite treaty. We know there was an American link and possibly a Russian link through Gorski, but we don't know whether he was working on his own or in an official capacity. You have to get me something I can use, Peter". There was an urgency to Daniel's voice.

"I'll see what I can do and, as always, I will be discrete".

Peter was now sitting on the edge of his bed, fishing around the floor for his slippers. There was a thoughtful pause from Daniel.

"I don't think we have time for that, Peter. Let's not keep it quiet, clatter around a bit, let them know that we're looking for them. I've had enough of tiptoeing around".

"Are you sure that's wise, Daniel? It seems a bit like poking a hornet's nest".

"Sometimes, Peter, the most dangerous thing you can do is to play things safe. Call me when you have something".

23. The Bull's Head Pub

Sunday 26th January 2020

The air between them was thick with tension as they huddled together in a discreet corner of the Bull's Head. The traditional black and white painted coaching house was a short drive or a healthy walk away from Shady Fields. It was set back from the main road and had the obligatory painted picture of a Bull hanging from a wrought iron signpost above the doorway. Inside was not the faux beams and lacquered horse-brasses that some breweries 'instant history department' adorned pubs with these days. This was authentic. There was a welcoming inglenook fireplace with a real wood fire crackling in the hearth at one end of the room and a well-used dartboard hanging on the wall at the other. Highly polished tables and chairs were arranged around the room, and an upholstered bench seat followed the contours of the wall in the bar area. It was quiet for a Sunday lunchtime, but that was common for this time of year.

Dowie-Brown and Sharon sat at a corner table, lost in their intense discussion. Their attention was so focused on each other that they failed to notice two men enter the bar, order two pints of Timothy Taylor's Landlord Bitter and seat themselves at a nearby table.

Bill and Ben often strolled down to the pub after Sunday lunch to get a bit of exercise and some fresh air into their lungs. Bill had chosen the table while Ben ordered the drinks. He had spotted Dowie-Brown and the woman, and was intrigued as to why these two had chosen to meet here, and he wondered what they needed to discuss that should not be overheard by fellow residents. Ben joined his friend and placed the pints down on cardboard coasters.

"You could have sat anywhere; the place is virtually empty, and we end up behind a pillar and next to the toilets. Let's move".

Bill pulled at his friend's sleeve.

"There's no rush, I sat here because I wondered what those two might be plotting".

Ben glanced at the couple.

"You stagger me. Why does everything have to be a plot or intrigue? Sometimes people just want to enjoy a quiet drink".

Bill smiled.

"I would agree with you, but then we would both be wrong. There's something going on here that we're not seeing. Your man over there suddenly has a rush of blood to the head and tries to strangle the ex-head of the Secret Service, and nothing happens to him! He is still under the same roof and no charges have been bought, no police involved at all. You were given the job of baby-sitting him for a few days, but now it's all forgotten. I'm not buying any of it. There's something we are missing and if you had any natural curiosity, you would have pumped him for the lowdown on what it is when you had the chance".

Ben took a gulp of his beer.

"Oh, I did, I knew exactly what was going on. Dowie-Brown blamed Celia for his best friend committing suicide and wanted revenge. He told me it was an instinctive response to something she said in the heat of the moment, and he lashed out. He was filled with remorse when he realised what he nearly did, but she refused to press charges, and there you have it. Nothing to take any further".

Bill nearly choked on his drink and spluttered incredulously.

"What the f... Why didn't you tell me this before?"

Ben blinked innocently.

"You never asked me".

Dowie-Brown watched as Sharon, who had been fixated on her coffee cup, absent-mindedly ran her fingers around the rim of the cup.

"So, what was made to look like a tragic suicide, was actually a sanctioned murder? My God, I knew we operated in a murky world, but I honestly believed there was some sort of ethical code. Your father was one of the best men I knew; principled, intelligent, and ethical. I should have known that he would never bow to pressure like I did. Of course, he would have stood up to them. I realise now that if he'd blown the whistle, not only would our government have suffered a catastrophic collapse, but the Americans would have lost their home support too. They clearly learned nothing from the Vietnam War". Dowie-Brown leaned towards Sharon,

"So, what's your next move?"

Sharon casually pushed her cup away.

"There are a couple of people I need to track down if they are still alive. There was the unknown woman who was spotted behaving suspiciously in the vicinity. She was in a wooded area on a windy autumn day wearing a business suit and court shoes. Who was she, and what was she doing there? I don't believe they even tried to look for her. Witnesses said she had quite a distinctive birthmark. Then there was the man who found Dad's body. He headed the Special Branch dog unit, and because of the questions we have about where Dad was killed and where he was found, he might have the answers we want".

Her voice carried easily in this quieter area of the bar, and Bill's ears pricked when he heard the description of the mysterious woman, who he recognised immediately as Kitty Oliver.

"Did you hear that, Ben? They're talking about Kitty".

Ben shook his head.

"Christ, Bill, that's a bit of a leap. It could have been anybody".

"Yes. But it is a coincidence that an operation that reeks of MI5 should have a woman with a distinctive birthmark, who also has a reputation for being useful in covert operations, at the centre of it. Not that much of a stretch, as it turns out".

"What would have warranted such a star-studded cast of Kitty and Celia, then Bill?"

"Shut up a bit and I might find out!"

He shifted in his chair so that his good ear was closest to the two in conversation.

Dowie-Brown, whose face was partly in shadow, spoke with a sense of remorse.

"I know it's in the past, Sharon, but they will have done what they did to protect their interests and close ranks. The likelihood of getting to the truth of it is impossibly small, you know that, don't you? Robert had to be silenced, and they did exactly that".

Sharon gathered her bag as Dowie-Brown finished his coffee.

"I know he didn't take his own life. I also know that there are lots of unanswered questions about his death and the circumstances surrounding the discovery of his body, but every path we take to get to the truth leads to dead ends. All I need is someone to break ranks, but everyone is doing what authority always does at times like this, they are concealing the truth, and I am not having it!"

Bill scowled as he heard those chilling words. This woman's father had not taken his own life, he had been murdered. He gestured to Ben.

"A bit of a leap, eh?"

Relief washed over Dowie-Brown, a strange sensation considering the gravity of the revelation. At least Sharon now knew the truth, and he could draw some comfort from the fact that he had not let his best friend down and had not been there to prevent him taking his own life. But that also meant the mystery had only deepened. Who had ordered this murder? And why?

Sharon's voice wavered as she asked,

"But why did it have to be him? Why my father?"

Dowie's voice was cold, detached.

"It was a matter of trust. He knew too much, and he was becoming a liability. They would have had little choice if they wanted to protect themselves. Robert had a stubborn streak a mile wide, but you know that, and I'm guessing that that's where you get yours from".

Dowie-Brown saw Sharon's hand trembling on the table, her eyes betrayed her bewilderment.

"The murder of your father to protect a dirty secret is not an easy thing to accept".

She nodded in agreement. On one level, it was what she had always suspected, but the details made it somehow unbelievable, like it wasn't happening to her.

Bill had hardly touched his drink, he was too busy eavesdropping. He was all for going across to join them, but Ben put his foot down.

"If we are going to get involved, we need more information. Daniel will know what's going on, perhaps we can offer to help in some way?"

They would have to tread carefully from here onwards, Ben understood how easy it was for them to get in over their heads, after all, it wouldn't be the first time.

24. Hunt Foundation Geneva

Monday 27th January 2020

The elegant, subtly lit conference room at the Hunt Foundation conveyed an air of secrecy and power. It had become a sanctuary for the Tripartite Treaty, a place where the future was sculpted behind closed doors. Adam Hunt, Adam Hudson, and Vladimir Gorski, the architects of the sinister Tripartite treaty, had convened for a clandestine meeting. Stewart Pearson hung around in the shadows, happy just to be here to see the contribution he had made begin to bear fruit.

The main players sat at the polished mahogany table; a colour-coded world map projected on the wall behind them indicating their global reach. Each man bore the weight of their shared responsibilities, the memories of the bold decisions they had taken, and the power they held over the world's energy markets.

"Gentlemen, we have a problem that requires our full attention". Adam Hunt said, his voice firm and determined.

"This hacker, Vector 10, is becoming an annoyance. The documents he is releasing now about our treaty are buried in the sheer volume of his mischief-making, but he's getting too close".

Hudson, a man whose face was etched with experience and cunning, nodded in agreement and replied in a low but powerful voice,

"We can't afford any embarrassment, not with what we have planned. Our timetable could be compromised, and that would have a knock-on effect that our backers would not tolerate. What went wrong, Adam? You assured us that you had this under control when we last spoke".

Hunt shifted uncomfortably in his seat; he was not used to being questioned in this way.

"I had hoped that our diversionary tactics would be enough. We have all sought to divert attention away from our domestic issues and boost our approval ratings. War has a way of doing that. While the people were focused on the common enemy, it left us alone to get on with the real work. The Middle East targets we selected gave us the ability to hide our strategy in plain sight. By choosing a nation with perceived ties to terrorism and nuclear ambitions, we were able to rally public support and justify military action. But if what we did ever comes to the attention of the general populace, it will be terrible for us all".

Gorski laughed.

"Not bad for me. You two will be held responsible for that, and people will laugh at the way the West painted Russia to be the warmongers. That apple will fall much closer to the tree".

The enigmatic Russian leaned forward, his eyes as cold and calculating as ever.

"We need to find this hacker and silence him for good. If I could do this, what would it be worth to you?"

He looked directly at Hunt as he spoke. The other men exchanged cautious glances. It was clear they were determined to maintain their upper hand, but this hacker had become an unexpected obstacle. He was unearthing their dealings, exposing their crimes, and unravelling the intricate web of deception they had woven for years.

Adam Hunt's voice dropped to a near-whisper.

"I've reached out to our contacts in the intelligence agencies, but we can't rely solely on them. This hacker is elusive, cunning, and has successfully evaded our efforts so far".

Hudson, ever the pragmatist, interrupted,

"We have to consider the possibility that he might have inside help. He can't be so good that any system he targets he can access at will, no one is that good. He must be getting help from someone, somewhere. We can't trust anyone".

Gorski's eyes narrowed.

"I may have a way of identifying him. He's a threat we can no longer ignore, but it will be expensive, I think, to track him down".

Silence hung in the room, heavy with the realisation that their secret world was teetering on the edge of exposure. A decision had to be made, one that would secure their power and protect their future. Finally, Adam Hunt broke the silence, his words firm and chilling.

"What do you need and how expensive are we talking?"

Gorski's eyes narrowed and he gave a sly smile.

"Ten million should be a good start. I will use my own people, at least I know I can trust them".

The Tripartite members exchanged brief nods of approval; a feeling of cold determination settled in the room. Vector 10 had been a thorn in their side for months, and in one quick discussion, he was marked for eradication. The secrets of the past were catching up with them, and they were willing to do whatever it took to ensure that their vision for global energy dominance remained intact.

Hudson had been listening to the exchange and thinking through their options.

"If he is getting help, it must be through the security services, your lot or, God forbid, mine. Sadly, the CIA is not the organisation it once was. There are three myths that the public labour under, and they undermine the work of the security agencies across the globe. The first and biggest myth is that there is a difference between 'intelligence' and 'fact'. Intelligence analysts are tasked with understanding situations that are often multifaceted, forming a judgment about that situation and informing policymakers. Therefore, they frequently pass off intelligence as fact. I think that's a good defence for you, Adam from what you have shared, it's unlikely that they will be able to produce hard facts. That gives you breathing space. Myth two is that intelligence can predict the future. No amount of intelligence could have stopped 9/11 and the twin towers because the US security services would have found such an audacious attack inconceivable. The same is true of the war in Iraq. We couldn't know that our actions were shaped by less than perfect data. Hindsight is a wonderful thing. That's our defence. Even Russia failed to foresee the rapid collapse of the Soviet Union".

The jibe was accurately aimed at Gorski who grunted but did not rise to the bait. Hudson continued.

"Myth three is that the intelligence community is composed mainly of spies. Since the majority of intelligence requirements can be addressed through open sources, the real need for spies is relatively low.

Currently, in the CIA, less than 10% of their employees are covert operatives. Ninety percent are analysts, managers, scientists, and support staff. Most intelligence employees work at a desk and often possess high-level expertise in geopolitical issues, history, and international relations. Very few actually play James Bond in foreign countries. It makes sense then that if Vector 10 is getting help, it must be from one of those low-profile people. I am currently looking at potential weak links in our security services, Adam, I suggest you do the same".

Gorski said,

"I shall do the same".

With a look of irony, Hudson smiled.

"Russian traitors have very short life-spans, Gorski. We all know that it takes more courage for a Russian soldier to retreat than advance".

Unknown to them, on the other side of the digital divide, Vector 10 was closing in on them. The next release would leave no room for interpretation or denial. The game of shadows being played had intensified, the stakes were higher than ever, and everything was now in place to bring them all down.

25. Shady Fields

Monday 27th January 2020

Kitty wondered what she'd done to deserve a visit from Daniel Grant. He had taken over the reins from her old boss, and in her opinion, he was a lightweight. His career had been cut short by a schoolboy error. His adversary had set a trap, and he'd walked straight into it and almost paid with his life. Sloppy! She suspected that it had been personal, and anyone in the game knew that emotional involvement played havoc with your judgement and decision-making.

She prided herself on having a laser focus because emotion was something she was simply able to switch on and off. It was what had kept her in the game for so long. She had been involved in many missions, some sanctioned, some not, some were based on her own judgement about the right solution for a particular problem. It did mean that you had to have a good insurance policy. Information valuable enough to trade as a get-out-of-jail-free card if things became difficult.

Daniel had arranged to meet her in the garden room at 10 am. It was quiet in there at this time of year. No one liked looking out onto the drab lawn and empty flower beds. Even Ken the gardener and Jenny, his wife, spent December and January every year visiting their son on the Costa Brava, until the weather improved, and their work could begin again.

In the summer, these windows looked out onto a riot of colour, but the winter was a reminder of dormant decay. Not a thing you wanted to dwell on when you were in the last years of life. She wondered if his choice of location had been intentional, and if so, maybe she had underestimated him.

Daniel carried a folder which contained a document that held the power to upend governments and shatter the foundations of national security. It had taken Peter a while to track it down, but it was worth it.

Among other truths, it clearly implicated an agent called Kitty Oliver, who had served the interests of the government with unwavering loyalty throughout her long career. Now, however, the secrets of her past deeds threatened to expose a sinister government plot to orchestrate a war in the Middle East.

When he had fully scrutinised the document, the implications it held were only too clear. The names and signatures of high-ranking government officials stared back at him. There was undeniable proof that Kitty Oliver had been sanctioned to assassinate an eminent scientist, a key figure whose knowledge had the potential to expose a conspiracy that was earth-shattering. And he was convinced that Peter King possessed some mystical power to be able to find something that had been buried so deep.

Daniel had known Kitty for years, and he knew her to be a brilliant and ruthless operative, but someone who had frequently operated on the other side of the official line, executing her missions with unwavering precision. He had never considered her a friend, and she was considerably older than him, but she was a legend in the world of espionage. Now, her actions had cast a shadow of doubt over her entire career.

He entered the garden room and saw her sitting on one of the soft, thickly padded armchairs facing the French windows. She was no longer the young, agile operative she once was, but the intensity in her eyes remained undiminished. She was ageing, and not well if Dr Arnot's reports were to be believed, but he could see that her determination had not wavered.

"Kitty," he began, "I won't beat around the bush. This document details a mission to eliminate Professor Robert Crane that you carried out".

She started to protest.

"Please, let us not waste time denying it. I know you were following orders, and I know who gave you those orders".

She was silent, her gaze locked onto the document he held in his hand.

"It holds the names and signatures of those who sanctioned your mission. It could expose a grave conspiracy within the government, namely, a plot to push us into a war in the Middle East".

Kitty spoke, her voice low but steely.

"What do you want, Daniel?" He met her gaze.

"Kitty, I want to hear your side of the story and who was willing to hang you out to dry if things had gone wrong?"

Kitty looked into his eyes, as if searching for signs of deception. She had spent her life immersed in the world of deceit and secrecy, and trust did not come easily. The consequences of her actions, the lives she had taken, and everything she'd done was beginning to weigh heavy on her, and now her body was starting to give up on her too. Where were her just deserts? She thought quickly, could the document he held be her redemption?

"I want a guarantee," she said, her strong voice unwavering.

"Protection and a new identity, and a fresh start somewhere warm with lots of home comforts".

Daniel thought for a few seconds and nodded solemnly.

"I'll see what I can do, Kitty, but you must understand the risks involved. The world you knew has all but disappeared. You may not be able to ride off into the sunset scot-free".

She took a deep breath, a lifetime of decisions and consequences spinning around in her mind.

"I'm happy to take my chances, are you willing to make a deal?" Daniel nodded,

"I will, but it won't be everything you want; I can tell you that much. What I want to know, is who gave you the mission and how you did it". Kitty took a deep breath.

"You won't like it. It was your mentor, darling Celia. It wasn't the first time she'd handed me a job like that, and it wasn't the last. It was the usual process, no paperwork, nothing in writing, no records. I was given the target; the means and methods were left to me to choose. It was fairly straightforward; I knew him, so getting close wasn't an issue, and he was so naive he never suspected a thing. All I had to do was see if he was willing to give up his crusade, and if so, he could live. They could have called it off if he'd been willing to 'take a bullet for the team'. He wasn't, so he didn't".

She blinked in a matter-of-fact sort of way before continuing.

"I had to confirm the kill, then the clean-up crew were supposed to go in and do the rest, but they made a complete pigs-ear of it. They needed time to search his house, so the body had to be hidden overnight. They couldn't leave it out in the open because it would have been found, so they concealed it in the undergrowth. The problem was that he died before he could bleed out. By the time they staged the suicide scene the following day, any idiot could tell he'd been on his back all night. So, they added the thing with the tablets as a last resort. Then the cretins wiped everything down and removed all the tell-tale signs, including his fingerprints and his bloody jacket, which they were ordered to leave at the scene. It's a good job I put his suicide note in his trouser pocket, or they would have got rid of that too. The woodentop dog handler who found him decided he would look more comfortable propped up against a tree, so he moved the body again".

She shook her head in disbelief.

"My God, how we got away with it at the time is still one of life's great mysteries!"

Daniel swallowed; the distaste he felt for this elderly woman was making him feel nauseous.

"You knew him, you had worked with him. He trusted you, Kitty". She looked puzzled.

"Sometimes you have to hug people to know how big a hole to dig".

"You don't regret it, do you? Killing Robert Crane?"

"Daniel", she said in a patronizing way.

"There are no regrets in life, just lessons".

Daniel shook his head.

"We have looked at your financials, and it's clear that you have been receiving regular, substantial sums of cash from somewhere. I'm going to hazard a guess that you have been practising a little blackmail, and I think I know who with".

Kitty smirked at him.

"Good luck with proving that! It was always in cash and untraceable. You can't do that with the way the banking system works now. Do you know who and why, though, Daniel?"

"I can take a good guess, I think you were probably milking Pearson because you knew he had ordered Cranes' death, am I right?"

Kitty looked directly at him.

"You may think that, but I couldn't possibly comment".

Their meeting was over, Daniel left, and she returned to her apartment. She had been left out of sorts by the conversation with him. It had reinforced the loss of power and influence she had once enjoyed. Kitty felt like she owed herself a little treat.

In readiness for dinner that evening she showered, carefully applied her makeup, and selected her little red dress. If it was fun she deserved, then it was fun she would have.

Kitty was on a mission; a little distraction, and she had chosen Bill Tandy as the lucky man.

She wore the red jersey wrap dress because it hugged her hourglass-like figure and revealed an impressive cleavage. Her heels were small and the black stockings she wore showed off her still shapely legs.

It was 6.30 pm, people were gathering in the bar for a pre-dinner drink. Not everyone entered into this ritual, but Bill and Ben were always to be found here at this time.

Ben was seated at a corner table with Jon Dowie-Brown, who had set up the chessboard.

"A quick game before dinner?" Ben was opposite him waiting for the game to start.

"Can't wait".

It sounded to Kitty like he was just humouring Dowie-Brown. Bill was standing behind Ben, patiently looking on.

Kitty approached him with all the subtlety of a peacock in mating season.

"Bill, darling! Are you an aficionado of the game?"

"No, not really. I like something a bit quicker," His eyes were trained on the board.

Undeterred, Kitty leaned in, her perfume so potent it could wake the dead.

"Bill, shall we go into dinner and leave these two to their game? I was thinking we could grab an early slot, then maybe watch a film afterwards".

"Thanks, really kind, Kitty, but I'll wait for Ben".

Kitty, interpreting this as the usual coy resistance, purred,

"Oh, Bill, you're such a tease!" Bill looked at her and blinked.

"Am I, I was going for disinterested".

Kitty slipped her arm through his and rubbed his sleeve.

"Are you flirting with me, Kitty?" She batted her mascaraed lashes at him.

"I'm not flirting; I'm just being extra friendly to someone who is extra attractive".

"That's very nice, but I'm no good at that stuff. My version of flirting is telling you that if you were a potato, you would be a good potato".

Kitty was made of sterner stuff; she tried again.

"Is there no one special in your life at the moment, Bill?" Bill laughed, "I don't do relationships, Kitty; they never end well. Romeo died because of Juliet; Jack died because of Rose in Titanic. The moral of the story is simple, stay single if you want to stay alive".

Kitty's perfectly painted eyebrows arched in surprise.

"Oh, Bill, that's really sad, and a bit cynical if you don't mind me saying".

"Kitty, I don't mind you thinking I'm cynical. I prefer to think of myself as realistic. I'm happy with my life and the freedoms I have. I don't need a woman in that way. If you're looking to meet the love of your life, then I suggest you buy a big mirror". The message finally got through.

"Well. I never took you for someone who batted for the other team, Bill". Bill chuckled,

"No worries, Kitty, it happens all the time. Perhaps you're not as intuitive as you think you are".

26. Wayne Priestley's cottage

Monday 27th January 2020

Wayne Priestley averaged ten miles a day walking his beloved German shepherds. He estimated that Maisie, Gus, and Milo must do at least twice that because of the constant trotting ahead and doubling back that they did. It was unavoidable really, there were so many scents to track, squirrels to chase and even occasionally, the odd ball to fetch. His dogs were his friends, no, not just his friends, they were family members. Gus had saved his life twice and taken a stab wound in the process, and Maisie had alerted him to an ambush he was about to walk into, at the very least saving him from a good beating by the drug dealing gang they had tracked down.

Milo was the youngest, and a gift from the Special Branch Dog Search and Rescue Unit when he retired eighteen months ago. No active operations any more, but old habits die hard. He still worked his dogs, keeping their tracking skills finely tuned because he really couldn't imagine not doing it.

Wayne was tall, slender, and wiry with excellent muscle tone that defied his 56-year-old body. His retirement had been on medical grounds due to a back injury which left him with limited movement, fine for walking, but not so good for chasing villains.

As they walked down the lane towards his house, he was surprised to see a car parked partly on the grass verge by his gate. Whoever it was, they were either lost, or here to see him because there was no other property along this track. He was not used to unexpected visitors, and the dogs also sensed a new presence. They slowed their trot to a stealthy walk; they had instinctively switched to stalking mode. He could see over the hedge that no one was waiting by the front door, so whoever it was must still be in the car.

He slid the three dog leads from around his neck and wrapped them tightly around his right hand, ensuring that the metal clips dangled loose. They would make a decent makeshift weapon. You couldn't be too careful, with his history.

When he was about twenty yards away from the car, both front doors opened, two women emerged and stood by their vehicle, not offering to venture closer. Sensible, thought Wayne, you never knew if you needed to take quick action with three adult German Shepherds moving towards you. There was something familiar about the passenger with the flowing dark hair. A spark of recognition stirred in him, and she was the first to speak.

"Hi there, I'm presuming they are friendly?" She motioned towards the pack.

"It depends on what you want" Wayne answered curtly. She tried again.

"Wayne Priestley? My name is Sharon Louca, and this is Hilary Geddes, we want to ask you a few questions about an operation you were involved in a few years ago".

Wayne studied the woman's face. As he got closer, there was definitely something, but he couldn't recall what it was. He watched the dogs' reactions. Maisie could spot a 'dog person' a mile off, and her body language was always telling. If she sensed anything off, tension or aggression, her hackles went up. Maisie cautiously approached the woman, then nuzzled her hand. She was okay. The blonde woman spoke.

"Mr. Priestley, we want to talk to you about the search for Robert Crane in 2002, anything you can remember about the events surrounding the discovery of his body".

He had often wondered when this visit would take place, but strangely, he had not predicted that it would be by two unassuming women.

"And who are you?" Sharon took a step forward,

"Robert Crane was my father Mr. Priestley, you probably don't remember, but we did meet briefly, I was there on the day he was found, you were the one who discovered his body".

Wayne shifted his weight as his back twinged,

"I thought there was something familiar about you, but that was twenty odd years ago. I'm not sure what I can tell you". He hesitated,

"Would you like a coffee?"

Without waiting for an answer, he turned and headed for the back door. The dogs, anticipating what was going to happen next, started to dance excitedly around his legs.

"I need to feed these three first, then we can have a chat".

They followed him into a tiled boot-room vestibule decorated with the trappings of a dog handler. A coat stand with various dog leads and harnesses hanging from it was also home to a long wet-weather wax jacket. A pair of heavy-duty walking boots sat beneath the coat. A door off to the left was open showing a wet room, presumably to hose off muddy paws, the door to the right opened into a large but cosy farmhouse kitchen. He ushered them into the kitchen, which was gratefully warmed by an ancient Aga. A sturdy oak table surrounded by four high-backed wooden chairs occupied the centre of the room, and a well-used Ercol armchair, upholstered in faded chintz, surrounded by an array of dog beds sat next to a tall Welsh dresser which filled the far wall of the room.

"Have a seat, I'll put the kettle on while I feed the dogs".

He flicked the kettle on and opened the cupboard door below to reveal the biggest sack of dog kibble Sharon had ever seen. He deposited a large scoop of biscuits into each of the three bowls on the floor, and as one, the dogs sat down, watching for his signal. He took a plastic container of chopped beef heart from the fridge, adding a large handful to each bowl, replaced it and crossed the room to the old Belfast sink to wash his hands. The tense dogs watched his every step, but never moved a muscle. He busied himself making three mugs of coffee, placing milk, sugar, and teaspoons on the table. He took a biscuit barrel from a shelf, removed the lid and gesturing to the women to help themselves. After he joined them, taking a seat at the table, he clicked his fingers and the dogs immediately leapt on their bowls, devouring their meal.

"It was a long time ago, and I really don't know how I can help. Presumably you've read the official report, so you know what happened. I remember that your father had been missing for something like twenty hours when my unit was called in to commence the search. We wouldn't normally be involved in a search for an adult after such a short period, but there were concerns about his state of mind considering what was happening at the time. I led the dog unit to trace his journey from his house, and after forty minutes or so we located his body on one of the paths in the woods. A young couple of hill walkers saw his dog guarding something, but they'd been unable to get close enough to find out what it was. They decided to walk down the hill to notify someone, and we met them as we were about to start a sweep of the woods. They directed us to where they had seen the dog, and we went to check it out, unfortunately, we found his body. His dog was protecting him, and it took me a while to gain his trust so that we could get to your father to examine him. When I did, it was obvious that he had been dead for some time. I sent one of the team back down to the house to fetch the police officers, and I waited with the body. Thirty minutes later it was a three-ring circus, plain clothes detectives, local woodentops and SOCO's taking photos and stuff. Our job was done, so as soon as we got the 'all clear', our unit withdrew and returned to base. That's, it really".

He absent-mindedly dunked a thick digestive into his cooling coffee, popping the damp biscuit whole into his mouth.

Sharon looked at Hilary for some sign of how to proceed next. Giving too much away too soon could scare him into clamming up, and that was the last thing she wanted.

Hilary fiddled with the handle of her mug,

"The couple you met who directed you to Professor Crane, can you remember what they said?"

Wayne threw his head back and laughed heartily,

"You can't be serious; it was almost thirty years ago. How am I supposed to remember something like that?" But the hard stare in his eyes betrayed his laughter. Sharon stepped in,

"We just wondered if anything unusual stuck out in your mind about them, or what they said".

Wayne got up and took his mug to the sink, swilling it under a running tap.

"They were a young couple out for a walk, the lad said there was a dog behaving strangely, like he was guarding a bundle of clothes or something. They tried to approach him, but he began to growl at them, and they thought he might attack if they persisted, so they decided to come down the hill and report it to the police. We walked back along the path in the direction they had come from, and after about ten minutes we came across the black Labrador pacing around a tree. I approached him to get a better look, and he came straight across and sat down in front of me. He seemed to know I was there to help. I walked around the back of the tree and found the body propped up against the trunk. I knew he was dead, but I still checked for a pulse and when I couldn't find one, I sent Gibson to alert the Inspector heading the investigation. That's it really".

Hilary drained her mug, swallowing the last of her coffee and said,

"So, you say he was propped against the trunk of the tree when you found him?" Wayne nodded.

"Yes, that's right". Sharon interrupted,

"Yet my brother distinctly remembers that he was lying on his back when he saw him".

"Well, he'd just suffered a terrible shock, he may not have remembered things correctly". Hilary continued,

"But if they had been walking along that path, the body would have been clearly visible to them. He was only wearing a white shirt and trousers when he was found, and his sleeves were bloodstained. I can imagine that it would have been quite a distressing scene to witness. Yet, they didn't spot Professor Crane, they only mentioned the dog". Both women waited for his reaction.

Wayne paused, trying to recall the events in detail,

"I never thought about that. Perhaps they didn't want to get involved, and they knew we would find him if they pointed us in the right direction. Or perhaps they shouldn't have been there in the first place, there could be a hundred reasons why they said what they did. All I know for certain is that we found him, job done!"

"When you found him, was there much blood at the scene? The report mentions that his shirt sleeves were bloodstained, but did you notice any on his hands or the ground surrounding him?"

"No, not particularly, but there were lots of empty pill packets dotted around, so I assumed he had overdosed. I do remember a knife close by though, I guess that's what he used to cut his wrists, just to make sure". He looked across at Sharon uncertainly,

"I'm sorry. This must be hard for you to hear. Why are you asking about this case now after all this time?"

Sharon gave him a direct gaze.

"It is quite simple Mr. Priestley; I do not believe that my father committed suicide. There are many inconsistencies in the official report regarding the events of that day, things that don't make sense, things that contradict each other. At the very least, the police investigation was seriously flawed or was manipulated. I don't know by whom, or why, but I do know that there was more to it than what was stated in the records. I intend to find out what really happened, and who was involved".

"I can assure you that what I've told you is exactly how it happened. There was nothing strange about the discovery of his body, and I stayed with him until the main party arrived. Nothing happened during that time, no one interfered with the scene or the body. I can understand why you might think that, but based on the scene I witnessed that day, I'm sure he really did take his own life".

The women glanced at each other, Sharon nodded, and they both got up to leave. Hilary said,

"We thank you for your help, Mr. Priestley. We can see ourselves out".

Wayne watched from the doorstep as they walked to the car, he didn't close the door until he could no longer see the tail lights of their car in the lane.

He hoped that would be the end of it, but he had a sinking feeling that it may just be the beginning.

In the car, Sharon said,

"Well, considering it was such a long time ago, his memory seemed surprisingly good. In fact, it sounded almost like a direct lift from the report we read".

"Yes, almost as if he had been rehearsing it for 20 years".

27. Shady Fields

Monday 27th January 2020: Late afternoon

They were largely silent on their journey back to Shady Fields. They were each lost in their own thoughts, Sharon focused on the account the dog handler had given them and Hilary focused on the bigger questions of why standard procedures had been flouted in the way that they had. Sharon interrupted the silence,

"We have to take his word for all of that, but I think he was being evasive, and I don't think he was telling us everything". Hilary nodded.

"I agree. We should check out the full Special Branch case report. There will be additional details of the events that we haven't seen yet. Daniel said there will be a hard copy waiting for us when we get back to the office".

"Can you to drop me off at the Bull's Head please, I feel exhausted, and I think I may have a migraine coming on?"

"Of course, the report will keep until tomorrow. Have a good night's sleep and let's start fresh tomorrow".

True to his word, Daniel had arranged for a courier to drop the document off, and it was waiting for her on her office desk. It was quite late by the time she arrived back at Shady Fields. She took a quick bath, ate sandwiches from a tray that the kitchen had sent up, and settled down with a glass of whiskey and the report.

It was after 10 p.m. when she finished making notes about the report, and the results were pretty explosive. It was clear that the body had been moved. When Sharon's brother and Priestly had originally found the body, Crane had been lying on his back, but the photos of the scene clearly showed Crane propped up against a tree.

There was no mention of the investigators trying to identify and locate a woman who was seen leaving the area, and yet Hilary knew who that woman was. From the description given by the young couple who had seen her, a woman with a distinctive pale red birthmark on her left cheek could only mean that Kitty Oliver had been there that day.

But the clincher was how Special Branch had issued a missing person alert at 12.30 pm on the Thursday lunchtime, when Crane hadn't left the house with Nero until 1.30 pm.

Hilary had tried to rationalize how that might be possible. Maybe human error, someone noting the time down incorrectly. The local police had not been notified of his absence until 4.30 pm, but they refused to respond because they said not enough time had elapsed to make it a 'missing persons' case. That was clearly stated in the report. The response at 9 pm to send officers out to the house was also clearly documented. But there was no explanation of how they knew he was going to go missing before he actually had gone missing.

She decided to call Sharon, who answered after the first ring.

"I wasn't sure if you would still be awake, I would have left a message".

"No that's fine, I had a shower and something to eat, and I feel better now, but it's been a hell of a few days and I think it's all catching up with me".

"I'll cut right to the chase, we need to speak to Dowie-Brown, he was your father's closest friend and a colleague. He would know what Robert's frame of mind was at that time, considering what was happening". There was an embarrassed silence.

"I already did. He came down to the pub yesterday and we chatted. I know exactly what dads' frame of mind was like, he was looking forward to me coming home. He was not suicidal; it wasn't in his nature. Everything we've uncovered so far just reinforces the inevitable. He was murdered, and it was made to look like suicide. I have no idea who would have the power to do such a thing, but it must be someone with the authority to make things disappear. The risk they took was huge. It was a high-profile case, and it would not have stood up to scrutiny, so it must have had government involvement".

28. Moscow

Monday 27th January 2020

Marina glanced across at Mitch as they stepped out of the anonymous saloon car, his face was hidden beneath the brim of a fedora style hat, the collar of his coat upturned. Mitch was totally different from the men in her life up to now. He was big and physical, with a sharp intellect and unwavering resolve. From the first moment she met him two years ago, he had fascinated her. He had been the one to encourage her to transfer to MI6 from the relative safety of the CDC, the Centre for Disease Control and a life of lab testing and reports. Now here she was, her training complete, a fully-fledged operational agent in the middle of Moscow, ready to meet a contact who may be able to help with their search for Vladimir Gorski. To add that extra dimension, they were here on Daniels' direct instructions and completely off the grid.

They made their way through a labyrinth of alleys, following the instructions their contact had provided. Gorski the Russian, suspected of being a linchpin in a conspiracy to manipulate global oil prices and supplies, had been declared dead in a suspicious car crash five years ago, but their intelligence suggested otherwise.

As they approached the derelict building that served as the meeting point, Marina began to feel the weight of this mission bearing down on her. If what they had discovered so far was true, then the fallout could be catastrophic. Doubt gnawed at her, and she couldn't shake the feeling that this might be an elaborate ruse, and that nothing was what it seemed to be. Her senses heightened, imagining a trap, an ambush or worse.

Mitch cautiously approached the dilapidated warehouse door, peeling paint and a broken lock suggested that it was no longer an operational site. He took out his firearm and switched on a tiny but powerful LED torch. He signalled to Marina to check the rear entrance, and watched as she disappeared around the corner of the building.

Mitch quietly entered the building; his senses tingling as he stepped into a long, gloomy corridor. He could see a pale light coming from a room near the end of the passage. He kept his torch pointed at the floor, he didn't want to raise the alarm, but as he silently edged his way along the corridor, he heard a metallic click, like someone readying a weapon. He paused outside the dimly illuminated room before entering, listening intently. He slowly pushed against the door. The rusted hinges betrayed his position with a silence-shattering creak. No shots fired; he waited, silence resumed, Mitch entered the room. It was lit by a single flickering bulb, his contact Sokolov was seated at a battered wooden table. He appeared older, more weathered, but there was an air of confidence about him. That may just have been the Mauser pistol he held casually in his lap.

"You took your bloody time".

His accent was thick, but his English was excellent.

"Welcome, Mitch; you can come out now, Marina"!

Sokolov's voice was cold and emotionless. He used their names like he had known them all his life.

Marina's heart was pounding as she joined them in the room, replacing her service weapon into its discrete holster and taking up a position behind Mitch. Mitch began,

"Sokolov, I understand you have some information for us on the whereabouts of Gorski, or are we too late?"

Sokolov's lips curled into a cynical smile.

"Not too late at all. He is very much alive, even if he doesn't want the world to know it. He escaped an assassination attempt, but we think his cousin didn't.

The wrath of his boss was satisfied, and he took the opportunity to disappear. He had taken too much for granted and became embroiled in a dubious enterprise with the British and the Americans. That was never going to end well, regardless of his motivation".

Mitch took off his hat and laid it on the table.

"Was his motivation money?"

Sokolov shook his head in disappointment.

"Espionage is an imbecilic way of getting rich. He was doing it through some misguided belief that he was securing Mother Russia's place as a world power for the future".

"And how did that work out?" asked Marina, stepping out from the shadows behind him.

"It didn't. The glorious leader thought he had turned traitor and ordered a state funeral for the ex-minister for the interior. As I say, we think it was his cousin they buried, but it was definitely not Gorski".

"How can you be so sure, Sokolov?"

"Because I had dinner with him four weeks ago. He's working with them again, but this time for his own advancement rather than for Russia's. If the Politburo finds out, then he is a dead man for real".

"Do you know what he is working on exactly?"

"No, he did not say, but I do know that he is very keen to find out who Vector 10 is. We know Vector 10 is out to embarrass you and your American allies, and normally, we would be enthusiastic spectators at such a spectacle. But this is different, it's like he has a stake in what is happening. Sokolov was playing his cards close to his chest". Mitch pushed a little harder.

"If you had to hazard a guess, what might it be about?" Sokolov shrugged.

"A catastrophe involving oil prices and supplies. It's a matter of global stability, my friends. There's a plan to destabilize oil markets, and it's being orchestrated by a shadowy organisation with deep pockets and disreputable ambitions".

Marina's disbelief was giving way to curiosity.

"Tell us who's behind this, and what your role in this thing is?"

"It's simple, he contacted me because if Vector 10 continues to leak these documents, it will jeopardize their whole project. Rumour has it that Gorski has put out an eight-million-dollar bounty on Vector 10. That's more money than any spotty teenager hacking from their bedroom can ever hope to see in a lifetime. He is turning the poachers into gamekeepers, and they will catch him without Gorski lifting a finger".

Mitch leaned in, studying Sokolov's eyes for any sign of deception.

"Why should we trust you, considering your track record?" Sokolov's voice grew solemn.

"Mitch, I may walk a thin line, but my loyalty to my country and the world has always been steadfast. You have the same duty. Trust, in this world, is a luxury we can't afford. If the energy resources are controlled by one organisation, we are a hairsbreadth away from a global government, where no country is sovereign, and we all end up living on an insect diet in 15-minute cities".

"If this information is true, then we owe you".

Sokolov stood and gathered his coat around him.

"My request is a simple one, never contact me again".

29. Shady Fields

Tuesday 28th January 2020

Hilary looked at the group assembled around the meeting table in her office. Sharon had provided copies of her papers for everyone and was waiting to present her case. Marina looked intrigued as she flicked through her pack. Daniel sat back in his chair, slightly detached from the group, as if he was waiting to be convinced. Hilary had placed a pot of coffee and mugs in the centre of the table and people were helping themselves.

"If we are ready; Sharon, over to you".

Hilary reached for her coffee and sat down. Sharon was clearly nervous. The revelations they had uncovered in the last week had sent her normally balanced and composed appearance into a spin, even though they had confirmed her worst fears. It was one thing to hope and believe that your father's death was not a suicide, but when you had definitive information that clearly established that he had been murdered, and the authorities had conspired to cover it up, it turned everything you believed sacred on its head.

Hilary had told Sharon that she would have to present her findings in a logical and factual way if Daniel was going to be convinced that he needed to act. Letting her emotions get the better of her would not help. Sharon had turned the findings into a set of questions, hoping that it would minimise her association with the evidence they had uncovered. Sharon took a sip of coffee and began.

"OK, so looking at the coroner's report and the official records of what happened on the day, we have produced the following summary and identified several questions that we are unable to answer.

Firstly, SIB, the Special Investigations Branch, appointed the Special Coroner, stating that it would not be appropriate to put the case through normal channels because of the high-profile nature of the case. Once appointed, Mr. DeBeer made the controversial decision not to hold a formal inquest. When he was asked to justify his decision he said, *'My duty was to determine whether there are exceptional reasons that warrant an inquest, and if I had thought there had been, I would have ordered one.'*

Daniel raised his head and looked directly at Sharon.

"He was simply following protocol. There are three reasons you hold an inquest. First, if you don't know how the person died. Second, if you suspect it was at the hands of another person, and third, if the death was caused by medical negligence or as the result of medical treatment. The fact that his suicide was widely accepted, means there was no obvious justification for an inquest".

Sharon took a breath to offer a counter to his argument, but he continued.

"I'm playing devil's advocate, Sharon. If we are going to open this can of worms, our arguments have to be watertight". She nodded and replied.

"There is a fourth reason for ordering an inquest, Mr. Grant, and that's when it's in the public interest. And we know that it certainly was not in the Government's interest to have this incident aired publicly. If we look at the Scene of Crime report describing the discovery of the body, it says he was found propped against a tree, surrounded by empty pill packets and with his wrists cut. The conclusion drawn was that he had committed suicide by taking approximately fourteen Temazepam tablets, then, just to be certain, he had cut his wrists and bled to death.

No prescription was found to say how he had obtained the drugs, no one in the family took them and the blister packs were scattered around, no box was found. No identifiable prints were found on the foil packets or the knife that was used to make the cuts. And he was not wearing gloves. Also found near the body was an unopened bottle of water, again with no fingerprints".

Daniel interjected.

"Blister packs are notoriously difficult to get prints from, given the nature of how fingers slide around when applying pressure to get the tablets out. Temazepam are tiny, he could easily have swallowed twelve or more without water. It's also possible that he cut his wrists before taking the tablets and that he wiped the knife himself. When people are in that frame of mind, logic isn't the first port of call, they make strange decisions that are out of character and make no sense".

Sharon took a deep breath and forged on.

"The lead SOCO concluded that he 'probably' bled to death, but if that was the case, why was there no significant blood loss evident at the scene. Most coroners agree that cutting your wrists is the least effective way of killing yourself, unless you do it in a warm bath. Given the size and depth of the wounds, it is more likely that the blood would have clotted before sufficient loss occurred. Also, in the pictures taken at the mortuary, there is clear and significant evidence of lividity present on his shoulder blades, buttocks, and heels. That suggests he was on his back long enough for the blood to pool. He was found propped up against a tree, the lividity pattern would have been different if he had died in that position and anyway, lividity cannot take place in someone who dies of blood loss because there is no blood left to pool".

She held her breath, waiting for Daniel to counter her argument, but he simply nodded his head. She was relieved that he didn't challenge her, she continued.

"Next, the photographs show evidence of vomit trails from the corners of his mouth, like you would expect if he had been lying on his back. There was no corresponding vomit residue found anywhere near the body, and if he was sick, was that because he was expelling the tablets? The only conclusion you can come to after reading this report was that the body was moved by someone after he died. A dead man cannot move himself, so who moved the body?"

She took a sip from her cooling coffee cup.

"From the account we were given by Wayne Priestly, the dog handler in charge of the search, when they found Crane's body, he was wearing a white shirt that was blooded across the front and on the sleeves. There was also mud staining evident on the knees of his trousers, but no identifiable blood stains, which I find significant". Daniel seized on the statement.

"Why is that surprising, he could have knelt whist he was taking the tablets before he cut his wrists". Sharon smiled.

"You miss the point, Mr. Grant. It was a chilly and blustery autumn day, and he was walking his dog. Where was his coat? He would not have gone out with Nero on such a day without his coat".

Sharon had saved the ace up her sleeve until last.

"All of this is enough for any decent coroner to call for an inquest. There are too many unanswered questions and anomalies for this to be waved through on a whim, but the two strongest indicators that this does not add up, are not linked with his body, or where or how he was found. The suicide note that was found in his pocket is not in his handwriting, and I can provide samples that would categorically prove that".

She waited for Daniel to speak, but he stayed silent. She continued.

"And no one has been able to explain to me how the Special Branch enquiry was recorded as starting on Thursday at 12.30 pm, when my dad never left the house until 1.30 pm that day. We didn't report him missing until 4.30 pm, and yet the digital signature on the file clearly shows 12.30 pm".

The room was silent.

30. DG's Office Thames House

Thursday 30th January 2020

Pearson had been checked in by security and was now being escorted up to the 8th floor of Thames House to the Director General's office. Daniel had thought about where the meeting should take place, but eventually the decision was simple. He had come across men like Pearson before. They invariably had a reasonable intellect and were competent communicators, but their stock-in-trade was manipulation. People, situations, power plays, it didn't matter because they never played a straight game. They were always playing an angle of some description and treading on people to get to where they wanted to be. The civil service was filled with these tinpot empire builders. These types of people often built their careers in the media or politics. He had decided it was time to rattle cages, and Daniel wanted to be on home territory to do that.

The low hum of the lift mechanism was the only noise as they travelled up in an atmosphere of dread. The doors opened and Ann-Marie, Daniel's personal assistant, gestured for them to follow her. She stopped at the tall wooden doors, knocked twice, then waited. After a full three minutes of waiting, Daniel called 'enter,' she opened the door and ushered Pearson inside. His security escort returned to the lobby to wait for the call to escort him back out.

The impression Daniel wanted to create for this interview was as the enigmatic head of the world's oldest intelligence agency, positioned behind his huge mahogany desk. He was generally a man of few words, but his reputation for ruthlessness would come in very handy this evening.

He looked up at Pearson, standing, shifting nervously from foot to foot, like a naughty schoolboy in front of the headmaster, he was sweating profusely. Daniel was surprised at how shabby his appearance was, he stared at him with an icy gaze. He did not offer him a seat.

Pearson's eyes darted around the room, taking in the framed commendations and modern art that adorned the walls. He was not sure why he had been summoned to this place. It had not been a request, it was an order, and he was under no illusion that he was in no position to refuse. He couldn't shake the feeling that he had crossed a line of no return.

"Mr. Pearson...... Stewart," Daniel began, his voice calm and deliberate.

"I am sorry to tell you that you have been caught with your proverbial trousers around your ankles. You've been playing a dangerous game, and you seem to have forgotten just who you're dealing with".

Pearson cleared his throat nervously, struggling to maintain his composure.

"I don't know what you mean". He tried to muster some bravado but failed.

Daniel gave him a sardonic smile, leaned forward, and placed his hands on the desk. His fingers drummed lightly on the polished wood, creating an unnerving rhythm.

"Please don't fuck with me, Mr. Pearson. It could be argued that what you and your boss orchestrated in the nineties could be constituted as corruption at best, treason at worse. Now, I'm a man that values loyalty, Stewart. Although, it's a malleable concept in the world we inhabit today. Loyalty to power, to influence, and to one's own survival. Are you loyal to those principles, Stewart?"

Pearson hesitated for a moment, sensing the weight of Daniel's words.

"I... I do what I have to, to protect my interests, and those I work for".

Daniel's smile widened, revealing a hint of amusement that sent shivers down Pearson's spine.

"Interests, you say. Well, Stewart, I have a unique way of ensuring that everyone's interests align with mine and those of this country".

As he spoke, Daniel pressed a concealed button on his desk. A panel in the wall behind Pearson slid back to reveal a screen filled with several recently taken views of Pearson, at train stations, an airport, shopping in his local Tesco express, and more unnervingly, speaking to his researcher in their office earlier that morning.

"You see, Stewart," Daniel continued, his voice now a whisper,

"This is my realm. I have access to everything that you have ever been or are now involved in. I know who you work for and with. Furthermore, I also know those you have betrayed, and those who have betrayed you. And with a keystroke, I can feed you and your ex-boss to the dogs if I choose to".

Pearson's face paled, beads of sweat glistened on his forehead. He realized that Daniel was not bluffing. Daniel continued.

"Although I have never met Vector 10, I am familiar with his work, as you are, I'm sure. He was a minor inconvenience for a while, until I began to examine what he was really up to. Now, if you want to hide a tree Stewart, where would you do that?" Pearson heard himself answer.

"In a wood".

"Well done, Stewart, excellent! I began to wonder what you would hide in a bunch of state secrets that you uploaded to a public server, and do you know what I found, Stewart? I found a seed of something so big and so cynical; that I didn't quite believe it. So, I thought I would invite you up here this evening to share it with you and see what you think".

Pearson now looked scared. Daniel leaned back in his chair, his eyes never leaving Pearson's.

"Remember this, Stewart. Loyalty is a two-way street. You can serve your interests, or you can serve your country. The choice is yours, but know that crossing that line might be the last decision you ever make. Your researcher Ally is a lovely girl, bright and eager to please. She has found some of the material that Vector 10 has kindly shared, but what she will not have found are the markers that Vector 10 left specifically for me, pointing in the right direction to fill in the blanks. So let me show you some of what we know".

The screen changed and a series of slides accompanied the disclosures Daniel made.

"We know the truth about the dossier that Adam Hunt compiled using manipulated data from the CIA to gain the country's support to invade Iraq. We also know that the weapons inspector who authored the original report tried to get it changed to reflect the real situation but was silenced. We even found a tape of him confessing to a journalist that it was him who falsified the information in the dossier. Luckily, you didn't need to use it, as technology has moved on, and it would have been shown to be a poor fake. That might have been very difficult to explain away. You had a lucky escape there, Stewart. And you were also lucky that he committed suicide before that could happen. And yet, if he did commit suicide, why have you been making regular and large payments to keep the person who staged that suicide quiet? We have the whole sorry incident, signed documents and all. Oh, we even have a copy of the original dossier with your handwritten notes and your signature".

Daniel flashed up an image of Pearson's doctored report and watched the look of shock appear across his face.

"None of it's true. I wasn't aware of what went on. I was just an aide at number 10". But even he thought he sounded unconvincing. Daniel ignored the outburst and continued.

"Next are the redacted reports that we have managed to 'un-redact', of the deals to select who the civil engineering contracts would go to when the war was over, and the country needed rebuilding. That's a lovely photo of President Hudson and Adam Hunt, isn't it? No wonder the American Construction industry had a bumper few years. And here are the share certificates showing the investment Adam Hunt made into five of those companies. I have lots more, but I don't want to bore you".

"Is what I am saying hitting home, Stewart? We have enough to take you and Hunt out of circulation permanently. You know who I am and what I do. You know the resources I can call on, but what you may not know is that I am not a man who makes idle threats. I am a man of my word. When this is in the public domain, your boss can say goodbye to his special envoy posting, and I am not sure his global foundation will survive a PR crisis of this magnitude. And as for you, well………"

Daniel rose and walked over to a side table, where he poured two considerable measures of scotch into tumblers and offered one to Pearson.

Pearson took it and swallowed half of it in one go. He took a deep breath, and when he was sure that the alcohol hit had steadied his nerves, he said quietly

"What do you want?"

Daniel gave him a piercing look and said simply but with absolute conviction.

"Well Stewart, I want you to tell them their time has run out, their scheme ends now".

31. Shady Fields

Monday 3rd February 2020

Daniel was satisfied that things were now back under control.

Celia was insistent that she was fine and had no intention of taking the incident with Dowie-Brown further. He had realised how close he had come to doing something unforgivable and was making preparations to go back home. There was nothing else he could do.

Daniel had taken advantage of the anonymity of Shady Fields to conduct the debriefing with Mitch and Marina, fresh from their recent Eastern 'fishing trip'. They needed to capture Gorski and that would be the beginning of the end for the Tripartite Treaty and the Hunt Foundation.

Right now, he needed to get back to London, and Marina was going back with him to check on Peter's progress on the hunt for Vector 10.

Daniel was extremely aware that his meeting last week with Pearson had stirred a hornet's nest, and they needed to be ready for any repercussions. Mitch was chasing down a suspected sighting of Gorski, so it felt like they were finally getting somewhere, and they were on the home straight.

When Daniel walked out to the car park, Marina was already standing at the passenger door waiting for him. She was chatting with Bill and Ben, who were obviously taking their latest health kick seriously. They looked like an odd grouping, her tall angular frame wrapped in a camel coat with a large fur collar, sporting a pair of knee-high brown leather boots, and the two older men in running shorts, vests, and trainers. It was already 11 am, yet the temperature had struggled to get above freezing. Clouds of condensing breath escaped their mouths as they talked. Daniel was still twenty yards away. He reached into his pocket and clicked the central locking release button on the remote key fob. Immediately, there was a secondary clicking sound from the car after the door locks released.

"Come on, Marina, we haven't got time for idle chit-chat; we need to get a move on if we're going to get back to HQ before lunchtime". He said jovially.

As she opened the door to get into the car, the clicking sound increased in speed. Unexpectedly, Bill rugby tackled Marina, lifting her off her feet. He was half pushing, half carrying her towards the workshop doors. At the same instant, Ben shouted to Daniel to 'hit the deck'. Five seconds later, the car was engulfed in flames and smoke as a deafening explosion shattered the early morning quiet. A searing orange fireball scorched the air around them. Laminated glass windows shattered into thousands of tiny pieces and flew through the air in all directions. The shockwave of the explosion knocked them all to the ground, rendering them senseless. It seemed like the world was operating in slow motion.

Daniel tried to roll over to see what exactly had happened. His ears were ringing from the shock wave, his overcoat, which had protected him from the worst of the blast, was scorched and smouldering. Where his black Audi A9 had stood just a few seconds ago, now a mangled ruin burned fiercely. He struggled to a sitting position; high-pitched white noise was the only sound he registered. There was blood on his hands, and he could feel a trickle of blood running from his hairline down his cheek.

Marina was protected from the worst effects of the blast because Bill, having carried her several yards from the car, had thrown himself on top of her. She had lost consciousness for a few seconds and, as she regained her senses, realised that she was now lying by the workshop doors. Bill must have carried her twenty yards in a few seconds. She was dazed and unable to move, and felt like she'd been punched in the chest. She wasn't sure if it was the explosion or the impact of the tackle that was making her gasp for breath.

People came running from the house to see what the explosion was, burning debris was still falling from the air.

Daniel struggled to his feet and stumbled towards Ben, who was lying face down on the tarmac. The back of his running shirt was tattered and coloured with flecks of blood. He checked for a pulse, it was fast and strong. As he bent over Ben, he could see that he was beginning to come around. His eyelids fluttered, then the big man let out a groan and pushed himself up to all fours, coughing vigorously.

"What the fuck was that, Dan?"

"Are you okay, Ben? I need to check on the others". Ben nodded and a cloud of dust fell from his hair. He rasped

"Go…. Go…"

Daniel skirted the wreckage, looking for Marina and Bill.

Two of the kitchen staff who had been on their morning break came out of the side entrance to see what was happening. Layla   Strong   followed   closely behind. She rushed to Daniel's side.

"I've called the emergency services; they are on their way. Are you okay?"

Daniel nodded, more in response to her manner because her voice sounded as if she was talking through wads of cotton wool.

"Check Marina and Bill, they may be hurt," he shouted.

As the smoke drifted across the car park, he caught sight of them. They both lay crumpled up against the wooden workshop doors, he thought he saw some movement. He wasn't sure if they'd reached the workshop doors under their own steam, or if the force of the blast had deposited them there. A huge wave of relief swept over him, knowing they had survived.

He coughed and his chest hurt, but he made his way over to them. By the time he got to Bill, the older man was sitting up, looking dazed and ashen faced. He tried to stand, but Daniel put a restraining hand on his shoulder.

"Wait until the medics get here to check you out". Bill looked around in a panic.

"Where's Ben, is he alright?"

"Yes, he's okay, I just spoke to him, his ears are ringing a bit, he's got a few cuts and bruises, and he'll definitely need a new shirt, but apart from that, he seems fine. I'll make sure the medics check him out too". Bill breathed a huge sigh.

"Thanks Daniel".

He turned his attention to Marina, who was still lying on the floor. There was a blood smear across her cheek that trickled from her ear, the lenses in her glasses were cracked, but she was conscious. Her breathing was laboured, he bent over her, checking for injuries and spoke reassuringly.

"Marina, it's Daniel. There was an explosion. I need you to stay still until the medics arrive, can you do that for me?" She nodded her head gingerly. Mitch came careering round from the front of the house, he looked frantic.

"Marina!" He called out. Daniel raised his arm, wincing as he did so.

"Mitch, over here".

Then suddenly, Mitch was on his knees in front of her, holding her hand and stroking her face.

"Marina, are you okay?"

She gave a small nod and attempted a smile. Mitch sat back on his heels, visibly relieved.

"What the hell happened, Daniel?" He looked at the tangled wreckage, "Was that a car bomb?"

"Yes, and a big one. Someone definitely means business. Thank God, Bill and Ben were here talking to Marina. I unlocked the doors as I came into the car park, so Marina could wait in the warm, and they heard the detonator arm itself. Ben called out a warning to me, but Bill physically carried Marina out of the way of the blast zone, it all happened so fast".

"Hilary is checking everyone inside is accounted for. Are you okay?" Daniel nodded. The sound of sirens could be heard in the distance. Mitch looked at Daniel.

"You have seriously pissed someone off. Who would be desperate enough, or stupid enough, to try to assassinate The Director General of British Security Services in broad daylight?" Daniel suddenly felt exhausted, the adrenaline high was dissipating.

"This could only have been the Russians, they are the only one's stupid enough to try, and barefaced enough to front it out, and they will". He slumped down into a seated position.

"I've had enough, this stops now!"

Two days had passed since the powerful explosion that shook the car park at Shady Fields. Windows on the side of the house facing the car park had been blown in and a couple of nearby cars were damaged in the blast, but it was nothing that couldn't be fixed, the repair work was already well underway.

Marina had been taken to hospital with minor cuts and bruises and a perforated eardrum, Mitch had insisted.

They had also taken Bill and Ben, but they had discharged themselves after a couple of hours. Daniel escaped with a mild concussion and a chipped tooth, not bad considering someone had tried to kill him.

A forensic team had conducted a fingertip search of the car park, and what was left of the car had been taken away on a low loader under a tarpaulin. The scorch marks on the ground where the car had stood were the only tell-tale sign that anything had happened. At some point, it would need resurfacing. The windowpanes had been replaced and things at Shady Fields were already returning to normal. A fresh coat of paint, and you wouldn't know anything had happened here.

Back at HQ, members of Daniel's team were scouring all available CCTV footage of his car over the last few days to see if they could pinpoint where and when the bomb was planted. Daniel wasn't optimistic.

"They will have planted it when it was out of sight of CCTV. We are checking footage from the multi-storey where it's parked overnight, but I am not holding my breath". Mitch agreed.

"If it was the Russians, they will deny it even if we have got footage. I have asked the investigators to share the photos and forensics with Bill & Ben. They will nail it if there was Russian involvement, with their knowledge and connections".

Bill and Ben were in a strangely buoyant mood. The two bomb disposal experts were incensed that a skilled bomb maker had attempted to kill their boss and on home turf, and now they had a problem to work on that made use of their expertise. Bill in particular was warming to his task. The renowned "Dynamite Men," were back in the game! They were determined to discover who was responsible, and they had agreed with Daniel that it had Russian involvement plastered right across it. It was no secret that he had been investigating the activities of Gorski, a man suspected of being involved in various covert operations across Europe. Daniel was obviously poking into things that people would rather remain undisturbed. An act of retaliation was to be expected, but this was audacious. A car bomb wasn't a warning, it was a direct attempt to put a stop to the investigation. Their methods may have lacked finesse, but if they had wanted to be subtle, their choice was more likely to be poison. If they wanted to send a direct message that the gloves were off, then it was a car bomb or a shooting.

The morning sun was shining through the small side window of the workshop at the rear of the car park. Illuminated by the shaft of light, stood a large white board that Bill had 'acquired' from the main meeting room in the house. The pair were sifting through the evidence, carefully arranging pictures of fragments of bomb casing, wires, and images of what looked like debris to the untrained eye. Ben squinted at the photo in his hand and shook his head. It was an extreme close up of what looked like fragments of greaseproof paper.

Bill, with his meticulous eye for detail, inspected a picture of the burnt-out remnants of the car. They were mentally piecing together the puzzle.

"I'm leaning toward Semtex," Ben said, rubbing his chin thoughtfully.

"That blast was too powerful for C-4, besides, Semtex is more the Russians' style". Bill nodded in agreement.

"Agreed. It would give them the extra kick they'd want and take up half the space. Maximum impact with a limited blast zone. Injuries would have been fatal if this had exploded in a confined space. It would have contained the blast force and done more human damage".

"Oh, I have been meaning to say, nice rugby tackle on the Doc. She would have been a goner if you hadn't been so quick". Ben nodded his head at his friend as a mark of respect.

"Yes, well……..,"

His voice trailed off, partly with embarrassment from his friends' praise and partly because something had caught his eye.

"Ben, have a look at this. Is that Cyrillic text?"

He was looking at an image of a fragment of singed brown paper. Ben squinted at the writing, tracing his finger under the characters.

"I'd say this confirms our suspicions, but it also ups the ante. This is a deliberate calling card Bill; they want us to know who it is".

Bills' focus shifted to the wiring and triggering mechanism.

"It's a professional job, beautifully constructed, with multiple redundancies designed to ensure detonation. If we hadn't recognised the arming tone, none of us would be around to tell the tale".

"This isn't just some hired thug," Ben said.

"This is the handiwork of a seasoned explosives specialist. Gorski's got connections, and we know who they are".

"Bogdanović!" They both said in unison. And gave each other a triumphant high-five! Ben raised an eyebrow, contemplating the implications.

"So, what do we do next?" Bill leaned back in his chair.

"We need to find out where he's operating from. If we can trace the Semtex and the components back to him, we might find a thread leading to Gorski or his superiors, but we've got to be careful. This is high-stakes, and Daniel will not want us getting involved". Bill looked defiant.

"I'll be buggered if someone's going to take a pot shot at us in our backyard and get away with it. We know how Bogdanović works, Ben, and we can locate him quicker because we know the stones he hides under".

The room grew quiet. The enormity of their task had hit home. Identifying the location where Bogdanović worked from would be tricky, but a train of events had been set in motion and unless they were stopped, people would die. They knew they had to tread carefully, getting involved with this meant they would have a target on their backs as well.

"I'll make some calls, and then we need a plan".

32. Marseilles Docklands

Wednesday 19th February 2020

Marina was quite surprised at the level of trust Daniel had shown in the Dynamite Men. He had listened to their investigation and how they had tracked down the current location of Bogdanović. What had surprised her even more was their assertion that Gorski was probably using it as a base too?

It all seemed too convenient, but Mitch and Marina found themselves navigating one of the shadier suburbs of Marseilles, looking for the Russian bar on the dock. There had been a sighting last night of someone answering the description of Gorski, so tensions were high.

If she wanted to create a better stereotype of a Marseilles bar, Marina would have failed. It looked like a wooden cricket pavilion perched on top of a row of makeshift garages, and she doubted the whole structure would survive if a strong gust of wind blew in off the sea. The corrugated tin roof looked flimsy, and yet these buildings had clearly stood here for decades. A faded neon sign advertised that they were open.

The harsh glow of one of the few street lights that still worked revealed an intricate labyrinth of packing crates and boxes in an area that looked run down and neglected.

To his trained eye, Mitch recognised that what appeared to be haphazard clutter was strategically placed obstacles to slow down any attempt to raid the place. A small group of drunken sailors staggered out of the bar, and prostitutes cruised for their business.

The information Bill and Ben had provided led them to this clandestine headquarters. They had it on excellent authority that the dealer Bogdanović, who had likely supplied the Semtex for the car bomb, operated from this establishment. He was a Chechen of dubious repute and a skilled bomb maker, and who absolutely could not be trusted.

The stakes were high tonight. If their other target was here too, and they captured both, it would be a real coup for the intelligence community. They knew Gorski was a cunning, once high-ranking Russian official, and a man who had betrayed his own nation.

He was involved in something big enough to fake his own death to protect himself. He would trust no one and take no chances, and that made him very dangerous.

They led a small but highly trained extraction unit. When both marks had been identified, the team would move in and round them up. If all went well, they would be in an interrogation unit on the outskirts of London by the following morning. Daniel's orders had been precise. Track down Gorski, bring him in for questioning, and present him with evidence of his involvement in the conspiracy they had uncovered. Daniel and Peter had built a compelling case that consisted of documents, eyewitness statements, intercepted communications, and a damning collection of photographs, all linking Gorski to the Tripartite Treaty and more recently, the Hunt Global Foundation. If they could get him to turn, they could bring down the house of cards they were constructing.

They stood in the shadows waiting for the people milling about outside to move on. Marina adjusted the Kevlar protector she wore under her jacket; she was clearly nervous. Mitch smiled at her,

"No one else I know could make a stab vest look that sexy". It broke the tension. He nodded at her, and they moved off towards the entrance.

The bar smelt of Bouillabaisse and Gitanes. Their footsteps echoed off the bare floorboards as they walked up to the bar. Marina's fingers wrapped firmly around the handle of the service weapon in her pocket. Mitch ordered two shots of brandy. Marina wasn't aware that Mitch spoke fluent French. She was impressed. The dirty glasses the bartender served them could, quite frankly, have contained anything. They raised their glasses in a salute to each other. Almost immediately, the sound of approaching footsteps behind them made Marina stiffen, ready for action.

"I hear you are looking for me?" The couple turned to face Gorski. He was flanked by what Marina described later as two gorillas. Huge men both in height and width, their necks and hands covered in distinctive Russian prison tattoos. They stood in silence.

Gorski's cold, unblinking eyes surveyed Mitch's hands before fixing his gaze on Marina.

"Take your hands out of your pockets where I can see them. You've come a long way to confront me, I would hate anyone to get jumpy". He sneered. Marina met his gaze without flinching.

"You are looking surprising well for a man who died in a car crash five years ago". He smiled at her.

"So, you are the comedian, who is he?" Gorski gestured towards Mitch.

"I am the one who is going to stop you in your tracks". Mitch's voice was low and menacing.

"We have enough evidence to ensure that you rot in a Russian prison for the rest of your life".

Gorski chuckled, a chilling sound that echoed through the now empty bar.

"You think I'm alone here? You think I'm the mastermind?" Mitch spoke, in a matter-of-fact way.

"We know you're involved Gorski, not the mastermind, but we know there are others. I can see the company you keep; they look as sharp as a sack of soup. We also have company, and we are not leaving alone".

Gorski's eyes narrowed, for a moment, he seemed to be weighing his options. He laughed,

"Are you waiting for me to look behind me? Don't hold your breath. You are here on my territory, and you come here to insult me. You will be lucky to leave with your life. Though, I think I might keep her here for a bit. Give the dogs something to play with".

He gestured to his men. Mitch looked unimpressed.

"Look, Gorski, I would rather we took the pragmatic approach. We want the people you are working with, and we know you can deliver them for us. You could get out of this without adding to your collection of tattoos if you cooperate. We can help you disappear for good this time, after all, if we found you, Putin can". Mitch paused,

"We want the others from the Tripartite Treaty, and we think if the price is right, you will give them to us".

With a sinister smile, Gorski delivered a message that sent shivers down their spines.

"Has it not occurred to you why we have been able to operate for so long in the shadows without raising a single suspicion? The reality is, Mr. Bennett, yes, I do know who you are, we have inside help. A mole within the UK security services. You've been chasing the wrong shadows".

Mitch struggled to conceal his shock. He exchanged a quick glance with Marina. The revelation caused her to take a sharp gasp. A mole within their own ranks? It was unthinkable. Mitch's jaw clenched as he muttered,

"Who is it?"

Gorski laughed, a mirthless sound that echoed around the bar.

"It's the man you're all hunting, the one you call Vector 10. He's been feeding me crucial information, and you've been dancing to his tune. He is clever and sly. No one else has ever breached your systems the way he has. He has proved a valuable ally".

The revelation hung heavy in the air, a bombshell that left them reeling. The hunt for Vector 10 had been a high-profile but fruitless pursuit for months, now suddenly, they knew how he had accessed so much information, it was an inside job. It was a nightmare come to life.

While they'd been talking, another three more of Gorski's men had joined the troop. This stand-off was escalating, Mitch and Marina were becoming outnumbered. The tension was becoming intense and unless they acted now, the situation could spiral out of control. They had no choice but to make a move. Gorski began to retreat into the ranks of his bodyguard as Mitch thrust his hand into his jacket pocket and began firing through the fabric of his coat.

Marina dropped to the floor, firing at the man who was taking aim at Mitch. He dropped his weapon and fell to the floor squealing, clutching a shattered knee. She used the corner of the bar as a shield as a volley of bullets chewed up the wooden floor in front of her, splinters of wood stinging her face. Her damaged ear began to protest at the noise, sending shooting pains into her head and setting the room spinning. She heard another two gorillas hit the floor when the room was suddenly rocked by the blinding flash and thunderous blast of a powerful G60 stun grenade. The 'flash-bang' was intended to disorientate and distract hostiles giving the entry team a few moments to enter a room and neutralize threats. Using the flash bang grenade as cover, their team burst through the door, and it was all over. Mitch was still standing, but there was no sign of Gorski. A team member emerged from a door at the back of the bar and approached Mitch.

"Sorry boss, we got Bogdanović, but the others got away". Mitch slapped his foot soldier on the shoulder.

"That's fine, we've got what we came for. Let's get the hell out of here before the Gendarmerie turn up wondering why we've just destroyed their bar".

The revelation of a mole within their own ranks meant that their every move had potentially been compromised, the rules of the game had changed in a blink, and they could trust no one. The conspiracy had just taken a more sinister turn, they had no idea who knew what or who they could trust.

33. Thames House

Friday 21st February 2020

Daniel had gathered his team in one of the old conference rooms in Thames House, situated several floors below ground level. Mitch and Marina had briefed Daniel as soon as their plane had landed. They had said very little to each during the flight because they were reluctant to talk about the revelation of a mole within their ranks in front of the others. They had no idea whether what Gorski said was true or not, he could have been bluffing in an attempt to aid his escape. Though Mitch knew that what he said made perfect sense. And it explained how the hacker had been able to avoid detection for so long. The mole had clearly used sleight of hand to divert attention from their activities. Could it be that the document releases were an enormous smoke screen that concealed Vector 10's true identity in plain sight?

The group muttered among themselves, and Daniel waited for them to settle before he began.

"Mitch, can you please share with everyone the conversation you had with Gorski on Wednesday evening"?

He briefed everyone on their encounter and delivered the disturbing news that Vector 10 was actually a mole within MI5.

Daniel's expression darkened as he considered the fallout of such a discovery.

"We have to act quickly. If Vector 10 has been feeding our secrets to our enemies for God knows how long, all of our classified information is in jeopardy". Peter shook his head.

"I can't believe it. Right under my nose, I should have picked something up, I should have been one step ahead, but it feels like I've been two steps behind all along". Daniel was curt.

"Recriminations waste time. We need to test this allegation and find out if it is true". Mitch nodded.

"I've assembled a team, the best in the business, to help us identify and neutralize the mole. Time is of the essence".

Marina chimed in, her voice resolute.

"If the intelligence is correct, then Vector 10 is a high-ranking operative within our organisation, which makes this hunt even more difficult because he is either technically able himself, or working with someone who is guiding him in and out of our systems. Either way, he has intimate knowledge of our protocols and some sort of undetected back door. Peter, any ideas?"

Peter leaned back in his chair, deep in thought.

"However he's doing it, this is no predictable hack. He's using something that leaves no trace or signature on the system. My knowledge, understanding and instincts are unmatched in this field, and I have nothing, no real idea at this stage where to start, or how he could be doing this".

Marina had been thoughtful, listening to Peter, who was unaccustomed to being on the back foot. She looked thoughtful.

"It makes sense for us to build a profile of Vector 10 like we would any double agent. There will be characteristics we can predict that might give us a clue to who he is. Meanwhile, Peter should concentrate on identifying the technical access. I also have a connection to Forrest Selznick, probably better known as 'States'. He could prove useful". Peter looked at Marina with fresh respect.

"You know 'States'?" Mitch interrupted them,

"As in the States of America?" Marina smiled.

"No, as in 'Enemy of the State' with Will Smith. He chose the 'handle' because he was a fan of the film. He is one of the world's leading authorities on computer hacking and the dark web. A reformed character after a five-year stint as a guest of the California Penal System for numerous computer related crimes. He set up a private consultancy firm in 2012 offering cybersecurity services".

Peter added,

"You're not giving him enough credit, Marina. He's the guy who hacked into Microsoft in 1999 and copied their millennium patches, then put them in the public domain as shareware, rendering their marketing campaign void and losing them an estimated $1billion in expected revenue. The millennium bug was rendered as harmless as a stubbed toe".

He could not disguise his obvious admiration for a fellow tech-genius.

"So how do you know him?"

Marina warmed to her newfound 'cool' status.

"I went to a conference in New York, and we met in the hotel bar after the session finished. He was a good laugh, and he was fascinated by my Scottish accent. I was intrigued by a convicted felon that had turned his life around, and we just hit it off. We've stayed in touch, and I really think he might give us a few ideas about where to start the search".

Daniel interjected.

"I'm sorry to interrupt this stroll down memory lane, but we need to focus. If you think he can be of some help, Marina, reach out, but be guarded in what you tell him. He may be a poacher turned gamekeeper, but the fewer people who are read in on the details, the better". She nodded her agreement.

He turned to Peter.

"Peter, I trust your instincts, so let's do this methodically and discreetly. No one outside this room can know what we're doing. We'll start by gathering all the information we have on Vector 10".

"Let's meet back here on Tuesday morning. I don't have to labour the point about the need for secrecy, but we need something to go on". Daniel was hoping they would provide it for him.

They knew that identifying Vector 10 would be like searching for a needle in a haystack, and that every resource at their disposal would be required. They needed a plan, and this had to take priority. It was pointless trying to establish a link to the Tripartite Treaty or The Hunt Foundation until they knew Vector 10's role in it and exactly who he was. The meeting broke up and they went their separate ways. Marina made a call and within the hour, 'States' was on board.

Mitch and Marina returned to Shady Fields together, and set up a 'war room', They also knew they would find two sets of extra hands they could rely on.

Peter went back to his office and considered these latest developments. He was desperately trying not to feel concerned, but he did feel strangely exposed. He was used to being the go-to person and the solution provider for all things technical. He was getting older, but had never really considered a succession plan or what he would do if he didn't work here. Not only that, but he'd carved out a very specific niche for himself, and he wasn't sure how it felt being usurped by a younger and possibly more knowledgeable man like Forrest. On one hand, he was excited to be working with such a formidable peer, but 'States' definitely represented the new world and was a reminder to Peter that he had a limited shelf-life and may soon become surplus to requirements.

At Shady Fields, the search for the mole was like peeling an onion, revealing new information layer after layer. They combed through classified documents looking for patterns, inconsistencies, and connections that might lead to Vector 10's real identity.

The benefits of having the dynamite men on their side were fresh eyes, and someone unafraid to ask the obvious questions. Sometimes, if you were deeply involved in a mission, it could be difficult to tell the wood from the trees. Thinking creatively was their speciality. So far, their investigations had led them to multiple dead-ends and red-herrings, but they were determined to leave no stone unturned.

They faced an unusual contradiction. They needed to uncover the mole before he could cause further damage to national security, but they also realised that they wouldn't be aware of the Tripartite Treaty, without the help Vector 10 had provided.

They worked day and night, breaking for food and a little sleep. They were not going to be the ones who failed to produce anything new when they reconvened in London on Tuesday.

As the weekend progressed, the pressure intensified. Their tireless dedication and diligence was unwavering. But each passing moment was another opportunity for Vector 10 to compromise their operations, leak more classified information, and endanger lives.

The initial breakthrough came late on Sunday evening when Marina presented the profile she'd been working on to the group. She had an audience who were keen to hear what her expertise had produced.

"There are two distinct approaches we use for psychological profiling. The American system uses data gathered about the suspect, usually from a crime scene, and the investigators identify characteristics of the suspect, like their lifestyle or personality traits. It labels them as either an organised or a disorganized suspect and fits the details of the crime to one of those typologies. We prefer a different approach, starting with small details of the crime, looking for patterns and trends to create an overall picture".

Marina personally favoured this approach as it didn't make any assumptions about the suspect. It was the software that crunched the data to build a likely picture of the suspect. She continued,

"Because of the nature of the problem, I decided to use both approaches to see what it would throw up, and I got some interesting results. The suspect is likely to be highly organised and shows signs of having planned the document release for some time. That would suggest they are patient but persistent. They are likely to be personable, socially adequate, humorous, quite charming and have a very high IQ. The data also suggests that they could be hiding in plain sight. The suspect would be quite businesslike in their approach, not engaging in small talk, would pose a laser-like focus and possibly be prone to outbursts of frustration if things don't go their way. Our suspect is clearly an analytical and strategic thinker, able to see the big picture, and would be drawn to strategy games like chess. The more interesting aspect of this profile suggests that our suspect may return to the scene of the crime several times and volunteer information when questioned, appearing to be compliant and helpful. Any questions?" Ben smiled.

"And you got all of that because he stole and released some documents over the internet?"

Marina blushed and nodded.

"Jesus" said Bill, "Remind me not to lie on your couch".

"Have you ever tried therapy, Bill?" Marina was genuinely interested, knowing his career choices.

"I tried it once," said Bill. "But when I asked her how my lack of progress made her feel, she refused to see me any more". Marina ignored the joke and added.

"I also got an update from Forrest, who offered a few suggestions, the most likely being that Vector 10 may be using a legacy system to piggyback onto our network to divert and download the documents. This approach would be ideal because he wouldn't need to hack into the system to do it. He may be using an old protocol that he has repurposed". Mitch looked confused,

"Do you want to run that past me again but this time in plain English?" Marina smiled,

"Imagine you had a maintenance programme that did a housekeeping task on your computer, like deleting old files to free up disk space. You could put any file you wanted in that folder, then download it at your convenience when deleting the files. It might be written to a USB stick or even uploaded to the cloud for you to pick up remotely later. The point is that because the programme is doing what you expect it to do, it wouldn't attract attention". Mitch nodded.

"That's quite clever and simple. You wouldn't need to be highly technical to do that, either".

Bill shot a grin at Mitch.

"Okay, Vector 10, the game is up!"

Mitch wasn't amused.

"Very funny Bill". Marina interrupted the banter,

"Forrest was going to call Peter this morning to see what he thought".

Daniel thanked Marina and the team for the fresh insight their profile had offered them and brought the meeting to a close.

"We have plenty to be going on with, so let's get to it".

Peter King's instincts kicked in. He was surprised that 'States' had come up with a possible solution so quickly. Hiding something in plain sight was always effective. It was how MI5 worked all the time. He would need to prepare a response for Daniel. He could see a subtle inconsistency that had eluded everyone else. It was a small breadcrumb, but it could point to a high-ranking operative who had access to the most sensitive information they possessed.

Now they had a means and a method, but they were missing a name and a motive. No one knew what the endgame might be, and the mole was still operating. Tomorrow they would meet again and share what they had. Peter knew he needed to make a significant contribution; otherwise there was a possibility that 'States' would be bought in to help. He remembered a conversation he'd had years ago with one of MI6's top agents, she had told him "age and treachery will beat youth and exuberance every time". They had to act swiftly on this new information, people would be watching and waiting. The race against time had never been more critical, and Peter's resolve had never been stronger.

34. Thames House

Tuesday 25th February 2020

The investigation into Vector 10 had accentuated the fact that the mole had made fools out of them all.

This clever hacker had convinced everyone that it was an attack from outside, no one had suspected that it was an inside job, so audacious and so risky were their actions. It was only a matter of time before Vector 10's identity was exposed. However, MI5 did have a history of missing what was right under their noses, Kim Philby being a case in point. It only took them twenty-five years, countless agents captured and killed and a very public defection to realise he might have been a spy.

The team assembled again in the basement meeting room at Thames House, this time there was more than just a sense of excitement in the air. The group sat around the large wooden meeting, staring at the image a ceiling projector was throwing onto a plain cream wall. No hi-tech LED displays down here.

Marina had constructed the profile of Vector 10, and she talked to the image on the wall, describing the attributes and personality traits that made this person tick. The team gave her their full attention.

"It all points to one person who had, or still has, virtually unrestricted access to our network. If Forrest is correct, then they're using a legacy system as a back door. They could easily gain access to restricted files from any remote server, all they would need is a login that's still active". She said, her voice heavy with implication. She nodded to Peter, and he took over. Peter's analysis had led him to the conclusion that it must be an experienced agent, someone who would have high-level clearance and who knew their way around the system.

"We've drawn up a short list of five possible suspects that fit the profile; one current serving agent, two terminated agents, and two retired agents".

The list appeared on the screen. Daniel scrutinized the list.

"Why the terminated and retired agents, surely their logins wouldn't still be working?" Peter shot Daniel a guilty look.

"I don't quite know how to put this, Dan, but our investigation has identified a major flaw in system management. Our understaffed Tech Department has been too busy focusing on the Vector 10 files, to keep up to date with maintenance procedures. It appears the protocol to cancel old login credentials has not been implemented in all cases".

"Christ on a bike! Don't tell me that. So, ex-agents can still access files proportionately to their clearance levels after they've left? Vector 10 isn't the crisis around here; it's our own incompetence". Daniel's face was flushed with anger.

"Er, it gets worse, Daniel". Peter ventured.

"It's possible that if they held a grudge, they could have sold their access credentials onto a third party, namely Vector 10, to give him access".

 Daniel's eyes opened wide. He took a deep breath to control his anger. He summarized what Peter had just told him.

"Potentially, there are five logins that fit Marina's profile, which could be how he's getting into the system, but he could also be using anyone's login that he's acquired, and they may not fit the profile because Marina has not profiled the other account holders. Is that really what you are telling me?"

"Yes" said Peter with confidence.

"Right, as of now I'm ordering a full audit of all system logins and their current status, and I want to know who has accessed the two key files that Vector 10 released onto the internet. Peter, please lead on that with the tech unit". He slid a piece of paper towards him.

"I want it done by 5 pm today, and I wish to see the section head in my office to present the findings to me personally. Whoever's responsible for this has had unfettered access to the most sensitive information and the keys to the kingdom, we have held the door open, and he has left with the spoils. If this gets out, we will be a laughingstock".

Mitch nodded in agreement.

"I'll do a deep level security check on the five names, to see what that throws up. There must be a link somewhere".

"Thanks, Mitch, I think that's a sensible idea. Peter, can I also ask you to include all of us in the login audit? If he's got hold of someone else's login details, we could all be possible targets, so let's double-check". Daniel's mind was racing.

"And I want the system passwords on every major database, server and storage device changed right away. Triple encryption protocols implemented immediately. I want the tech' team to run the hacking protocols daily until further notice". Peter looked unsure.

"Daniel, that will be really difficult to do because…" Daniel interrupted him.

"Do I look as though I give a shit? We've spent the last twelve months or more half asleep on the job. We have gifted our nation's secrets to Vector 10, whoever he may be. We have been lax in closing an open door, and we still have no idea who the traitor is who's selling off the family silver. So, forgive me Peter, but I really couldn't care less who finds this inconvenient or time-consuming. It will be done, and I will have Vector 10's head on a stick, along with anyone else whose laziness or incompetence has enabled him to do what he's done. Do I make myself clear, Peter?" Peter nodded despondently.

Daniel looked at Mitch.

"I want you to add a couple of names to that list, Stewart Pearson, and Adam Hunt. I want a full security rundown on both of them. If they are of interest to Vector 10, then they should be of interest to us. I want everything from their shoe sizes to which scouting badges they got. ASAP please Mitch, schedule a call tonight to bring me up to date. Right, let's get cracking".

The meeting broke up and they each went off with their to-do lists, no one felt the need to linger.

Back in his office, Mitch decided to start with Pearson and Hunt. He'd met them briefly when he had been assigned to the PM's security detail at an EU Summit years ago. At the time Hunt was struggling to survive as PM, his own party was orchestrating a night of the long knives, and Mitch remembered thinking '*we are far more vicious and underhand with each other than the intelligence community is out in the field*'.

He had found Pearson to be a thoroughly untrustworthy, snide little creep. His sense of self-preservation was unmistakable, and Mitch suspected that nothing would be out of bounds for him to achieve his goals.

As he went through the security protocols, pulling intelligence from a dozen or more sources, it became evident that they were indeed an impressive double act, Hunt issuing the dictates and Pearson making them happen. Pearson was not only cunning but well-connected, with allies in the shadows who were willing to do his bidding, a great many of them were not exactly law-abiding citizens themselves. Hunt was the consummate politician whose only allegiance was to his goals and his agenda, and he did have a beautiful smile.

Hunt's financial history was significant and complex. For a man who had supposedly come from a council estate in North Shields, his accent and his business interests appeared far more upper class. The Hunt Foundation that he promoted everywhere was a shell corporation that had amassed vast financial resources before it had even established a purpose as an organisation. It wasn't just cash rich, either; its property portfolio was hugely impressive, with buildings in all the world's major cities and a share portfolio growing by the day. The latter was loaded with shares in oil producers, refiners and distributors, massive investment in green energies and a number of other related subsidiaries aligned with electric vehicles and Giga plants. If you wanted to see what an attempt at world domination looked like, then the Hunt Foundation would make a pretty neat model.

Mitch needed some results, and algorithms are wonderful things. By programming some clear rules or markers, they can analyse truly vast quantities of data, identifying commonalities and patterns to provide possible solutions to a problem. They don't always perform perfectly, but they crunch data a lot faster than a person could do manually. He flipped through a document for a few seconds and added known associates to the search field. Within seconds, a list appeared on-screen, weighted by the type or level of contact, it produced 12,557 results.

Scrolling back up the list he was surprised to see his own name appear at 11,903, obviously from his time on the PM's security detail, but what he wasn't expecting was to see Celia Browning at 2047 and Kitty Oliver at just 969. He ran a second, more refined search looking at these two specific links, which produced some very interesting questions. Celia's link dated back to when Hunt had been Prime Minister in the late 1990s and early 2000s, which was predictable, but what he struggled to understand is why the link to Kitty was still active in 2018, five years after she'd left the service.

Marina had taken the suspect agent list and was working her way through the names. The two retired agents on her list were now both residents at Shady Fields: Kitty Oliver and Celia Browning. If felt awkward rifling through these lives, knowing who they were. Celia's reputation was impeccable, having achieved some impressive innovations and accomplishments during her time as Director

General. When Marina transferred into MI5, Daniel had only recently taken over the DG role, but the legacy Celia had left was still evident, it certainly wasn't the misogynistic monolith that she had expected. Daniel himself was the first to admit Celia's contributions as their leader for almost a decade, had improved the culture of the organisation, even if there was still a lot of work to be done.

Kitty, though, was infamous, and although Marina had never met her, she was the stuff of legend. Tales of evading capture by biting her own tongue to make it bleed and faking tuberculosis on a mission in Sierra Leone were the one most people talked about, but the incident of planting pubic lice in the underwear drawer of a Russian Minister who had rejected her advances in a honeypot sting was probably Marina's favourite.

She called up their login access details and was alarmed to see that Celia's account was still active. Celia had retired six months ago, yet the activity log showed entries that went right up to last month. By comparison, Kitty's access was still live, but access had been spasmodic and nothing at all for the last twelve months.

Marina was perplexed, she refined her search to cross-reference the date of the document releases that Vector 10 had made, and the dates when the Tripartite and Robert Crane files had also been accessed. Sure enough, Celia's name appeared on both, but disturbingly, so did Peter Kings. Marina called Mitch over,

"I think I may have something here, Mitch".

He came straight across and looked at her screen; he did a double take.

"No" He said incredulously, "That can't be right?"

"Think about it for a second and look at the profiling". Marina was warming to the idea forming in her head.

"The suspect is highly organised, patient, and persistent. They are personable with a high IQ, businesslike, an analytical and strategic thinker, and they volunteer information to appear helpful. The only thing missing is his physical description". She waited for Mitch's response.

"Peter has legitimate access to the archives; it's what he does, so his access is easier to explain than Celia's. She retired more than a year ago". He argued.

"Why would Peter King, the gatekeeper to the nation's secrets for nearly four decades, suddenly want to leak thousands of documents to the public. I can't see it myself". He shook his head, almost as a gesture to rid himself of the image this had planted in his mind.

"What if he was disillusioned with the whole thing. He's been in the same job for years, never promoted, probably not recognised for everything he has done. He's getting older, and what does he have to show for it? You would have expected him to be a senior section leader by now, not stuck in the basement where no one knows what he does or even who he works for. The rest of the team work on the fifth floor, why isn't he with them?" Marina was becoming animated.

"Did you see the face he made when I mentioned 'States', and getting him involved, he looked like he'd been sucking a lemon. What if he was worried about being found out by someone younger, brighter and more tech-savvy than him". Mitch looked unconvinced.

"Daniel trusts him, and his instincts are so sound that I can't believe he wouldn't have known if something was off". Marina was reluctant to let it go.

"Perhaps he's too close to him. He just couldn't imagine him doing anything like this, it would be a personal betrayal. Friendships can blind you to what is going on".

Mitch considered the suggestion that one of the most trusted analysts in the service had turned rogue.

"I think if we are going to put two and two together and come up with six, we need more concrete evidence". Marina suddenly had a thought.

"What if Vector 10 is Peter, and he is using Celia's login to throw us off the scent?" Mitch shook his head.

"Sorry, Marina, but you're barking up the wrong tree. If it is Peter, he knows the system architecture so well he could get in and out without being detected".

Marina gave him a petulant look.

"But no one detected any breeches until 'States' gave us an idea where to look. Daniel asked us to pull this together and give him our findings. We have to tell him that Peter has come up as a 'person of interest'. He can decide how to proceed, but we can't make that judgement call just in case we are right". Mitch reluctantly agreed.

"You're right, but I don't look forward to having this discussion later".

35. Thames House.

Sunday 26th February 2023

They were closing in on Vector 10 and Peter King's instincts were unwavering. He had to finish what he started. Time was of the essence, and he had one chance to get this right. He needed to see it through to the end, otherwise what had it all been for?

It had been the only way he felt he could bring it all out into the open without risking his own life. He knew what had happened to others; cancelled, discredited, turned into a pariah in their own profession by their peers, and in one case, permanently silenced.

The real traitors were Hunt and Pearson, who had used their positions to create a conspiracy so fantastic that people would dismiss it out of hand until all the pieces were in place, and by then it would be too late to stop it.

Mitch decided to give Daniel the 'heads up' before the scheduled meeting.

"We couldn't believe it when his name came up in the search, but you did say leave no stone unturned, so we haven't. All I can say is that at the time of the recent leaks, Peter was accessing all those files. There is no evidence that he downloaded them, moved them to a different file location or even copied them onto a USB stick. The activity suggests that he opened them, read them, and returned them to their correct location. Marina checked Celia's login, and it seems that hers was the account that was used to gain access then leak the information to the public. There's even trails of direct correspondence traceable to the journalist Rufus Hurst".

The conversation left Daniel deeply troubled. Everything in his being told him they were wrong, but he'd been in the service too long to ignore these sorts of signs. He had to tackle this head on and speak with Peter. He needed to know if the person he trusted most in the organisation had turned rogue and risked everything to reveal some dirty secrets. If it was the case, then Daniel needed to know why.

He rode down in the lift and found himself in the familiar basement corridor once again. He didn't bother knocking this time, he just entered. Peter was sitting in his usual position, overseeing a bank of monitors, the same ghostly blue light illuminating his face. He didn't look up from the screen.

"Hi Daniel, I thought we were meeting in your office?" Daniel's voice was quiet and devoid of emotion.

"I've come down here, Peter because what I have to say needs to remain confidential". Daniel watched him carefully for any tell-tale signals. Peter caught some inference in his voice and looked at him.

"That sounds ominous".

"I am just going to say this, and I want you to do me the consideration of answering me honestly".

Had he seen a flicker of fear cross Peter's face? Daniel took in a deep breath and asked,

"Peter, I need to know if you are Vector 10".

It felt as though the air had been sucked from the room. Daniel couldn't read the expression on Peter's face. He remained silent for what seemed like an age, eyes fixed on his screen. Daniel was about to repeat the question when Peter stood and turned to face him.

"It's not what you think, Daniel". Daniel exploded!

"Jesus Christ Peter! Why?"

Daniel felt a physical sensation in his chest that was not quite pain, more like a sharp punch. He shook his head disbelievingly.

"I can't believe it. We've known each other for years. What was it? Because I know it wasn't the money". Daniel couldn't bear to look at him. He looked down. Years of trust smashed beyond repair.

"Daniel, please, let me explain". Peter had lost his composure and sounded urgent, almost pleading.

"Tell me why, Peter. Why betray your country?"

"I am not Vector 10. But, I have released some documents under the same umbrella. I'm the one who's been feeding the documents about the Tripartite Treaty into the open. I knew what they were trying to do, and I was worried that no one was challenging them because we were all looking in the other direction, so I decided to act".

Peter scanned Daniel's face, trying to read a response.

"With all due respect, Peter, that's crap! You could have come to me if you had suspicions. You've leaked highly sensitive documents in breach of the Official Secrets Act, you've put this Nation in jeopardy as a result, you've thrown your career away and risked a serious jail term based on what? A concern you had! Do you know how lame that sounds?"

"Of course I do, but I know what they are planning, Daniel, and it will be catastrophic if they pull it off. It could completely destabilize the Middle East, maybe plunge us into World War Three. The architects behind this are doing it based on some ill-conceived ideology, but their financial backers are doing it purely to take control of those financial energy markets and wipe out the competition in one fell swoop". Daniel could tell he was being deadly serious. He shook his head.

"Why didn't you come to me? We've worked together a long time; we've taken on the system before. Why do it in such a destructive and reckless way?"

Peter shuffled his feet, then looked Daniel squarely in the face.

"I didn't know if I could trust you".

Despite the gravity of the situation, Daniel laughed out loud.

"You have got to be kidding me. You don't trust me? What have I ever done to make you think that? I've always played it right down the middle with you, Peter. I've stuck my neck and my reputation on the line time after time, so exactly why did you not trust me?"

"This is so big Daniel, it must be happening with the highest level of support, not just from our government but the Americans and possibly even the Russians. I know Celia was involved in some dubious activities when this plan was first formed. And you were her appointee, even though you were not the one everyone was predicting as her successor. I wasn't sure if she had appointed you because you were complicit in the whole thing". Daniel studied Peter'face,

"And if that were true, why tell me now? If you think I might be complicit, what do you think my next move will be?" Daniel was conflicted and angry.

Peter looked at him and said,

"Honestly, Daniel, I don't know, but I've reached the end of the road. I've played the last ace in my hand, and it's not enough. I've used all the ammunition I have, and I still can't stop what's happening. I knew that you were not complicit after the car bomb, but by then I was in so deep I didn't know how to tell you what I had done. I know what's happened to others who knew too much, they are no longer with us. I knew what I was risking when I started this, but I had to try. Our whole way of life is at risk, this global control of energy markets could change every aspect of how we live. Governments will be undermined, our ability to trade with whom we choose, or be a self-directed power will be controlled by some faceless bureaucrat holding the purse strings. If nations decide not to play ball, these people will have the power to cut them off, literally. No energy, no commerce, no internet access, no freedom of speech, no liberty. I am watching us sleepwalk right into this and no one is doing a damn thing to stop it". Peters' shoulders slumped, but he continued.

"I love my country; I have given a life of service to it, and I will not stand by and watch a faceless group of megalomaniacs sell it out from under us without a fight. I'm sorry I didn't trust you Daniel, I know now that I was wrong, but honestly, carrying this millstone around my neck for the last year has left me paranoid. I knew as soon as you bought States in, he would find out how the information was being accessed, and the backdoor would be slammed and bolted. I was on borrowed time".

Daniels' brain was racing with everything that was unfolding.

"So, if you are not Vector 10, do you know who is?"

"Oh yes," said Peter. "Didn't I say? Vector 10 is Kitty Oliver".

Daniel did a double take, his jaw dropped.

"Whaaaat! How...... What... Why...?"

Peter blinked matter-of-factly.

"She was the simplest and most obvious piece of the puzzle. She was selling documents purely for the money".

Peter sensed there was a window opening where Daniel was prepared to listen. He had one chance to explain everything, and then his fate would be in Daniel's hands. He had nothing to lose.

He laid out all the documents, plans and recordings that he'd been gathering for the last year. He presented the whole plan beginning with the formation of the Tripartite Treaty, the conspiracy to destabilize Iraq and the subsequent murder of Professor Robert Crane to protect their plan. He was able to outline the real purpose of the Hunt Foundation and the web of conspiracy, fraud, and deception it represented. He explained the power and influence Hunt would have if he were appointed Diplomatic Envoy to the Middle East by the World Bank.

Daniel listened without question, his face etched with a mix of irritation and disbelief, he pored over the documents Peter presented. It was clear that the conspiracy ran far deeper than anyone had imagined, in fact, it was truly monumental in its ambition. High-ranking officials in the US security services were implicated, their names appearing in confidential reports and encrypted messages. The conspiracy had ties that stretched across the Atlantic, connecting powerful players on both sides of the ocean.

"The scope of this plot is staggering," Daniel muttered, his voice laced with grim realisation. "The Tripartite Treaty is just the tip of the iceberg. It's a global scheme, and the energy markets are at the centre of it all". Peter nodded in agreement, and continued,

"They have everyone eating out of their hand. Hunt is the darling of the media, almost like he's the next messiah. Everyone wants to be in his orbit and wants a piece of this mesmeric power he has. He is the epitome of the world we are living in, where image and brand are accepted at face value, and no one bothers to look any further. The Hunt Foundation is nothing more than a front for continued profiteering on a global scale. They've manipulated energy markets, raking in billions while the world remains oblivious. The proportion of the world's population living in poverty is increasing, even in developed countries, and still, we worship at the altar of sustainable energy without questioning the cost of it or who is behind it misrepresenting the science. They have hijacked responsible stewardship of the planet, and they are using it as a cloak to disguise their real intentions".

Daniel nodded; his jaw firm with resolve.

"This is an unprecedented conspiracy, Peter, one that involves individuals in the highest echelons of power. The fallout from this revelation could be catastrophic. You're right, we do need to stop it, and preferably still be alive at the end of it".

Peter took a deep breath; he felt the weight lift off his shoulders.

"Daniel, I am truly sorry. I should have trusted you with all of this, I was wrong. Is it too late? Is there something we can do to take them down?" Daniel looked at Peter.

"We need to balance the need for justice with the potential diplomatic fallout. That is not just a fine line, it's a dangerous one to cross. The exposure of the conspiracy could fracture international relations, incite political turmoil, and plunge the world into chaos. These disclosures could bring about the very situation we are seeking to prevent".

Daniel knew that with the evidence laid out in front of him, they held the power to expose the truth, to bring the perpetrators to justice, and to dismantle the global profiteering machine that had been created. But he also knew that they had to tread carefully, this would make them targets, and previous experience showed that those involved were not beyond rubbing out their enemies.

Instead of rushing to expose the conspiracy, Daniel opted for a strategy of quiet diplomacy. He would discreetly reach out to foreign counterparts, heads of the CIA and the Russian intelligence agency, to share their findings in confidence. The goal was to gauge the other agencies' knowledge and intentions without causing an immediate international incident.

"We have to do this right. The world must know what's been happening, but it must be done in a way that prevents a total breakdown of diplomacy. The team will have their work cut out for them. First, I need to deal with Vector 10, I think she can help to bring this to a satisfactory end, but I'm not sure how cooperative she will be. Let's get to that meeting, we have a lot of explaining to do".

In Daniel's office, the plan had been laid out and the identity of Vector 10 revealed. Daniel looked around at the stunned faces. Marina was the first to speak,

"But she's an old lady, why would she do it?" Daniel suppressed a smile,

"Firstly, sixty-one is not that old Marina, and although she may be slowing down physically, mentally she's as sharp as anyone of us. Secondly, have you ever seen Kitty's psych evaluation? She's a borderline narcissistic sociopath. She's arrogant, lacks empathy, and manipulates others for the fun of it. She has little sense of danger and is reckless in her actions, a master of deception, a born liar, and highly intelligent, plausible, and personable. She was one of our most successful agents in her day. I would guess that the lack of admiration for her work in the paid assassin world and the physical difficulties she is experiencing meant she had to look for other ways to reinforce her status. Money would do that every time for a woman like Kitty. She thrived on dangerous games, and if, as I suspect, she was blackmailing Pearson and selling secrets to Gorski, you can't get riskier than that". Marina nodded

"So, what do we do with her?"

"Well, now we know how she's doing it, we simply cut off her access. This has Kitty's fingerprints all over it. It was not born of her technical genius; it was simply opportunistic. My guess is that she stole Celia's access codes not really believing they would work and when they did, she couldn't believe her luck. There was no rhyme or reason to the data she stole, it was a mishmash of documents that were sold to the highest bidder, in this case the journalist Rufus Hurst. He would have gone through the haul, picked out the more salacious items, not fully understanding what he was looking at. The majority of the first two leaks were low level and mundane, with a few juicier morsels buried among them. It would have been like a raccoon digging through the trash. But what she did find was the information about Robert Crane's death. She had known at the time that Pearson was complicit, may even have had the suspicion that it was he who ordered it, plausible deniability, to keep Adam Hunt clean. She wouldn't have blackmailed him while she was still an agent, it would have been too risky, but as soon as she became self-employed, she could. It may have been going on for years. It's my guess that she found the surveillance reports from the Kremlin hacks in the first haul and approached Gorski. He had some tentative links with Hunt and Pearson because of the Tripartite Treaty, and she saw another opportunity to make more money.

Gorski assumed that Vector 10 was still an active agent, which is why he referred to a man when he spoke to you, Mitch". Peter interjected,

"What is to stop her warning them to get a final payday?" Daniel looked a little sheepish.

"What I haven't shared is that I had a discussion with Pearson and made him an offer he couldn't refuse". Mitch said,

"How do you know you can trust him?" Daniel was serious.

"I know I can't. It was that discussion that prompted the car bomb. They felt backed into a corner and lashed out, but in doing so, they showed their hand. Their plan only works if they can operate in the shadows. Once we shine a light on it, their anonymity will be gone, and they will scuttle for cover like a colony of woodlice".

"So, how do we tackle this then, Daniel?" Peter said.

"We have to be realistic. I want Pearson because his fingerprints can be tracked back to serious crimes, the attempted murder of Marina and me to name just one. With a bit of well applied pressure, I think we can get Gorski to roll over on him as the one who organised and paid for the bomb. Realistically, I think the likelihood of bringing Hunt to account will be much more difficult. We may have to be satisfied with taking him out of the game as a player, I have got tech working on something that might help". Mitch looked at Marina then at Daniel,

"What can we do?"

"I have a great job for you two. I want you on the next flight to Washington, DC to visit an old friend, Bruno Gomes. He's going to decide what the CIA is willing to do to tackle the American association in this fiasco". Daniel paused,

"Did I mention that the American arm of the Tripartite Treaty is former President John F. Hudson?"

36. CIA HQ, Washington DC

Friday 28th February

Mitch and Marina's journey to Washington, D.C. was a long flight filled with tension about the task they faced once they had landed.

. They were aware of the heavy burden that had been placed on them. They had a plan, but it would require a significant amount of bravado, some skilled diplomacy and some technical sleight of hand. They were, carrying some questionable evidence of the vast international conspiracy that implicated a former President of the USA and a couple of high-ranking supporters within the US Treasury. The implications of the revelations they were about to make were staggering, and the delicate negotiation that lay ahead would test the strength of the UK-US alliance. They would both need their best poker faces to pull this off because there was a huge amount at stake.

Inside the secure, soundproofed and surveillance protected room of a bland government building, Mitch sat across from his US counterpart, Director Bruno Gomes. Their paths had crossed last year when Phil Santos had been revealed as a renegade senior agent involved in the assassination of a foreign president simply to gain better funding for the security services. To say this meeting was awkward was an understatement.

The grey metal walls and tubular steel chairs were utilitarian and designed to make people feel uncomfortable. They were arranged around a table that had an obvious anchor point for the cuffs and shackles favoured by American law enforcement. Bruno offered them coffee, it was black, strong, and served in corrugated paper cups. The atmosphere was intense and there was an 'elephant in the room' that they were doing their best to ignore. Bruno was keen to establish superiority. His accent contained a trace of a sneer,

"Can you tell me what is so important that you request an interview with me in a secure facility without disclosing why? Is it just the British tendency to overreact, or do you just love the cloak and dagger stuff?" He laughed, but it was humourless.

Marina looked on, her role was to observe and detect whether the Americans had an appetite to handle the disclosures they were about to make.

Mitch was not an easy man to intimidate, and Bruno had failed massively.

"Honestly, Bruno, I thought you had cleaned house. I didn't expect to be here again with another loose cannon problem so soon".

Bruno could not conceal his embarrassment. Mitch continued with more than a touch of glee in his voice.

"Well at least this time it's a politician not a serving agent. That should make you feel a bit better". The joke fell short.

Mitch placed a folder containing the collected evidence on the table, but Bruno studied his face carefully, as if the answer was written there.

"What's this all about?" Mitch slid the folder towards him.

"We have uncovered a scheme of unrivalled fraud and corruption that has sought to manipulate the worlds' energy markets, and one of the key architects is a former US President". Mitch waited for the weight of the statement to land and be absorbed. Bruno screwed up his face in disbelief.

"That's outrageous, what evidence do you have?" he said, with a combination of unease and curiosity.

With a deep breath, Mitch continued,

"Director Gomes, we've come here today with information that is so sensitive and damning that it warrants this level of secrecy and then some. It concerns a very real threat to global stability. Our two nations have been implicated in a conspiracy that threatens our collective security and economic standing in the world".

Gomes leaned forward, his brows furrowing.

"You can't be serious. The US would have no involvement in such a conspiracy".

Mitch tapped the folder, encouraging Bruno to examine the evidence.

"What is contained in here proves otherwise. We need to act swiftly, and in a manner that limits the damage to the fallout from this". He looked directly at Bruno, who had acquired an anxious look.

"Please, Bruno, just read the file".

The tension in the room grew as he scanned the documents, his face reacting dramatically to each revelation. The weight of the truth began to descend, and the implications were impossible to deny. Mitch threw Marina a look of disbelief and said under his breath. "I hope he's given up poker".

After a long silence, Gomes finally looked up and met Mitch's gaze.

"This... this is deeply troubling, Mitch. Is there anything else, or is this it?" He tapped the folder.

"Yes, there's some video footage and a transcript of a meeting that took place in Geneva in early January detailing the scheme and their next steps. We can give you sight of that, but we were not prepared to transmit that digitally for obvious reasons. Its voracity would be easy enough to confirm with flight details of Former President Hudson". Bruno swallowed hard.

"I can assure you that this was done without the knowledge or authorization of the present US Government. I am sure these individuals, acted on their own". Mitch's voice was measured, but resolute.

"Whilst I appreciate that assurance, you will understand why I expect you to conduct a proper investigation to confirm that. We need to root out ALL the individuals responsible, bring them to justice, and ensure that such actions never occur again. The alliance between our nations depends on it".

"Will you be doing that with your ex-Prime Minister and pin up boy Adam Hunt?" Bruno asked pointedly.

"We wouldn't be here sharing this with you now unless measures were being taken as we speak to tie up matters at our end". Mitch relaxed.

"You know what's at stake here, Bruno. This is not the time for one-upmanship. If we fail to put a stop to this, can you imagine the fall-out in the Middle East? There's always been an uneasy peace in the region, but if representatives of the west were found to be guilty of price fixing and market manipulation to this extent, there could be war. It's in all our interests to do this as quietly as possible. The repercussions for some of the oldest banking institutions in the world would be significant if their involvement in financing this were to come out. There's enough will to do this with a low-key approach, but we have to smash the organisation and its infrastructure to ensure it cannot be revived". Bruno nodded slowly,

"Yes, I see that".

The negotiation that followed was delicate and loaded with complexities, with both sides working to preserve their partnership while holding those involved accountable. Trust had been strained, but both Mitch and Bruno understood the necessity of this alliance, particularly in a world filled with climate fears and net-zero targets. The revelation of the conspiracy had shaken the foundations of their special relationship, but it had also brought about a renewed sense of purpose.

The meeting continued for another three hours until, finally, they had an agreement to collaborate on a thorough investigation and to share intelligence with the goal of dismantling the conspiracy. The negotiations were fierce, but they both had the same objective, namely that the alliance between the UK and the US remained intact. They knew if they were to be successful, they had to be honest with each other and face whatever the investigation uncovered with a united front. Bruno had the unenviable task of informing the current President of the threat to energy stability, knowing that a former President was clearly implicated.

As Mitch and Marina left the government building, they carried with them an undertaking to do what was necessary to break the organisation that The Hunt Foundation was building and to take down the three key figures fronting it.

The world had changed, and the delicate balance between justice and diplomacy had been tested. The fight to expose the truth and protect the global order needed to continue, and the strength of the alliance would be put to the ultimate test in the days to come.

Mitch looked exhausted as they travelled back to their hotel. Their flight to the UK was early tomorrow morning, and it couldn't come too soon.

"Do you think you can trust him, Mitch?" Marina asked with genuine concern.

"If I'm honest, Marina, I don't know, but I'm sure that Bruno is as committed to seeing this through to the end as we are".

"How can you tell?" she asked.

"It's the first time I have seen him put outcome above his ego".

37. Shady Fields

Friday 28th February 2020

Whilst Mitch was tackling their transatlantic counterpart, Daniel was orchestrating a more public take down of the British contingent of this nefarious scheme. He was about to unleash a very public revelation of the global conspiracy masterminded by Hunt and his allies that would send shockwaves through the international community and the energy markets.

Daniel had instructed Peter, Hilary and now Professor Evelyn Anderton to conduct a forensic analysis of the financial transactions, shell corporations and money trails, to build an accurate picture of funding and beneficiaries. Peter had already mapped the encrypted communication channels they were exploiting and although some of the content was beyond reach, the connections between the players were evident. They revealed direct links between the ex-US president, the ex-British Prime Minister, and the Russian double-agent Gorski. They were building an irrefutable case. Professor Anderton's job was to track the sequence of events that had created the control of energy supply markets. That evidence would provide powerful motivation for America and Russia to cooperate.

Daniel had decamped to Shady Fields for this stage of the operation. Thames House was too visible, too accessible to parliament, and he didn't want word to spread before he was ready to launch his Coup de grâce.

He needed to tackle Kitty and put that part of the plan into operation, but he knew that would not be straightforward. She was a devious and master manipulator. He needed her to think the plan was her idea. If he presented this as a done deal, she would automatically rail against it, he needed to box clever. The Kitty Oliver offensive was born.

Daniel knocked on her door and waited. He knew she was there; her habit was to eat a three-course evening meal washed down with a half-bottle of wine at least, then retire to her apartment to watch TV. He had given her just fifteen minutes to settle down before calling on her. That way she would be relaxed but not ready to retire and turn him away. Of course, the bottle of her favourite Laphroaig whiskey he carried with him might also help.

The door opened and she stood blinking at him.

"What do you want, it's late?" Her tone was flat and disinterested. He looked at his watch, displaying the bottle he was holding.

"Really? I hadn't realised it was that late, I've just been finishing some work, and I thought I'd see if you fancied a tipple. No problem, I can make it another time". He turned to leave.

"No, no, of course you can come in, Daniel. I'll get a couple of glasses". She walked over to the console that held an empty decanter and a couple of crystal tumblers. She blew the dust away and placed them on the coffee table that stood in front of the fireplace. Two recliner armchairs were positioned to give a view of the TV in the corner. She moved stiffly towards her chair and sat down gingerly, using the remote control to mute the TV sound, but didn't switch it off. Daniel poured her a triple measure and placed it in front of her, and poured himself less than a single. He was not a fan of the peaty, iodine flavour of Laphroaig. He found it bordering on unpleasant, and had always believed that fans of that particular spirit were quite perverse. He felt it suited Kitty down to the ground. He took the other chair and raised his glass in a toast, "Cheers".

She took a gulp from the glass and felt the warming effect of the spirit work its way down her throat.

"What's this all for then, Daniel? Have you thought any more about our conversion?"

"I have Kitty, but things have moved on a pace in the last couple of days. We know that it was Pearson who floated the idea of Robert Crane's elimination, possibly sanctioned by Adam Hunt. We think you know this because we know that he has made payments to you to stop that information becoming more widely known". Daniel watched the woman carefully to see if he could read anything in her expression. She remained emotionless and said,

"Presumably that's what the bomb was for. Whatever's going on, Daniel, you're getting too close for comfort? They clearly want you out of the way. Personally, I would have been more subtle, but these people have little finesse and even less class". Daniel agreed with that point at least. He wanted her to see the big picture.

"What they didn't disclose was that it was part of a bigger plan. They pressured Celia to act, and she used you as the instrument who wouldn't question an order. They needed Crane out of the way to get their plan off the ground, and you both obliged". He could almost see her processing what he was saying.

"It was an insurance policy because they needed parliament to agree to the Iraqi invasion, and they did it by generating a climate of fear that had people believing an attack on the UK was imminent. Crane couldn't find the weapons because he played a straight game. They were lying to him, running rings around his team. They said those weapons were there and that he just couldn't find them. With him out of the way, the government decision would go through on a nod". He could see her disbelief grow as she spoke.

Daniel looked at her seriously. She frowned,

"But if that was true, why didn't they find anything after they invaded?"

The truth began to dawn on her, and she realised they had manipulated her. That was her role, and they had played her, getting her to do the dirty work so that they could reap the rewards. Daniel needed to pile on the pressure.

"The scheme was always to manipulate the energy markets and make billions, and that's what they've been doing. Once the war was over, the Americans carved up the private contracts for rebuilding Iraq's infrastructure. Our Prime Minister and a few well-selected friends and family invested heavily in those companies, making millions in share dividends. That was just the beginning. Every conflict and uneasy peace in the Middle East since, has been exploited to build massive share portfolios of oil suppliers, renewable energy technologies and battery making plants. We are a hairs' breadth away from global energy price control, and it is being fronted by Adam Hunts' Foundation and his cronies. That's why Pearson has been so generous over the years, he is not protecting them from what happened twenty years ago, he is protecting what is happening right under our noses. In fact, he's probably having a good laugh at your expense thinking how cheap it was, knowing what's really at stake".

He reached across the low table and filled up her glass, which she had emptied. Kitty picked up the glass and took another gulp, a slight tremor visible in her hand.

"Did Celia know what was going on?" Daniel was clear.

"No, Kitty, she knew nothing about the real reason. She was Head of the Operations Desk at the time. Government Ministers would have pressured her into acting, but they wouldn't have shared any of this. It only worked because they sold everyone the perfect lie. Once she was appointed Director General, she conducted her own enquiry into the matter and found out the truth. She's in no position to act now, so she placed it in my hands, but I'm not sure if I can do anything; too much time has passed, and they seem to have powerful connections. I think we may just have to accept our fate". The small woman almost exploded!

"Jesus Christ, Daniel, when are you going to grow a pair? We are not going to let them get away with this. They need to be held to account for what they have done".

"But we can't do that without implicating you. Unless……"

"What, unless what?"

"Well, it occurs to me that the only reason they've got away with this for so long is their anonymity. They operate in the shadows and can do what they do because no one can see them. If we could find a way to expose them very publicly, make sure they were well and truly in the spotlight, then their game would be up. People would see them and their deception, and their power would be neutralised". Kitty was warming to the idea.

"So, if we 'out' them publicly, it all comes crashing down around their ears?"

"Yes, but it doesn't come without risks Kitty, you know first-hand how ruthless these people are. You are not an active agent any more; those days are behind you. No, it's too dangerous to get you involved".

"Daniel, I'm still my own woman and make my own decisions. I am perfectly capable of taking care of myself. We need to take these people out before they cause any more damage, and I think I know exactly how to do that".

"Does it have anything to do with your role as Vector 10?" He expected her to be angry or deny it. To his surprised, she just laughed.

"Well, it took you bloody long enough. I thought you would be on to me right after the first leak. I couldn't believe my luck when the login still worked. I assume you know how I was doing it?"

"Yes, we found the programme that deletes duplicate files, and the tell-tale signs of a USB download. It was a very clever plan, Kitty, hidden in plain sight".

She preened like a cat filled with cream.

"It was clever wasn't it, and it earned me a pretty penny too, but that will end now. You know that it was Rufus Hurst that was publishing them, and I feel quite sure he will protect his source. His popularity was on the wane until I gave him a new lease of life with those documents. Well, perhaps we should give him the story to end all stories. Why don't we serve Hunt and Pearson up on a platter? I'm sure if you look, there will be other stuff that you have secreted away somewhere. We could put it all out at once, that way they won't be able to deny it because they will be being attacked from all directions".

"Kitty, the problem we have are media editors, they are so worried about litigation, they would struggle to get it approved by their legal departments, people would talk, and they would use the time to regroup and disappear, and they would just set up shop somewhere else and carry on". Kitty pondered this for a few seconds.

"What if we do it through Hursts' social media accounts, his Twitter account alone has a million followers. That is immediate and has the distinct advantage of being the home for every keyboard warrior here and abroad. Their faces would be everywhere, their reputations would be in tatters, they would be cancelled by huge sections of society. No one wants to be associated with losers or perverts. If anonymity is what they need, then we will take that away from them".

"Won't that be hard or take too much time?"

"Daniel, where have you been hiding for the last decade? It doesn't have to be true to be believed. It just has to offend enough people with large numbers of followers to work. Hurst is a case in point. You would struggle to find anyone who likes the man, but millions hang on his every word because he has a reputation for breaking sensational stories. We take them down using his reputation, not theirs".

"Kitty, you are a genius! If we do it that way, then it allows the dirty linen to be washed in public, while protecting the institutions to do their own house cleaning in relative privacy. It's perfect, a mixture of suspicion, misinformation, and prejudice will be their downfall. Meet me in Hilary's office tomorrow morning at 8 a.m. and we can make a start".

Days later, the world watched in disbelief as the truth unfurled, and the implications of the conspiracy began to ripple across the globe.

Back in London, Daniel and his team worked tirelessly to mitigate the damage, coordinating with intelligence agencies and governments to ensure that the conspiracy's reach was contained. Emergency meetings were held, and classified information shared to unravel the web of deceit that had threatened to destabilize the global economy and energy markets.

Yet, despite their efforts, the energy markets still fluctuated wildly in response to the news. Investors and traders around the world reacted with uncertainty, fearing the consequences of the audacious plot. Prices soared and plummeted, leading to economic uncertainty and chaos that impacted nations and industries alike. It would be six long weeks before things settled to pre-leak levels.

38. Safe House Enfield

Friday 28th February 2020

As the news of Gorski's reincarnation and his subsequent hunt for asylum unfolded, it became clear that powerful international players were vying for control of the situation. Diplomatic negotiations and covert operations blurred the lines between allies and adversaries, creating a complex landscape. Offers of asylum were made in a bid to entice one of the architects into the fold.

Gorski took the bait. He was on the run, but not from the British. He did not want to be captured by the Russian forces that were closing in on him. The realisation that he had been engaged in sabotaging their main export made him public enemy number one.

Fearing retribution, he made a desperate bid for safety by seeking asylum in a foreign country, ironically, he chose the UK. He contacted the British embassy in Marseilles to arrange a secret rendezvous; he said he wanted to come in from the cold. Little did he know that the entire operation was a meticulously crafted trap. Agents were ready to pounce the moment he showed his face.

The meeting took place in a remote location on a deserted road on the outskirts of Le Rove, far from prying eyes. As Gorski's vehicle approached the rendezvous point, Marina's extraction team, coordinated by Mitch's meticulous planning, moved into position.

By the time he realised what was happening, it was too late. He attempted to flee, and a short but intense car chase unfolded. Gorski was outnumbered, even so, his men put up a fierce but short-lived fight before they realised that they were outgunned and surrendered. Gorski's vehicle was surrounded, and he was captured by a team of well-trained British agents operating illegally on French soil.

The UK government were extremely aware of how the unfolding events would play with the rest of the world, and they were keen to do whatever it took to distance themselves from the once charismatic ex-Prime Minister who, unsurprisingly, turned out to be a serious megalomanic. They had already begun to offer the hand of conciliation to the main oil producers. Daniel had been instructed to do whatever he could to secure Gorski, and as usual, he was two steps ahead.

Daniel and Hilary were engaged on a different mission. They used diplomatic back channels to try to locate and engage in confidential discussions with Adam Hunt, intending to find out what he wanted. Not surprisingly, he had gone to ground, possibly in Switzerland, but no one could be completely sure where he was.

The Americans had been true to their word, and they had already convened a closed Grand Jury hearing and subpoenaed former President Hudson. They were keen to deal swiftly with this embarrassing incident and reassure the Senate that the current administration had no part in the conspiracy.

Gorski was being held in a secure location in Enfield, in one of the Secret Service's interrogation suites that were dotted across London, faceless on the outside and heartless on the inside. Daniel had asked Mitch to conduct the debrief.

In the featureless room with hard chairs and instant coffee, they began the process of understanding the extent of the Russian's involvement in the conspiracy. Gorski's mask of stoicism cracked, and he sneered.

"You know you are too late, what has been put in motion cannot be stopped. It will succeed even if none of us are around. It is unstoppable". In a moment of unguarded bravado, Gorski confessed,

"Power, money, influence. It was all there for the taking. I believed that we could reshape the world; every country bought into line for the greater good. You can only do that if you have a hold of the biggest bargaining chip. In the world as it stands, that must be energy".

"Where did it all start, Gorski?" Mitch was intrigued as he was under the distinct impression that it was Hudson and Hunt who were the main protagonists.

"Hudson had the idea from his predecessor, who had tried something like it before, but he lacked ambition. Hudson knew the scale of what was possible, but he didn't have the brain to work out the detail. He used the Special Relationship with the British to get his own way and invade Iraq because he knew that the Senate would never sanction the US going in alone. At least some of them had learned lessons from Vietnam". He took a sip of his coffee and grimaced,

"Tastes like old sock soaked in paraffin". He pushed his cup away.

"Once they had invaded, the train of events was set in motion. Do you know how hypocritical the west is? We go into countries that are Russian, have belonged in the Russian family for hundreds of years, and you call us warmongers, you say we are the aggressors. Yet, the West invades a sovereign power in the Middle East, and we are supposed to applaud and hail the liberators. It's a pile of crap!" Mitch was unconvinced.

"Do you really expect us to believe this whole thing was your idea? If they were serious about it being three superpowers leading this, why didn't they approach the Chinese? Russia was on the wane as a world power by then".

Mitch sniffed his coffee but pushed it away too without tasting it. Gorski rose to the bait.

"Our natural resources were attractive. Our leader had other priorities at the time, so I decided to enter into the Tripartite agreement to ensure we didn't miss out. I came along at exactly the right time. I had the vision and the ambition to see it through, and I could see into the future. I knew they had stumbled onto a plan that could offer power on a global scale into the hands of a single power broker. Hunt wanted it to be his Foundation, I wanted it to be Russia. I spoke with our leader, but he couldn't see it. He was too busy focusing on taking us back into a Soviet Union that involved unifying all the independent states, but the world had moved on. They valued their independence and were willing to fight for it. We had been through darks days with a drunk and a buffoon as leaders. Russia had lost her status in the world; we were no longer feared as we once were. In his bid to restore Russia, our leader was diminishing her further".

"What role did Pearson play in all of this?" Gorski gave a deep, guttural laugh.

"He was nothing, a puppet, a goffer. Hunt wanted someone to do the fetching and carrying to make him feel important. He was a snide little shit who took care of problems that Hunt had no stomach for, but this is a dangerous thing to do. The more people you involve in the chain, the more weak links there are. I told him to ditch the puppet, that he would bring us all down, but Hunt kept him around".

Mitch was intrigued to discover how much he knew about Vector 10, so to keep Gorski on his toes, he changed the line of questioning.

"Gorski, tell us how you came to work with Vector 10". Gorski smiled, stretched his hands behind his head and leant back in the chair.

"I saw the leaks from our internet alert system. I still have old KGB comrades who moved to the FSB. We were impressed with the information, and it confirmed what we already knew, that the Americans and British were surveilling other countries illegally and against diplomatic agreements. Until then, they had always denied it, yet there was the proof from their own files. We knew it had to be an insider because we have hackers working day and night to crack your systems. Occasionally, we got in, but they found us straight away, and we were kicked out. We smile when you accuse us and expect us to admit it. Do you not know that espionage is based on lies and deceit? We think you are very naive to believe others observe your British rules of chivalry. We don't". Mitch couldn't resist delivering the final blow.

"You may be interested to know who Vector 10 is". He pushed a photograph of Kitty Oliver across the table into Gorski's view. It was not a flattering image, she looked every one of her 61 years, a bent old lady with greying hair and that distinct birthmark.

"What is this?" He threw it back across the table. "This is not Vector 10!" Mitch didn't try to suppress his smirk.

"Oh, but it is Gorski. She's an old agent who stumbled across a backdoor that has since been slammed shut. She accessed what she could and sold it to the highest bidder. If you paid her money because you thought you had found the pinnacle of British traitors, then I'm sorry to disappoint you. This old lady has taken your money under false pretences. Some of what she leaked was unfortunate, but nothing that would cause lasting damage or even put active agents at risk. It seems you bought the equivalent of a second-hand car with no engine and flat tyres".

He saw rage flash in Gorski's eyes and continued,

"But if it's any consolation, you were right. Pearson was the weak link. If it hadn't been for a mistake he made decades ago, we wouldn't have been looking at her, and we would have missed her link to you and the Tripartite Treaty". Mitch picked up the folder and made to leave the room. He turned back to face Gorski,

"Oh, by the way, your leader has been missing you. A lot, judging by the amount of correspondence he's been sending us. He hasn't been that amiable in years. It's my guess that our government will re-examine our extradition arrangements, as we want to do what we can in the new spirit of détente, and we feel it's the least we can do in repayment for the attempt on Daniel Grant's life, which had your fingerprints all over it. We could prosecute you in our courts, but our current PM feels we would earn more brownie points by handing you back" Gorski was furious. He stood and slammed both fists down on the table. It was only the two pistols trained on him by the guards flanking the door that stopped him lunging at Mitch.

"You cannot do this" He spat.

"I have asked for asylum. You have to honour it. It is the British way". Mitch looked at him, his gaze, ice-cold.

"You asked Gorski, but we didn't grant it. That's why we used rendition. You were effectively abducted from foreign soil. No asylum. Call it the final thank you from us. You almost killed the Head of our Secret Services, a high-ranking agent, and two distinguished explosive specialists with your device, we will not let that go by without payback. The British are a tolerant bunch, we don't hold grudges, but we do remember facts".

He left the room, leaving a fearful Gorski behind. He walked a little way down the corridor and into the adjacent room with a two-way mirror where Marina had been observing the whole interview.

"That part about Pearson and Kitty leading us to them was not quite true, was it?" she smiled.

"Not strictly, but he doesn't know that, does he?"

39. The Aftermath.

Wednesday 15th April 2020

The fall out of the conspiracy sent shockwaves through the international community, leaving a trail of resignations and investigations in its wake. Daniel had been surprised at the effectiveness of Kitty's solution. The social media character assassination had been absolute. The number of people coming out of the woodwork, distancing themselves from Hunt and the foundation, was truly staggering.

An arrest warrant was issued for Adam Hunt, as well as other high-ranking officials in both the UK and the US, who had been implicated. Their names had been exposed in the damning evidence that had been gathered by Peter King and Hilary. Evelyn Anderton had proved herself particularly gifted in the forensic analysis of obscure paper trails.

Daniel held little hope of bringing Adam Hunt to justice. He had sought refuge in his Foundation Headquarters in Geneva. Britain has no formal extradition agreement with the Swiss, who defer to the Federal Act on International Mutual Assistance in Criminal Matters. However, that agreement does allow for extradition in exceptional circumstances, and in light of the magnitude of what Hunt had attempted and how it would have undermined the global banking system, the Swiss agreed to offer him up without a fight. It seems they take a dim view of what they interpret as 'embezzlement' on a grand scale. It just confirmed a truth that Daniel had always known. The establishment rallies against theft, it frowns on murder and the taking of human life, but it absolutely refused to tolerate anyone usurping the global power of money and investments.

The case being built by the Crown Prosecution Service was not murder or even attempted murder, but the unforgivable sin of insider trading on a monumental scale.

Daniel was back at shady Fields, once again knocking on Kitty's door. She answered it and invited him in.

"I was wondering when I would see you again. Have you come to whisk me off to some tropical island as thanks from a grateful nation?" Daniel shook his head.

"Not exactly Kitty". She slumped into her chair.

"They've shafted me, haven't they?" Her tone was resigned. Daniel nodded,

"I did say to you that the world you knew was gone and that I would probably not be able to negotiate the deal that you had in mind". She looked at him in a petulant manner.

"You said yourself you wouldn't have discovered what they were up to without me. I deserve to get something out of this". Daniel lowered himself into the opposite chair.

"Kitty, you killed a man, faked a suicide, and showed no remorse. You traded secrets with a Russian and extorted a former PM's aide for personal gain. Does the phrase 'two wrongs don't make a right' mean nothing to you? There must be some accountability. Crane's daughter always questioned the manner of his death, and it's highly likely, based on everything that has happened, that she will get her wish and they will finally hold an inquest. It will all come out".

"Then I may as well just give up. I'm too old and too tired to spend my remaining years incarcerated. I've had a good inning, but this is not what I want. I know you've done what you can, Daniel, and I thank you for trying. The likelihood is they won't let it get to court because they will not want me to tell what I know.

I am a dead man walking". Daniel knew where this was going.

"That's not the case, Kitty. I'm in charge, and I will ensure a proper trial with good representation for you. I will even mitigate for you to spend time in an open prison, you are hardly a flight risk. I would say you probably have twenty-four hours before the arrest warrant is served. Is there anything I can do in the meanwhile?"

"No, thanks, Daniel, I think you've probably done all you can. I just wish I could see my old home once more. You know, I grew up in Wales. We lived in a small village called Talysarn, it was wonderfully carefree. Strange that I ended up doing what I did". There was a wistful quality to her voice.

"Thanks for the heads-up, it allows me a little time to get my affairs in order".

As he left Kitty alone, he could not shake a strange feeling that was disturbing him. He would mention their conversation to Hilary, it may be an idea to keep an eye on her for the next few days, it would be a difficult time.

The following morning at Shady Fields, the dining room was filling up as normal with people going about their daily activities. Hilary had arrived back from London late last night and was taking the opportunity to have a leisurely start to the day. It was 10.30 am before she went down to the dining room to catch up with Layla Strong.

"Morning Layla, is everything OK?" Layla looked troubled.

"Not really, we can't find Kitty Oliver. No one has seen her since 8 pm last night. Daniel went to have a chat with her, and he left her in her room".

"Let's go and check her room". Hilary led the way up to Kitty's door and knocked firmly.

"Kitty. Are you OK? Can you let us in?" There was silence. Hilary gestured for Layla to use her pass key to open the door. As the door opened, she called out,

"Kitty, it's Hilary and Layla. We are coming in to check that you are okay". Still silence. They entered the room and looked around. Clothes were strewn around, her handbag was on the chair, a half-drunk cup of tea was on the bedside table. Hilary felt it, it was stone-cold. The light was still on, but there was no sign of Kitty. They checked the bathroom but still nothing.

"She must be somewhere in the house. Her coat is here, so it's unlikely she's out in the grounds, it's pretty chilly this morning".

"I'll check, you never know. Get the staff to check all the rooms just in case".

Hilary walked out of the main doors and around the side of the building to the car park. It took her a good twenty seconds before she realised that something was not right. Her car wasn't where she parked it last night, it was gone. She rushed back inside and up to her office; the keys should have been on her desk. She remembered throwing them there before she went to her room. Layla said,

"I can't understand it, her wallet and phone are still in her room. It's a bit of a stretch to assume that she has taken the car". But Hilary didn't really believe that.

She rang Daniel, who had gone back to Thames House, to tell him what they'd found.

"I have reported it as stolen. Layla looked at the CCTV footage, Kitty took it at about 3 am this morning. You can clearly see her leaving through the front entrance in ordinary clothes with a raincoat and slippers. I'm really worried about her, Daniel".

"The police will trace your car, and we'll soon know where she's gone. She knows time is running out, the arrest warrant has been issued. It could be her last-ditch effort to escape justice".

It was 3 pm that afternoon when the police called to say that the car had been found at the Dorothea Quarry near Talysarn in north Wales. It is the deepest water filled quarry in the UK and has claimed the lives of dozens of swimmers and divers.

There was no sign of Kitty, but there was a note found on the passenger seat suggesting that she could not face her imminent arrest and had decided to end her life.

Hilary was sitting in her office, feeling a mixture of sadness and shock at the news. The phone rang again, it was Daniel. She told him what the police had reported to her.

"I should have realised when she left without her phone or bag that something was wrong. I don't understand why she went to Wales".

"I can help with that. Apparently, it was where she grew up when she was a child. She told me that yesterday when we chatted". Daniel sounded unconvinced.

"I checked, and it's not what her file says, according to her records she grew up in Richmond. What did the note say?"

Hilary consulted the notes she had made from the call with the DI. It said,

"I am not going to fight any more. Time to say sorry and face the consequences. Kitty"

"Well, that confirms what I thought".

"Did you get a sense that she was considering taking her own life when you spoke to her?" Daniel's laugh shocked Hilary.

"No, but I know exactly how Kitty might fake her own death to escape, and it looks remarkably like this".

Daniel was telling the truth when he said the world had changed, but people like Kitty don't.

Now he faced another dilemma. They had exposed the conspiracy, brought the perpetrators to justice, and revealed the hidden undercurrents of power that shaped the geopolitical landscape. But there was one incongruent loose end, Vector 10. As far as everyone was concerned, the greatest hacker of the 21st century was a shadowy legend, but he knew she was really a 61-year-old woman with Secret Service experience and basic IT skills. When he thought about it like that, even Daniel had difficulty believing it.

They may well have underestimated the cunning and resourcefulness of their adversary. He had no doubt that Kitty would have stockpiled money and created an alternative identity. Her disappearance and suspected suicide had all the hallmarks of the Kitty Oliver that he had come to know.

As Daniel sat alone in his office, a smile crept onto his lips. It is funny that often, the best place to hide the darkest secrets is in plain sight.

40. Central London

Tuesday 12th May 2020

The pale oak panelled courtroom was filled with people. The royal blue carpet softened the acoustics, turning conversations to murmurs until the clerk announced.

"All rise for Her Majesty's Coroner, Lord Justice Simeon Bellingham.

A tall, distinguished man breezed into the court and sat in the largest chair on the dais. He looked around the court at the assembled faces, only too aware of what was at stake. He began.

"I call to order this public inquest into the death of Professor Robert Crane on Thursday 12th September 2002. The purpose of this inquest is to confirm the medical cause of death, and to answer three questions: one when did Professor Crane die? Two, where did he die? And, third and perhaps most importantly of all, how did he come by his death?

I will hear all the evidence including relevant witnesses and conclude with a verdict. I have issued the order of witnesses that are required to give their evidence. Each will be sworn in by the clerk of the court. Due to the sensitive nature of this inquest, there will be no press allowed in the courtroom during the proceedings, and everyone present needs to understand that if they speak about anything that happens in this court before my final public statement, they will be held in contempt and may receive a custodial sentence. I call the first witness, Ms. Sharon Louca".

The inquest ran smoothly, with Sharon the first to provide evidence. It seemed odd to her that the coroner wouldn't hear the evidence concerning the discovery of her fathers' body, but Hilary assured her they tended to hear family members' evidence first in cases like this.

Giving evidence and having the chance to explain her father's frame of mind, the sort of man he was and her concerns about the whole affair felt strangely cathartic. For the first time since it happened, she felt like someone was taking her seriously, not just dismissing her out of hand.

Her brother Colin was next on the stand, and the questioning for him dealt specifically with his help with the search and subsequent discovery of his father's body.

Justice Barrington was very specific.

"Can you please describe how you came across the body of your father?"

Colin took a deep breath and described the radio message saying they had found something.

"I realised where they must be from the description they gave, and we made our way back up the track. We met a couple of walkers coming out of the woods who said they had discovered a body. They seemed really shaken up; the dog handler on the scene asked them to go down to the house and give a statement. He was going to wait for help to arrive. As we walked along the path, I saw two more officers, one had a dog on a lead and the other was trying to calm Nero down; he was going mad, barking at him. As I got closer, I could see that he was guarding Dad. Nero saw me and rushed over; he was very distressed. I noticed he had his collar on, but there was no lead. I looked at where Nero had been and saw Dad. He was sprawled out, flat on his back. When I got to him, I could see his eyes were open. I knew he was dead. His shirt was splattered with blood and his wrists had horizontal wounds on them".

The coroner was making notes as he listened.

"And you are sure he was lying on his back?" Colin was certain and nodded.

"Yes, sir, he was".

"Can you recall how the deceased was dressed?"

"He was wearing a shirt and light trousers, but no jacket. I thought that was odd. Even in summer months, he didn't walk out without a jacket or cardigan because there would be nowhere for Nero's dog treats or bags to clean up his mess. He always wore a jacket".

"Thank you, that will be all".

Jon Dowie-Brown had been called as a friend and a colleague. His evidence detailed the extraordinary pressure that his friend had been subjected to, to alter the report he was working on. Justice Barrington had been quite pointed when he asked,

"Did that pressure affect his mood, his state of mind?" Dowie-Brown smiled,

"Oh yes sir, it made him mad as hell, and he was even more determined to see it through to the end".

"Thank you, you may return to your seat".

The next few witnesses were from the day of the discovery. Inspector Beech, who was now retired and in his early seventies, held himself with a military bearing. Justice Barrington asked him to confirm that he oversaw the Special Branch operation, which he did. He then went on to question him about the inconsistencies of the Special Branch reports, but the only response he got was that due to the passage of time, Beech could not recall the finer details other than what had been recorded at the time.

He then called Wayne Priestley from the Special Branch Dog unit to clarify his involvement on the day. He gave an account of finding the body, but in his version, Robert Crane had been propped up against a tree at the side of the track. Justice Barrington asked him to take his time and consider the scene.

"Are you sure Professor Crane's body was propped against the tree".

"Yes sir".

"How can you explain that the person with you at the time describes his father lying on his back"?

"Maybe he was in shock and misremembered?"

"Did you see a jacket at the scene or find one nearby?"

"No, sir, but I didn't search the area. We returned to the house so that the scene of crime team could gather evidence".

"Did you remember the couple who you met on the track going up towards the scene?"

"Yes sir, I remember there was a couple, but I don't remember much about them. By the time we returned to the house, they had left. I returned to headquarters with the dogs, they were tired out".

"One last question, Mr. Priestly. Do you remember seeing a mobile phone on the ground by the body?"

"No, sir, I do not".

"In the pictures taken at the scene, the phone is clearly visible, less than 18 inches from the body, the body that is propped up against the tree".

"No sir, I didn't see it".

"Perhaps you were in shock or are misremembering Mr. Priestly. Thank you, that will be all. I would like to recall Retired Chief Inspector Beech, please".

The old man arose, looking unsure, but made his way to the witness stand.

"I will remind you that you are still under oath, Mr. Beech". The old man nodded but looked nervous.

"I would just like to draw your attention to the times on the reports that were submitted. You will notice that the first police report from the initial phone call was recorded at 4.30 pm on Thursday 12th September 2002, and the first visit from officers was at 9 pm that same evening, is that correct?"

"Yes". He really wasn't sure where this was going.

"A brief search was made of the house and grounds but due to the failing light it was decided to postpone the search until the following day, is that correct?"

"Yes". He looked puzzled.

"And you conducted a search of the Crane residence for any 'confidential papers' that might be related to his work at that time".

"Yes" said Beech with slight irritation creeping into his voice.

"And the following morning, Friday 13th September, you resumed the search until Professor Crane's body was located at about 1.30 pm".

"Yes, but it's all in the report. If it's written down, then that's when it happened. We were most particular about our records; everything would have been entered into the time log for accuracy. It's so important if there's a court case or inquest that the details must be correct".

Justice Barrington nodded in agreement,

"Yes quite…. Then can you please explain why the time stamp on the original missing person report is recorded as 12.30 pm Thursday 12th September 2002, a full four hours before his family reported him missing and a full one hour before Professor Crane left the house?"

Beech looked stunned; he wasn't expecting that.

"Well Mr. Beech? The court is waiting. How do you explain that major discrepancy?"

"Er, I can't Sir. I would need to check".

"Clerk, please pass these documents to Mr. Beech so that he can confirm that the details are accurately recorded". The clerk took the documents from the coroner and walked them over to Beech, who had visibly paled. He made a show of looking at the sheaf of papers, but it was plain to see he was working out a suitable response. After what seemed like an age, he looked weakly at Justice Barrington.

"The only thing I can think of is that the time of him leaving the house was recorded as the time we started the file". He was working out if that sounded plausible and realised it would be challenged.

"Or sometimes we may decide to widen the window to ensure that when investigators are putting together a timeline, they would start before the disappearance, so they wouldn't miss something".

The coroner looked over the top of his gold rimmed spectacles and in his most patronizing voice said,

"Let me understand this correctly: a team that prided themselves on the accuracy of their timeline were given to guess work and estimates when starting a file of this type?" Beech nodded weakly.

"Thank you, Mr. Beech, I have heard enough".

The coroner called a recess for lunch, saying that the inquest would resume at 2 p.m.

Hilary, Sharon, and Colin walked across the road to a café to get a sandwich and a coffee. None of them had much of an appetite, but it would pass the time. Sharon spoke first.

"How do you think it's going, Hilary?" She looked quizzically at them both.

"It's difficult to say, but honestly, it doesn't feel like a whitewash to me".

They discussed the evidence that had been given. The coroner had been very thorough and seemed determined to get to the truth. At 2 pm they were back in the Court waiting for the coroner's verdict.

Again, Justice Barrington was announced, and he swept in, but this time there was clear irritation in his manner. He called the court to order, then delivered his verdict.

"In the matter of the deceased Professor Robert John Crane, it is with deep concern and a heavy heart that I deliver this verdict following a thorough and meticulous investigation into the circumstances surrounding his tragic and untimely demise.

The evidence presented before this court, including testimonies, forensic analysis, and expert opinions, suggests that the death of Professor Crane was not as a result of suicide, as initially indicated by the circumstances. Instead, it is the determination of this court that the cause of death was the direct result of actions taken by a person or persons unknown".

There was a murmur from several people in the court. And a cry of 'Yes' could clearly be heard.

The coroner stared disapprovingly towards the area of the disturbance and once they had settled down, he continued.

"The discrepancies and inconsistencies in the evidence, along with the absence of clear motive, indicate that Professor Crane did not take his own life. The circumstances surrounding this case raise serious concerns about the Special Branch team assigned to this investigation, the procedures they followed and the manner in which they conducted the original search. I conclude that, from what I have seen and heard today, there is sufficient evidence of the possibility of foul play".

He paused briefly, reviewing his notes.

"Given the limitations of this investigation and the unknown identity or identities of those responsible, this court must regrettably conclude this case with the verdict of 'death by person or persons unknown.' The court acknowledges the pain and suffering of the family and loved ones of the deceased, and the need for a thorough criminal investigation into this matter. Recognizing the passage of time, that may prove difficult, but should not dissuade Special Branch from undertaking a complete review of their procedures and processes related to this type of investigation in the future".

"It is our hope that the appropriate authorities will continue to pursue justice, to identify and bring to account those responsible for this tragic loss of life. Our thoughts and condolences go out to the family, and we express our deepest sympathies during this difficult time".

Outside in the fresh air, the three looked at each other, not quite able to take in what had just taken place. Sharon reached out and hugged Hilary.

"This would never have happened without you; please pass on our heartfelt thanks to Daniel. This vindicates our father and goes some way to restoring his reputation. I can't thank you enough". Hilary smiled.

"You do realise that this will probably end here, don't you. The likelihood of the culprit being found and prosecuted is highly unlikely. This whole situation was a bad political joke".

Colin put his arm around his sister's shoulder and gave her a hug.

"I don't like political jokes, too many of them get elected. But don't underestimate how important this process has been to us, Hilary. You have restored our father to us, and he is once again the man we always knew him to be. The stain on his character has been removed, we really could not have asked for a better result".

Press reporters clamoured to speak to the family about the outcome of the inquest. Tomorrow's papers would be full of speculation about the nature of the cover-up and the greater implications of the misinformation that was peddled by the authorities during that time.

The reality is that state secrets are never black and white but are the murkiest shades of grey, and evidence of them can always be found hidden in plain sight.

Epilogue

Global Syndicated News Corp

BREAKING NEWS

Lord Justice Simeon Bellingham today announced a verdict of Death by person or persons unknown at the inquest into the death of Professor Robert Crane OBE on 12th September 2002. Professor Crane led the weapons inspection team in Iraq in the late 190's and was instrumental in putting together the controversial dossier that launched the UK military action in the Iraq war.

Interpol tonight announced that they had arrested Former UK Prime Minister Lord Adam Hunt as part of an international investigation into Embezzlement and Insider trading. He will be returned to the UK on a private flight from his base in Geneva to face charges.

The UK is tonight in the throes of a constitutional crisis and more than 2 million people descended on the House of Commons in a mass protest against political corruption, bringing the City of London to a standstill for more than 4 hours today.

ABOUT THE AUTHOR

Wendy Charlton was born in Walsall in the West Midlands at the start of the 'Swinging' Sixties'. She describes her childhood as "happy and carefree" and spent most of it exploring books, spending hours in the local library.

By day, Wendy enjoys a broad and varied career in the public and private sectors, coaching leaders to develop their teams and helping small business owners to grow their businesses. The Personality Profiling aspect of her work has given her unique insights into what motivates and drives people to behave as they do. In 2023 Wendy won a prestigious business award, the Solopreneur – Woman Who Achieves.

In the evenings, Wendy swaps her "proper" job for one of author and novelist. Working from her home in a beautiful part of rural Staffordshire, she can pursue her passion for writing.

State Secrets is her third gripping novel featuring the unlikely duo of ex-Secret Agent Daniel Grant and civil servant Hilary Geddes.

Wendy's other Shady Fields Novels are:

Keeping Secrets – 2019

Hidden Secrets – 2022

Non-Fiction

Come out fighting – The Small Business Survival Guide

Secrets - Book 4 – Sneak Preview

The only weapon to hand was a craft knife, the type with a snap off blade. He extended the blade to its full extent and braced himself for the attack.

Dragonović rushed at him; he plunged the knife into his side and jerked his wrist up, feeling the blade break under the man's rib.

He lent forward and whispered,

"that will need to be removed surgically, so don't move about too much. I've missed all your major organs but if you make any sudden movement you could lacerate your liver, so if I were you, I would sit quietly in that chair and wait for medical help to arrive"

Printed in Great Britain
by Amazon